DANGEROUS GAMES

DANGEROUS GAMES

A JACK LIFFEY MYSTERY

John Shannon

CARROLL & GRAF PUBLISHERS
NEW YORK

Dangerous Games

Carroll & Graf Publishers
An Imprint of Avalon Publishing Group Inc.
245 West 17th Street
11th Floor
New York, NY 10011

AVALON
publishing group incorporated

Copyright © 2005 by John Shannon
First Carroll & Graf edition 2005

Library of Congress Cataloging-in-Publication Data is available.

ISBN: 0-7867-1543-X

Printed in the United States of America
Distributed by Publishers Group West

For Diane Stewart

Not to be aware of the natural light of California, nor even of a mountain fire that has been driven ten miles out to sea by the hot wind, and is enveloping the offshore oil platforms in its smoke, to see nothing of all this and obstinately to carry on running by a sort of lymphatic flagellation till sacrificial exhaustion is reached, that is truly a sign from the beyond.

—Baudrillard

The blood-dimmed tide is loosed, and everywhere the ceremony of innocence is drowned.

—Yeats

ONE

Drive-by

"Don't touch me there," she protested.

"Hey, kid. Did you know that's a song?"

She glared and rolled away from him. Covering her nakedness with the soiled bedspread, she clasped a hand against her breast, which he had reached out idly and touched, apparently just to fiddle. She felt as soiled as the bedspread, bewildered by the lights and activity around her. Not quite sure what she had got into.

"It was by The Tubes."

"Sure."

"They were a San Francisco punk band. Well, a sort-of art school band really. Before you were born, the seventies."

"What's going on?"

"On the set? Kelly's trying to fluff Kirk. This is known as waiting for wood, hon. If you're going to stay in the biz, you'd best get used to it. Guys can't always do the deed. Isn't fair is it? All you got to do is make a little noise, but we got to get it up. You want a boyfriend? I could be your boyfriend tonight. You wouldn't have to fake anything."

"Leave me alone."

He batted his eyelids a few times, and she had no idea what it was meant to imply. He was in his forties with a strange handlebar moustache and not too bad looking, but she didn't really trust him after he'd lied about what she'd have to do that afternoon. "You better not get yourself too stuck up, princess. It's a long, long road down blowjob lane, and somebody like me can ease the way for you."

Rod was the AD. It meant the assistant director, he'd told her—that much she remembered. Most of the rest was a blur. Too many people and too much happening in just her third week in the city, and then there was that pill they'd given her. They'd said it was to make her relax, but it just seemed to confuse her.

"Money is time! Money is time! Money is time!" The director stormed across the messy room, a huge man with a full beard and a shaved head with a tiny ratlike pony tail flopping down in back. He wore torn jeans, and his big hands were like ham hocks in her uncle's smoker up in the Owens.

"Ah shit! She's a mess. Make up! Get that lazy cunt in here!"

The director stormed away, and Luisa Wilson tried to lie still and cause no trouble, draw no attention at all. The AD came back with a clipboard and knelt on the mattress.

"You really an Indian, hon? You sure got the hair. And those black black eyes, I'll say that. Valley Talent says your name is Luisa Wilson, and that's fine with me, but I think you're going to want you a fancy screen name. Why don't you look these over while the big dog's hunting down Makeup.

She took the clipboard from him with a remarkably weak hand, almost dropped it. Something wasn't quite right about her muscles. He'd scribbled a number of ridiculous names.

Sleeps-with-Wolves
Princess Show-me-mo
Cat-on-back
Wild Beaver
Wiggling Bottom

She threw the clipboard down and said, "Call me Taboots."

"What's it mean?"

"None of your business."

"Sure, hon. You're only a feature player, remember. You still got time to change your mind."

"Time is money! Time is money! Time is money!" The director hove into sight again like a belligerent comet passing through the heavens, bellowing and gesticulating. Trotting behind was the makeup woman with hair so unnaturally red it gave Luisa Wilson a headache. "We're twenty minutes from golden time, Jess. Step on it!"

"Whoa, sweetie, you do need some work here." She sat on a corner of the mattress near Luisa and opened the accordionlike makeup box, then extracted several small square bottles and a brush.

"Here comes wood!" somebody cried.

"I don't know why they always say you guys are red. It's more like brown, isn't it?" The redhead held a bottle up for comparison. "Here. Sit up a bit if you can, sweetie." She had a nice smile, and Luisa tried to be ingratiating.

Boosting herself up against the wall, she readjusted herself for the woman but kept the spread clutched over her breasts. "Don't worry about it, hon," Makeup whispered. "That's why I earn the big bucks around here. Even some of the veterans cry the makeup off."

Dear Diary,
I was so hope-full of beginning a new life in this dreamy city, where I can begin completely anew with the aide of a person who cares for me, but little did I realize that this strange odissey of mine that began at the Greyhound bus stopping for me beside the Buy-Rite Market in Lone Pine & would end up in such a strange activity. One man here has tried to console me & I remain cheerful & hopeful inside, despite all. He is very handsome & looks a little like an overweight Brad Pitt. I dream of a handsome man like him who will become my protector. Since my first hope of finding a protector & sponsor in Little Deer did not pan out.

* * *

"I hear you hate cops."

Jack Liffey was indignant. "Does this look like hate to you?"

"No, it looks a lot like a penis. Only smaller."

They both laughed. It was hard to get the best of Police Sgt. Gloria Ramirez, even with both of them naked as jaybirds.

"I've had some bad experiences with the officers of public order," he told her. "You know how you guys react to anyone considered a private dick. I'm the partially chewed internal organ of a squirrel that the cat has left at the back door."

She shook her head, trying not to laugh again. She knew how Jack Liffey had lost his aerospace job just as the industry was hitting the skids in Southern California, and how he had found out by accident that he had a talent for tracing missing children. The truth was, she had a soft spot for lost kids and approved of what he did. Right now, they were in the big queen bed upstairs in her old frame house in East L.A., Boyle Heights actually. She owned the whole two-story house, which was unusual for the neighborhood where most of the bigger houses had been broken up into four apartments or more. Gloria had been living there alone until Jack Liffey had moved in with her.

There was a gentle rap at the door. "Are you decent?"

"I'm not into epistemology this early," he called out as Gloria flipped the sheet over them.

His nearly-seventeen-year-old daughter Maeve peeked in. "I'm making fresh orange juice, French toast, and strong coffee," she announced.

"Wonderful," Gloria said. "Any of the *pan dulce* edible?"

"I'll see, but I think they've gone pretty hard."

Jack Liffey knew his lover's favorite breakfast was machaca, a kind of scrambled eggs with chiles, peppers, and shredded beef, but Maeve was on a new vegetarian kick and wouldn't dream of serving up something with cow in it. Cows were destroying the planet. They were a tremendous drain on the earth relative to the calories they provided. Cows also committed the sin of farting more methane than the biota could absorb. Which was all probably true, but Jack Liffey liked beef enough to let the planet go ahead and die a little while he lived out his allotted span. For this attitude, Maeve claimed he was no better than an SUV owner—though she had to be careful where she said it because Gloria Ramirez drove a Toyota RAV-4 and Maeve was crazy about Gloria.

"We'll be right down, hon. Give us a chance to freshen up."

"Just don't be humping anymore. It'll get cold." The door shut quickly.

"Humping." He tested the word in his mouth after his daughter had gone. "Just how polite is that expression these days?"

"A few cents better than some others I know, that's for sure. You know what kids mean by 'hooking up'?"

He nodded. "Maeve's told me. I can't imagine a party where kids just pile in to choose up for meaningless sex, and then, when it's over, walk away."

"You're getting old, Jack."

"Boy, I hope that's not it. You're closer to the street than me, but not every kid's that jaded, or is it only wishful thinking on my part?"

She shrugged. "Yes, Jack. I wish I could tell you what you want to hear . . ."

He kissed her and gave it up. She was already putting on her work mood, he could tell, toughening up for her new partner, a hardnose who'd never even acclimated to having women in the department. "Okay, okay."

"I've got to shower. You go down and keep her company for a bit." As a consolation, she gave him a deep kiss with a lot of tongue, and for an instant she shuddered, pretending mischievously to be heading toward an orgasm.

"Women may be able to fake orgasms," he challenged as she pushed him away and jumped out of bed, "but men can fake whole relationships."

"If you're faking this one, Jack Liffey, I'll shoot your balls off."

You had to feel a little twinge when a woman who said that to you actually carried the new .40-caliber Glock that the cops had all switched to. He was the one who had proposed marriage about five times over the last year, though. Something—he wasn't sure what—was holding her back.

He even wondered if it might be his own anxieties putting her off. Over the last decade, he'd lost so many things important to him that he'd given up counting—the secure middle-class job, wife, beloved daughter (only back temporarily), comfortable house, money in the bank. It was strange living almost entirely without luck. It left you spiritually depleted, somehow, and a bit too needy.

He'd given up his psychiatrist, too, since he'd only gone to the blithering idiot under duress, and when he found out it wasn't going to get him back custody of his daughter, he'd quit. It was hard to know what effect moving to East L.A. was going to have on him. If it was like being a Commanche in Norway, at least he was studying Spanish to try to catch up. He wondered if he wasn't, in fact, too old to start over quite this thoroughly, but he really wanted to be with Gloria Ramirez, and he figured his fingernails were tough enough to cling to what little seemed to be left. It just couldn't help take a toll as he struggled to maintain that grasp.

Just before 9 A.M. was the perfect time at the big Coffee Plantation on Wilshire to catch the men's room full of pissers in business suits, semidisabled as they held up their big paper cups of latte in front of the long row of urinals. Surreptitiously, Rod Whipple slid a new cassette into the little digital video camera; his partner, Kenyon "Beanpole" Styles, had already done the same. They'd met in an extension film class, and the compilation video had been Kenyon's bright idea at a bar after class five months earlier.

"Are we set?"

"On some level."

"Well, on any level, what's the signal?" Kenyon asked. His nickname came from his being 6-foot-5 and thin as a pencil.

"I knock twice on the door."

"Sweet. Okay, I've got speed."

"Me, too." Rod stuck out his free hand and rapped hard on the outside swing door. They moved apart to give themselves different camera angles on the action.

There was a longish pause before anything happened. One man shook himself off one-handed and left for the basins.

Then the door flew open, and what was clearly a homeless old woman stomped in. She had only a few teeth in her big grin and wore a series of filthy skirts and shirts. Pink socks that had lost their elastic settled limply over laceless tennis shoes.

"Who's the richest cocksucker in the room!" the woman bellowed. Her scratchy voice echoed painfully against the tile.

Every eye and two cameras went to the woman, who stood with her wrists on her hips.

"Get out of here, ma'am. This is the men's room," a man in a suit said, with patronizing politeness.

"So it's *you!*"

She rushed at him and before he could turn away she punched him hard in the balls. He squealed and went down hard on his knees, spewing milky coffee from an oversized paper cup across the floor. "Ow! Ow! Ow!" he bleated. "Ow! Ow!" The woman turned immediately to a new target two stalls away, who was caught midstream with a panicky look on his face. She cackled and punched him even harder so that he went off like a steam whistle, bending over and clutching himself with both hands. He wasn't holding a coffee.

The old lady now approached a third man, also caught midstream, and he turned on her the only weapon he had, spraying her purposefully.

"You fascist!" she cried and went for him. But he managed to turn his back and absorb her blows on his hip as the other men in the room fled for the door, right past the softly purring cameras.

The woman reached around her new prey and grabbed his balls, squeezing until he screamed and threatened her.

"Go down, motherfucker, go down *now*," she commanded, and he did, falling to the side of his hip beside his still-writhing predecessor.

The old woman then turned to the camera and grinned broadly, exposing three widely spaced teeth lost in bluish gums. "Did I do good, boys?"

Kenyon handed her a hundred-dollar bill, and the two videologists fled the room, straight through the stirred-up coffee bar and out the front door. They sprinted up busy Wilshire and around a corner before slowing to a reaching gait.

"Jesus, was that sweet!" Kenyon exclaimed.

"You could of probably kept the second hundred," Rod said. "Fuck the bag lady."

"No, you fuck the bag lady. Let's be honorable. A hundred bucks is nothing to what we're going to make off *DG II*. We're gonna be *rich!*"

Jack Liffey was raking the front lawn, even getting in behind the plastic barrels that held geraniums and flicking out the leaves and crud caught there. It was some sort of completely gratuitous penance he was offering Gloria, who didn't demand it, yet always managed to keep him off balance. Still, he enjoyed the physical labor, and it had to be done. The yard had grown ankle deep in big papery orange and brown sycamore leaves. He didn't know why anyone planted deciduous trees in California, when there were so many attractive evergreens, from palms and pines to the live oaks that never dropped a thing but acorns. But he liked the look of sycamores, with their big arched boughs and the patchy beige and white bark that invited climbing, and this one was really huge, generations old. The hurricane fence along the sidewalk was also trapping leaves, and the chain-link grabbed noisily at the tines of his rattan rake. Used to the openness of Westside front yards, it hadn't taken him long to notice that every house in Boyle Heights had a wall or fence of some kind in front, often concrete block posts with forbidding wrought-iron spears in between.

A man in a straw sombrero pedaled past on his kid's banana bike, balancing two big shopping bags on his lap and yawing left and right. Two mariachis were hurrying somewhere in their maroon outfits glittering with silver. They sidestepped to give the meandering bike plenty of room. It was a little reminder that he was well out of his own pond.

One other good thing about that sycamore, he thought, was that it pretty much hid his view of the kids hanging out on the porch three doors up and across the street. In their uniform of T-shirts, dark glasses, and baggies, they were always accessorized with Budweiser cans. They were Greenwoods, and this was their turf. He'd talked a bit to the youngest one, Li'l Scooby, but basically as far as they were concerned, he'd simply dropped into their barrio one day from Mars. Li'l Scooby told him he thought only teachers and doctors were Anglos. The fourteen-year-old had never seen the ocean, never been west of the Harbor Freeway, and he immediately stiffened up into warrior mode whenever one of the older boys showed up. Two years back, Jack Liffey had befriended his old girlfriend Marlena's nephews, but he had no connection to these kids, and getting to know them was tough.

He'd tried to get close to the Balderamas in a tiny frame house just south of Gloria with the fridge on their back porch. The grandmother was home all day, and the place was crammed with colorful tawdry crap of all kinds, way more than the usual Virgins and religious artifacts. There were parrots side-by-side with polished brass icons and ash trays that looked like toilets. He'd read once that every collector was unconsciously creating some allegory, but he had no idea what this *abuela's* might be. His Spanish, despite the lessons he'd been taking doggedly, was even worse than her English. On the other side was a house that provided home base for a head gangbanger, so Gloria had warned him off trying too hard there. It was difficult to believe his bland condo was only ten miles away. At the same time, he was beginning to feel at home here.

Maeve came out and lay down on the grass with her hands behind her head, keeping him company.

"So what would be the practical consequences of being an existentialist?" he asked her, taking up a topic from breakfast. She was reading Sartre and having a hard go.

"I'd have to move to France and smoke a pipe."

"And die in an auto crash in the Alps, yeah, if you like Camus. But, seriously."

"Just like you, I'd have to find some way of building a viable moral system from scratch. Without the easy props."

"Don't you think you've internalized a lot of your mom's and my values already?"

She made a face. "You're talking psychology, Dad. That's different. I mean *principles*, the kind that are intellectually defensible."

The lawn looked a bit scraggly once the leaves had been cleared off, and he realized it might be a good idea to fertilize before winter hit. And buy containers for more flowering plants. The whole neighborhood was so awash with gaudy blossoms that Gloria's yard looked a little insipid in comparison.

"Is it really that hard to know what's right?" he asked. "I've never seen the need to rev up all that intellectual apparatus as a way of figuring it out."

"Well, there's always the kitten and the Rembrandt in the fire."

He smiled as he raked two heaps of leaves into one big one. He had begun to like the grating twang of the old rake. "I know you'd save the kitten ten times out of ten, no question."

"You wouldn't?"

"It always seems to me an artificial choice. You can't tuck the kitten under one arm, the painting under the other and haul ass? I mean, I know there are plenty of gray areas in the world, but they're usually a wee bit more complicated."

"A lot of yours seem to involve unzipping your fly at inopportune times."

He grimaced. "Not that again. Give me a *little* break. It's been quite a while since I strayed. Remember, Rebecca dumped me, and it was only after that that I started seeing Gloria. And you like Gloria better than her, anyway."

"Would you go back to Becky if she whistled—you know, just put her lips together and blew?"

He wondered how many teenage girls could summon up lines once uttered by Lauren Bacall.

"What was that movie?" she asked.

"*To Have and Have Not.* I would *not* go back. I'm completely crazy about Gloria. I don't even mind that she's a cop."

Jangly dancy *ranchera* music started up somewhere nearby.

"What about you and David?" he asked after a bit of reflective silence.

David was her—*beau* was the old-fashioned word he thought

she'd used the other day. Both of them were in their junior year at
Redondo High, and David had CalTech in his sights. Jack Liffey
supposed they were going steady, as he would have said in high
school. If he didn't like it, he still wasn't going to object and throw
her into overdrive. Everything happened too soon these days.
Divorce by eighteen, remarriage by nineteen, dark night of the soul
by twenty, midlife crisis at twenty-one. . . .

"What is it about 'what about' that you want to know, Dad?"

"How serious are you two?"

"Do you mean sex, has David got to home plate yet?"

That torched a whole bundle of nerves, but he tried not to let it
show as he came over to work on the southern side of the lawn.

"Not really. I mean, are you thinking long term? Is it going to
interfere with college?"

"How did we get here from existentialism?" she asked, and they
both knew it was only a diversion from talking about David.

"I wish I knew. Love gets a lot more mysterious as you get older,
and existentialism a lot less so. You can quote me."

He heard an ominous rumble and a lowered seventies Chevy
sedan with primer spots pulled near the curb and idled loudly with
ragged muscle-car belligerence. There were four shaved-head kids
inside, and he saw out the corner of his eye that the Greenwoods
had all disappeared from their porch and driveway.

"*Ese*, where you from?" a kid in the shotgun seat demanded to
know.

"Nowhere," Jack Liffey said. It was what you said. It meant you
weren't affiliated with any of the gangs. Normally, they didn't
bother with Anglos.

The boys on the near side of the car were making those complex
hand gestures out the windows—throwing sign—that were meant
to announce who they were, but he didn't have a clue. Little Valley
was to the east, where the city gave way to county. The Maravillas,
a sort of consortium of subgangs, commanded a barrio a few blocks
west. And even the Mara Salvatruchas, the citywide Salvadoran
gang, had an outpost, the Inez Locos, in an apartment building
nearby. That was all secondhand info imparted by Gloria. Jack

Liffey couldn't even read the spray-painted gang *placas* that came and went on walls and any other flat surfaces available.

He figured going on raking was his best bet.

"You dissing us, *pendejo?*"

"No, I'm not." He kept his voice as neutral as he could, but stopped raking and looked up to meet their eyes. He knew better than to try out even the politest of polite greetings in Spanish just then. He was sharply conscious of where Maeve had been lying on the grass, without looking toward her. He hoped by some miracle she had slipped back into the house.

The kid at the back window had a T-shaped moustache-beard combination and was mad-dogging him with fierce black eyes.

"I would never be impolite to anyone as powerful as you gentlemen."

"Well, fuck Greenwood, *lambiche, que watcha.*"

Too late he noticed that T-moustache in back was displaying a small black pistol.

"Insane respect, man," the *pistolero* said.

Jack Liffey dived for the leaf pile—feeling foolish and naked—as he heard three shots, one seeming to ping off the front fence, and then the squeal of tires as the lowrider accelerated away. He hadn't been hit, and he jumped up and ran out the gate after the car, focusing on the license plate to get a partial, JSP after three numbers, one of the very old gold-on-black California plates. It took only a second before he decided chasing after armed gangbangers carrying only a rake wasn't such a great idea.

His heart was hammering as he walked back up the street, panting, and he saw people appearing on porches up and down the block. He forced himself not to think of any racial epithets—even to vent internally—and to concentrate on the fact that they were really big wounded children, no-hopers, kids without jobs—grown callous and mean—but still just kids.

Then he saw Maeve lying in a strange position on her side. At first he refused to believe that the dark liquid seeping away down the grass was her blood. He turned and pointed straight at Señora Torres on her porch across the street. *"Call 9-1-1!"* he screamed.

She rushed inside, and Jack Liffey knelt beside his suddenly quiet daughter.

"Maeve, can you hear me?" He shuddered violently. "Maeve!"

There was no answer. He lifted her blouse, just enough to see the ugly entry wound in her abdomen. He ripped off his shirt to press against the seeping blood. His mind turned into a complete jumble of panic and guilt and rage. Off in the corner, an observer struggled for the meaning of *lambiche*. What had happened? He'd made every effort to be respectful, and how had it gone wrong?

Exit wound, a voice inside his head now cried out, taking him all the way back to his one day of medic training in Basic. Always look for that, too.

TWO

The Last Juvenile Delinquent

He was bent forward on the uncomfortable bench, holding his head with both hands as if it might spin off and fly away. The air in the busy room smelled of ether and ammonia and something else that he couldn't quite identify. Maybe just the odor of human fear and distress. L.A. County General Hospital, an immense Deco edifice on its own hill just north of the I-10 in East L.A., was reputedly one of the largest buildings on earth outside the Pentagon, though so badly earthquake-damaged that the framing was already going up for a replacement. Its ER probably handled more knife and gun incidents than any other hospital in the country, so he consoled himself with the expertise and experience of the doctors treating Maeve. The ER waiting room was the size of a bus station but remarkably quiet for a space holding so many wounded and terrified people.

It had been a long time since he had felt so panicky and guilty at the same time, and Kathy, Maeve's mother, wasn't helping much, sitting across from him in her own bank of plastic chairs with her arms folded, glaring at him. When he'd called the Harbor Station, Gloria had been out on a fraud case in Wilmington but he knew

14

she'd get the message and be there before long. He was counting on her to run interference with the Hollenbeck Division cops who'd already had a go at him once. First things first, though: he desperately required a visit from an exhausted-looking, blood-spattered ER surgeon resembling George Clooney who would assure him that Maeve was going to be just fine.

"I'm not mad at you, Jack," Kathy volunteered, none too covincingly.

"Well, I'm mad at myself, but I don't know why. I don't know what I could have done differently. I didn't challenge them, I didn't dis them." He knew what she was thinking: Her former husband's life had become so ragged, so caught up in the fringes of the city that he continually put Maeve in harm's way without meaning to.

"You sure you didn't bristle a little? You've got a temper."

"I *swear,* Kath. I'm not an imbecile. I don't pick trouble with gangbangers."

He looked at her trying to get a fix on her thinking. She'd aged, he noticed, but he supposed he had, too. Her typically Irish colleen look had taken on an artificiality now with the too-even red dye in her hair, and her face had gone wrinkly with worry lines the way a freckled complexion can, but she was still a handsome woman.

"You look healthy," he said.

"You don't. You look like a schizophrenic on work release."

They fell silent as an ambulance crew brought somebody moaning and gasping past them on a gurney. It was amazing how calm the EMTs stayed.

"Blood is always thicker than water," one of the EMTs offered carelessly as they disappeared through swing doors.

"Blood is thicker than water," Jack Liffey repeated. *¡Viva la raza! ¡Viva la familia! ¡Viva el barrio!* He shook his head. He was very tired and confused and couldn't sort out his thoughts, but "support your homeboys" was never a sentiment that sat well with him. It always seemed to lead to finding an "other" to hate.

Maeve had been in surgery for nearly five hours now. Four hours or so back, as he'd come through the archway into the waiting room, a guard had almost tackled him to relieve him of the Swiss Army knife that had set off a metal detector.

"It's like some huge open-air zoo," Kathy said.

"What do you mean?"

"I'm not sure. I just feel weird here, exposed somehow." She shrugged. She looked suddenly very drained. And very frightened.

He sighed. He figured *here* didn't mean the hospital, but the whole Eastside. He subsided into himself, but still aware of the babble around him and unable to completely ignore the sniffling of a preteen boy two seats away who waited with a friend, his arm cradled and wrapped in a bloody plaid shirt that had the handle of a kitchen knife protruding. Could he have dealt with something like that at the boy's age?

Then Gloria Ramirez stood there in all her impressive cop calm, and his heart lifted. Before speaking to him, she paused to kneel in front of Kathy for a minute, and the two women held hands and spoke softly. Jack Liffey could see Kathy begin to cry then stop. Gloria embraced her.

Eventually, Gloria came and kissed him on the cheek. She kept her face next to his as she whispered, "I'm so sorry."

Tears welled up suddenly, and he fought them back.

"What have they said?" she asked.

"Not a word. In four hours, more."

"Oh, for *Chrissake*." She got up and strode immediately across the busy room, decisively pushing past the double doors. He and Kathy watched her disappear like simpletons expecting a magic trick to occur there. *Tragedy makes us all primitives,* he thought.

It was about ten minutes before she came back. Again, Gloria went to Kathy first, and he could tell by the way his ex-wife's whole body lost tension that the news was bearable.

"I'm sure she's going to live, Jack," Gloria told him. "I've seen enough gunshot wounds to know. If she was going to die, it would have happened. One of the assistant surgeons was taking a breather, and he told me they're struggling to save her right kidney. She's lost a few feet of her intestine, so I'm afraid she'll have to wear an ostomy bag for a few months—which is no picnic for a kid—but she's tough. Her wound isn't critical. When they come out, prepare yourself—they won't be bright and cheery, and they'll say something like *serious* or *guarded* to cover their back. But it's okay."

"She can have one of my kidneys right now if it'll help."

Gloria shook her head. "It won't be necessary. You can live a full life on one kidney. And they may still save number two. Can you tell me the cops you talked to?"

He was unable to reply, trying to take in her report on Maeve's condition, but he dug out the card that the lead cop had given him. His partner, an obvious rookie about nineteen had hung back, listening and learning.

The card read, *Sgt. Dean Padilla, LAPD, Anti-Gang Unit.*

The gang detail had, until fairly recently, been called CRASH—the rather ludicrous Community Resources Against Street Hoodlums—until Rafael Perez and the Rampart Scandal had disgraced that acronym for all time.

"Padilla's okay," she said. "I know him. What did you tell him?"

"You're sure she's going to be all right?" It was hard to shift gears. The memory of Maeve unconscious on that blood soaked gurney was all he could think about.

"Trust me, Jack. The naked truth is they don't waste four hours of painstaking surgery in a public hospital on somebody who's circling the drain. Sorry, that's a lousy expression. Can you tell me what you told Padilla?"

He took hold of himself and repeated to her pretty much all of what he had told the cops a few hours earlier in the waiting room. Every word the gangbangers had said to him, as close as he could remember, along with the description of their car and the three letters he'd got off the plate.

"Describe the boy with the gun again, please?"

"It was a revolver. He had a shaved head, late teens, I'd guess. Chunky build, from what I could see. He had a mustache and one of those perfectly formed straight down exclamation mark beards

under the lip so it all made a 'T.' They were throwing those gang
signs with their hands, but it didn't mean anything to me. Maybe
one part of it was three fingers with the second-to-the-little-finger
tucked in, and the thumb tucked, too."

"Could be an M."

"He had on a black T-shirt as far as I remember. It happened
pretty fast."

"I understand. Don't blame yourself."

"I'm trying my best not to. What's *lambiche?*"

"Roughly, a kissass. I don't think it's anything special. Just a
random insult. Now what was it that you *didn't* tell Padilla?"

He watched her eyes, now as hard and flat as stones. She was on
the job. "You can't know me that well yet," he said.

"Yes, I can."

It took him a while. "Several years ago I was backed into a
corner." He wasn't sure he should say this, but the relief that Maeve
would live had pulled some plug in the side of his chest, and a lot
of emotion was rushing out without any exercise of his will. "I
killed a guy. He was unarmed. It changes you when it sinks in. It
rearranges the whole sense you have of what's normal for you, who
you are, what you're capable of."

"So?"

"So, if I see that kid again, I'm not sure I won't kill him. I'm just
telling you, Glor. Don't go ape on me."

"You need a dose of Father Greg Boyle."

"Unconditional love for the gangbangers, sure. He's famous for
it." Father Greg Boyle—G-Dog to the kids—was the patron saint
of the gangbangers and had made it his policy not to write off a
single soul for years. His parish had started Homeboy Industries to
give them jobs and refused ever to turn them into the police when
they came to him in trouble. "I try to appreciate the concept. I'm
just telling you how I *feel.* They shot my baby."

"I understand, Jack." She regarded him somberly. "You have any
idea how many of our neighbors are living with a loss like that?
Kids that died senselessly in a drive-by or just the result of poor
aim? Almost every family has one dead cousin or son. In the next

few days, they'll come to comfort you, bring you things like *chiles rellenos*. Ask them about it."

"I'd rather strangle the little fuck. Sorry, but that's the way it is."

Luisa Wilson went into the back bedroom and shut the door quietly so no one would hear. She had made it into her own private space, like that wonderful red-tailed hawk's nest she had watched for years from a taller hill back in the Owens. She had a single mattress with two sheets and an old blanket, her old army surplus B-4 suitcase laid out next to it on the floor as a closet, an upended red plastic crate for a bedside table that held her three romance novels. The only thing in the room not hers was a big poster on the wall that she couldn't do much about and was finally getting used to. It was from one of Rod Whipple's movies, *Coming Traction,* and showed a nude Amber Lynn driving a tractor away from three dungaree-wearing men in hot pursuit of her. Luisa had set one of the last of her Owens rocks in the corner of the room, a small rounded nondescript pebble, by its presence tying this place to the one she had left behind.

It was amazing, she thought, how little you really needed to create a refuge. She'd only been here three days, after crashing at various other unlikely L.A. pads, and yet she felt such an immense sensation of comfort in her nest. Rod didn't even insist on sex very much, just that first night when he was bored really, and he didn't ask for anything weird at all. She was coming to like him. He was lively and fun, when he wanted to be, and he seemed to be a protector.

She leaned back, turned on the light, picked up Treasure Chest Ranch and opened it where she'd sheep-eared the page.

> Ashton had dark hair that wasn't always tidy, thanks to his outdoor lifestyle as a rancher and broncrider. He seemed to be gittin' over his mother's messy divorce and his father's new 18-year-old blond trophy wife. His eyes were a piercing blue and steady as sapphire now. He was always active, squirming a little where he stood, and he had a great body— strong shoulders, muscular thighs, tight pecs and abs.
>
> Yum! Teresa thought. Oh, yum!

She was just sinking into it when a knock came at the door. "You busy, Lu?"

She didn't answer right away, but apparently it wasn't really a question because Rod came in and sat on the end of the bed, grimacing as he gave out a big theatrical groan. "Oooh. You have no idea, kid, the *headaches*. The director wants me to shoot second unit, no extra money. The editor complains we don't cover him. The cameraman says he can't stand shooting video, it's too flat and soapy, and he's never going to do it again. The famous Keith is gonna finally bring the money tomorrow. But, of course, Keith's *not* gonna bring the money tomorrow. "

She folded the page back over and set the book down.

"Whatcha reading?" He took a look at the cover, with its impossibly dimpled cowboy clasping a blonde beauty and frowned. "You finish high school? I'll get you something good to read."

"I was second in my class." She didn't tell him there were only twelve students in senior year.

"That's great. Why don't you save up a little money and start in at a JC? Look what it did for me!" He chuckled at his own expense. "But I'm serious, you know. Unless you're dumb. *Are* you dumb?"

"I don't think so."

"There you go."

She worked up her courage. "If you went to college, why are you making these kind of movies?"

He laughed. "You mean, why am I only AD on fuck films when I could be directing *The Godfather, Part IV*? You're wrong, kid. The system is crap—it's all killer robots and things blowed up real good. Why not bypass it altogether? We get to be the last rebels in the world. We film people going down on each other and how many Tarantinos out there actually dare do that? Who's the real indie filmmaker? I'm a cattle prod up the world's ass, and it's all a gas. Anyway, the *serious* feature I made on the cheap right out of college failed so miserably I dare not mention its title lest the movie gods hit me with a lightning bolt. I couldn't get a distributor. I couldn't even get a screen at Slamdance."

"I'm sorry," she said, though she understood little of what he'd just said.

"Aaah," he said dismissively. "It was pretentious crap. I mean it, I love what I do. I'm a juvenile delinquent writ large, and I get to stay this way as long as I want. I even get laid as much as I want."

She folded the covers down suggestively, though she was still dressed. "Do you want to now?"

He patted her knee. "Lu, I was wrong to jump your bones the other night. In my house, you only have to do what you want to, *when* you want to, though it did seem like you were into it 100%."

"It was just nice you didn't want anything weird," she said. "It was okay." The fact that she'd been giving it to boys on demand since she was thirteen, not figuring she had much choice about it, she kept to herself.

"All that acrobatic stuff we shoot is crazy, but it would get pretty dull without it. The girls doing reverse cowgirl, the poor guys having to stand on one leg like storks so the camera can see their weenies going in. Can you imagine middle America watching and trying to copy all that stuff. I bet I've personally made a million bucks for the American Chiropractic Association."

She couldn't help but smile.

"I mean it, Lu. You're your own woman here. When the money comes, I'll pay you, and then you can rent your own pad, do whatever you want."

"How come it's Keith who's got the money?" She didn't like Keith much. She'd met him only for a minute, and though she couldn't put a name to it, he had something about him you couldn't trust, like a guy with a habit of nasty surprises.

Rod shrugged. "I think he's just the messenger, the golden moneybags for the golden eggs. He claims it's his money, but I doubt it. You know what I think, I think he's found a group of doctors and dentists or something like that, and I just don't ask. He knows *somebody*. He hands us $25,000 to put together an hour and a quarter video in two days of shooting, and, as far as we need to know, that production money just falls from heaven, even if its far more likely it's come up from the other place."

"Why don't you save up and make movies for yourself?"

"Because it's not what I do. I don't have a clue how to promote or sell stuff. There's a lot of people doing this, three hundred tapes a month, and if you don't know the ropes it's just going to sit there on your kitchen table. And, to tell you the truth, it's just possible I could get my fingers broke in the process. This business used to be dominated by a lot of Italian guys with silver suits, and even though it's changed a lot these days, what with cheap videotape and all, I still think Keith's moneybags might have a vowel at the end of his name. Whatever, he's not somebody to mess with. Truth is, when I get ambitious, maybe I'll go out on my own and direct, but I've only been doing it a year, and I've got another iron in the fire, anyway."

"I think you're a nice guy."

"Nah, your standards are just too low. Look around you, everybody in this business is at least a little bit pissed off, a little crazed, everybody comes from some kind of dysfunctional family—moms ran off with a salesman, daddy used to do them, they had to lick the floors clean for the wicked stepsister. This pays the rent for now. It'll buy me a big Harley and a lot of coke. What you see is what you get, kid."

"I still think you're nice."

Dear Diary,
My protector came to talk to me & he didn't even ask for sex tonight. I wonder if this is a compliment to my dignified manner or if I look too Indian for him to want me. I was never very popular in school except when boys wanted you-know & the white girls didn't talk to me very much. I dont believe his real name is Rod but he just laughed when I asked him what his real name is. He could have any of these beautiful blonde women in his movies & he came to talk to me & then he bought me a hamburger at the Jack-in-the-Box. He even asked me to go back to school & said he would get me some books. My heart is filled with the warmth of gratitude for this kindly man. I wish I had someone at home to write a letter to & tell them about him. I live now mainly for the time at the end of the day when I can read about other times & places. Maybe one day I will go somewhere like that.

THREE

Put It Behind Me

The gang unit apparently liked its autonomy. They worked out of a nondescript storefront on East Third a mile east of the Hollenbeck station. There, amid the wanted posters and other notices, a mysterious bumper sticker was taped to the inside of the window: *There is a wide universe of love and pain and death.*

Padilla sat with his feet up on an open drawer, going over paperwork. Facing him was a big map with colored pins extending out of the City into County territory, with a key identifying the colors: Marianna Maravillas, Greenwood, Little Valley, Sangra, Lomas, 3 Innocentes, Inez Locos, Barrio Heroes, Quatro Flats, The Magicians, Dogtown, Orphans, Terrace, Obregon, Bluff Boyz. Gloria Ramirez studied the pastel shadings for a moment. Her house was well imbedded in the zone that had been cross-hatched with a light green magic marker—Greenwood. She noticed a white pushpin just about at her house on Greenwood Avenue and guessed it was for Maeve. White for *drive-by, nonfatal incident.*

Beside the gang map was the station's homicide board: forty or fifty Polaroid photos of the heads and shoulders of young Latino corpses, bloody and glassy-eyed, clearly deceased and lying on sidewalks or wood floors, although a few were shown still hanging on with tubes coming out of their mouths. There were others of some of the young men still alive, obviously taken by patrol cops. They stood looking defiant against walls or cars. Each photo had a typed caption with the boy's name and nickname—Popeye, Chivo, Stick, Largo, Huffy—then a date and the circumstances of death. One showed only a head, crudely decapitated. Gloria studied this one: *"Bad Dog" David Solis*—the date a few weeks earlier—*Veterano of Dogtown. Head found Pine Hill, north of minimart, fifty feet down culvert from body and machete. Presumably done by the Magicians, likely doer "Trumpo" Rodolfo Carillo.*

"Dean," she said. He looked up, and she showed her badge wallet casually.

"I know who you are," he allowed. "Sorry. It was your boyfriend's kid, wasn't it?"

"Yeah. Why do you think they hit a *gabacha?* They never do that."

"I don't know if they even realized she was there. Maybe the perp was just capping off a couple of warning shots, trying to freak the guy. The best thing we could do for this town is give everybody some lessons in marksmanship."

"So then it's just pure genocide," she said not caring how angry she sounded. "All the gangbangers kill each other off."

"That's super-duper in my book, Sergeant. These guys don't deserve to use up oxygen resources. Not one of these skells is gonna contribute shit to the world."

She decided to go easy. He had a Latino name, after all, and wasn't just another racist cop like her partner. "I hear Jack gave you a pretty good description of the car."

He rolled his eyes, then laughed. "Big old lowered Chevy. Yeah, that ought to narrow it down *a lot*. Guy inside with brown skin, T-moustache, used a revolver. Uh-huh, sure. Your Jack told us a gold-on-black plate and they went out in 1969, and from his description the Chevy had to be at least a 1973. The plate's just a junkyard special."

"You could consider it a family matter, a cop's daughter."

Dean Padilla raised a palm. "Hey, we're on it. We're talking to the Greenwoods, see what they might tell us. They can't like this happening in the middle of their tierra, real dis for them."

"Jack is really upset, and if nothing happens he might do something stupid on his own."

Dean Padilla stared at her for a while. "The girl isn't even dead, Ramirez. Can you explain the facts of life to this boyfriend? We're not gonna roll SWAT because an Anglo got hurt in Boyle. It's pattern, it's background, white noise, it happens ten times a night."

"Not at my house, it doesn't."

"And don't you horn in, either, Sergeant. You work in Harbor. I'm not coming down there trying to clear *your* 245s."

She left her card on his desk. "I'd just appreciate a call on anything you get."

"Sure thing."

"I mean it."

"Ay te miro, ruca."

Kathy came out of the hospital room, sniffling a little and blinking the tears away. She nodded to him. "Your turn. She's going to come home with me when she's ready. I just want that clear."

"Sure," he assented. But seeing Maeve was all he could think about. Kathy was a blur.

He went in slowly, full of trepidation. There was far too much apparatus for his taste, all of it attached in some way to his little girl, as if every one of her body systems required artificial ministrations—which was probably the case for the moment.

He peered down at her bleary gray eyes, her face colorless as parchment.

"Looking good," he said.

He noticed tears dribbling down her cheeks and wondered if it was something her mom had said. She wasn't convulsing with the emotion but something had left her steadily weepy.

"Hi, Dad. It's great to see you."

He rested a hand softly against her shoulder.

"Does it hurt, hon?"

"Uh-uh. I'm sorry, I just can't seem to stop crying. Nothing hurts. It's weird. It feels like I did something wrong."

"Good people always cry when they get attacked," he said mildly.

"Really?"

"Somewhere deep inside, you believe you live in a just universe, against all the evidence. So you can't help feeling you must have done something to deserve what happened."

She offered a pale smile. "Is *that* it?"

"Do you remember, we were talking existentialism just before . . . it happened?"

"Not really. I remember coming down the steps to talk to you while you were raking up the leaves. Then my memory's pretty much gone. There's a blank, is all. So I'm feeling guilty? Go over that part again about the just universe."

"Let's let it go for now, hon. You might get a wee bit angry, too, after the weepiness. I've seen it, and it would be understandable."

She tried to shake her head but ended up rolling it a little instead.

"Don't be too expressive—please." He moved his hand to her thin warm arm, and was reminded for the millionth time how delicate she was in this violent universe. He couldn't help thinking that a strong man could snap her arm like a carrot.

"What's wrong with me? Mom wouldn't say."

He thought about it for a moment, but the doctors hadn't issued any taboos. "The bullet hit one of your lower ribs and spun around inside you. You've got very tough ribs, it seems. The bullet tore up some internal stuff."

"Define *stuff*."

He grinned as best he could. "They managed to save the kidney, they're pretty sure. It seems to be functioning fine today. You lost about two feet of large intestine. You'll never have to have an appendectomy. I guess that's the bright side."

"Too bad it didn't get my tonsils, too."

He thought she was herself again at that minute, and he felt his face flush with the relief of it.

"Wait, what's this?"

She had lifted her right arm painstakingly, strapped as it was to a board to immobilize it for a drip, and he could see that she'd felt the bag attached to her side. Fortunately, it was under a sheet so she couldn't see it.

"While your intestine is healing, you'll have to wear a bag for a while."

"Oh, *gawd*." She closed her eyes and shuddered.

"Yeah, hon, I'm sorry, but it's only while you're healing."

"Oh, ugh. Double ugh."

"Triple ugh," he commiserated.

"Now I've got a reason to cry."

"You won't be doing any sliding into third base or boxing or jumping off the roof, but they say you can drive sled dogs just fine."

She didn't say anything. He could see she was shaken.

A middle-aged nurse looked in and called time. "Sorry, sir."

"Give me one minute," he told her.

Maeve lay there and watched him. He couldn't read her expression.

"Mom wants you home with her for a while. Let's not fight her on it. I'll come see you or take you on trips. She'll relent after a while, and things will get back to normal soon enough."

She nodded. "Yeah, and we won't say anything about Mom calling your neighbors gun–crazy trash."

"You know she didn't," Jack Liffey said. He knew Kathy wouldn't. She had subtler ways to say it.

"She might as well have."

"We'll get through this, hon. It's upsetting."

"I'll tell you one thing, Dad, I'll certainly be glad when I can put all this behind me again."

Until she started giggling maniacally, he didn't realize she'd made a horrible pun about the ostomy. His heart melted, the way it always did when he got a glimpse of her staggering strength. She was going to be okay.

"All the better saints did it," Kenyon Styles insisted.

The old wino leaned close and confided, "You know I ain't no saint. I been a mackerel snapper, and I know. For weeks I been

balling that girl with the torn red sweater." His breath gave off a
whiff of something fleshy and rotten, some premonition of the
grave.

"It's okay, you can do anybody you like. You just got to ask forgiveness for it."

"It's not right with the Lord. It's *fornication!*" The last word was
bellowed forlornly into the night, and the tall young man looked up
to see if his partner was rolling, and Rod Whipple flashed him a
thumb's up, his face buried behind the little Panasonic DC352.

"The Lord won't be so upset with stuff if you make it up to him
and do your penance. Look, there's the hammer."

As if suddenly discovering where he was, the old man noticed
the rough man-sized wooden cross construction on the park
grass behind him. "Anyway," he said, his gravelly voice suddenly
wistful and faraway, "balling's not the same as it was, not for
neither of us."

"That's tough." There was no real concern in Kenyon Styles's
voice. "The hammer, man. The nail's there. You want the hundred
bucks, don't you?"

"I guess."

"Go for it."

The old man picked up the huge galvanized nail and held it to his
eye gingerly, looking at it dubiously.

"Just your left. One moment of religious sacrifice and you'll
be rich."

Rod Whipple tried to hold the camera with its floodlight steady
as he took a quick glance around him. Their glow had scared the
dope dealers away from the northeast corner of MacArthur Park,
at least for now. A news team, perhaps, dogging some cops on a
sweep through the park. One of the hundreds of film or TV or ad
crews that infested the L.A. night. In any case *light,* something to
avoid.

The old man rested his left hand dubiously, palm up, on one
wing of the cross. "I wonder if me an' Erleen could get the ol' moon
river magic back."

A gunshot sounded not too far away, and Rod felt his anxiety level ratchet up a notch. He didn't have half the bravado Kenyon Styles did for stuff like this. But the money would be good.

The old man placed the tip of the 16-penny nail against his palm.

Rod remembered from somewhere deep inside him that nails were associated with St. Helena, the mother of Constantine, and with Joseph of Arimathea, of course, and St. Bernard, and St. Louis. It was all coming back.

The old man held the nail tip in place awkwardly with the thumb and little finger of his left hand and then raised the big roofing hammer. Oh, man, don't, Rod thought, despite himself. But the old man screwed up his face and drove the big nail straight through his palm with one blow.

His shrieking filled the whole night that hovered over MacArthur Park. "Aw Jesus, aw Jesus, aw Jesus!" he wailed on and on.

Gloria Ramirez got back to Greenwood late, and when she came in, she saw Jack crashed on the old sofa in the living room, his mouth open and snoring softly as if exhaustion had caught him all of a sudden. He hadn't even picked up the mail. Under the bills and catalogues, she found a postcard showing the sawtooth peaks of Mt. Whitney, with the roughened redder Alabama Hills in the foreground, and on the back there was a printed scrawl with the vertical strokes going every which way. She had to sit down in a kitchen chair to read after she realized what it was.

> **Deares Gloria**
> **I no you wasn real sure you was my for true Neese when you was here but I got to ask you now to help me. Luisa went and got real mad at Clyde and ranned away to the city. Im afraid Clyde went and touch her or something Please please can you find her and make her come home. Youre ant Nellie Wilson Emm.**

She read it three times, sighed and put the burritos she'd brought home from El Tepeyac in the fridge, noticing that he'd bought some, too. She wondered where he had gone. She knew it wasn't

El Tep because too many cops hung out there for his taste. She read the postcard again, very slowly, and once she recovered from the variety of emotions that assaulted her, she realized all at once that this was exactly up Jack's alley. Nellie and her family didn't have much money, but she could slip them some ahead of time to pay Jack's retainer, and it might take his mind off Maeve and finding the bangers who'd done it. It was almost perfect timing.

"You don't need to get married again, Jack. Who needs the official ceremony? Just find yourself some woman who yells at you a lot and give her a house."

He chuckled as she headed the RAV-4 east off I-5 onto the Antelope Valley Freeway. She always had a quip ready whenever he broached the subject of marriage, even lightly. Quite a reversal on the usual gender positions on commitment, he thought, but Gloria had some aversion to getting married—or to marrying him—and he still wasn't able to identify which.

In a weak moment he'd told Art Castro, an old friend from the anti–Viet Nam War movement long ago, that maybe he just wasn't cut out for marriage.

Art Castro had shrugged. "It could be just a matter of personnel, Jack."

His mind went back to Canyon Country and Gloria's aggressive driving, coming around the right side of a Porsche with skis on the roof.

"Have you ever been to Owens?" she asked, definitively changing the subject.

"A few times. I even came up here on a job once, the father of a girl I was looking for was directing a big-time film in the Alabama Hills. I like the little town there, it's like a snapshot of the past." He knew L.A. had stolen the water from the valley long ago, and growth there had pretty much frozen in place, leaving the town a tiny market, a general store, and a lot of cafes for the road traffic. "I think three-quarters of all the cowboy movies ever made were shot in the hills there."

"Remember, it's not really my home," Gloria said. "Even if my mom did die in the street in front of one of the bars. I was fostered out young."

The dying-in-the-street business was the story she had finally and grudgingly been told. What was acknowledged was that the woman had been drinking a lot and not very choosy about who she slept with. In the end, Gloria Ramirez had turned her back on the aggravating couple in East L.A. who had brought her up to hate Native Americans, sistered up with a rotating crop of Latino orphans brought in mainly for the state money. She had finally worked up her nerve to search for her birth mother, which resulted in a dismal trip up here on her vacation three years back.

"So this Nellie Emm is your mom's sister."

"I think so. She has an old photo of them as girls, and the one that's not her looks a lot like me. I wasn't stupid enough to go around the place offering money, or every warm body on the rancheria would have been my relative."

"What's a rancheria?"

"It's what they call a reservation when it's too small to be a reservation. And don't call it a rez, please, that's like saying Mex. One of my uncles, with a nice sense of humor, told me a rancheria is defined as soil erosion with a casino, but this one is even too small for that."

"I think it was General Sheridan, no friend of Native Americans, who said a reservation was a worthless piece of land surrounded by scoundrels," Jack Liffey said.

She was still speeding, and they overtook a big SUV with a ski rack on the way to Mammoth. They headed north through the high desert, passing another alphabet street every mile, the stretch where he and Maeve had once played their name-a-tree-that-starts-with, name-an-actress, name-a-city-in-Europe game. He wasn't in the right mood to suggest it to Gloria. Something big and soggy and unhappy was eating at him, like the hangover of a bad dream, but a hangover with the teeth to gnaw its way up his leg.

He'd never really got over the fact that years ago he'd had to accustom himself to seeing Maeve only at her mother's whim, and had little control over her fate. They weren't estranged, far from it, but in this litigious world, custody rights trotted along behind income.

FOUR

Nobody Runs Away From Heaven

Luisa had *Treasure Chest Ranch* propped up on her knees in her cozy nest, and again she was lost in its sweetly seductive delights, addled a little by a handsome stranger saying, "Hey there, Little One, you ever find out how far you could travel with your shoes off?"

There was a single knock, and Rod barged right in followed by Keith, a skinny guy who looked like a college kid in old Levis and a kind of maroon velour shirt. He had a shaved head and wore a goatee that really made him look like a goat. Rod seemed a bit skittish, like his companion was a bomb liable to go off at any moment.

"Hello, Luisa. I want you to listen to Keith, who's got some great ideas for us."

She hid away the novel, face down, but even the back cover with its purply look was a giveaway. Keith, though, showed no interest in her reading matter. His eyes were fixed on her like a laser beam, scanning up and down her body, and he seemed terribly intense. The only guys like this she'd ever run into before were deer hunters she'd hung around with back home for spending money, and just for a few days. But she'd gone careful with them after they'd shot up a poor town cat for target practice and then got a bit rough with her, as if their meanness had excited them.

"It's a pleasure to meet you, Luisa," Keith said, forgetting that they'd been introduced before. "I've seen the rushes of your work, and I've gotta say you're a natural. You look good, you act like you like it, and your smile is as good as Jewell Topaz's."

"Thank you." She didn't know if being a natural was good or not, and she had no idea who Jewell Topaz was.

"Your voice is nice and deep, too. That's always an asset."

"It's been like that ever since I had the scarlet."

"You look great, that goes without saying. Your tits are big and natural, and you're not covered with tattoos so we don't have to spend half the day painting you with makeup. How would you like to start earning steady money? No more iffy video shoots? Real money, so you can get your own place in town and buy a car or whatever you want?"

"What do I have to do?"

"It's easier than the videos, really," Rod put in.

Keith glanced over at him, and she could see Rod stiffen a bit under his gaze.

"Sorry, K. Your party."

He held his glare on Rod a while longer and then turned his goat-face back toward her. Luisa felt the hair rising along her spine. "Mainly, you'd be posing and talking on the phone."

She didn't know whether to believe him or not. Rod had promised there wouldn't be any sex in her first video, but it hadn't turned out that way. "You'd be an employee of a big corporation, with a steady paycheck and health benefits, and just like me you'd have to pitch in and do whatever was needed from time to time."

He came closer now and sat right beside her on the mattress. She wished she'd put on underwear, and she hoped it didn't show that under her oversized T-shirt she was naked.

"You'll have it made. You can make up your own name, too, be whoever you want. This is the big time calling, kid. It doesn't come around and knock on your door twice, so you got to move fast to stay in the fast lane. Most pretty girls show up in this town and wait tables and starve for years."

"I can't add very good," she said. She knew she'd never make it as a waitress.

"Well, then," Keith said, opening his palms. Instead of remaining there in midair, one of his hands reached out toward her and all of a sudden grasped her left nipple hard through the thin cotton.

"Oww."

"This is your big day, the biggest damn day of your life. This is Brittany getting her first break."

He wasn't squeezing hard enough to cause real pain, but enough to let her know he had the power to do whatever he wanted with her.

"Pack up now and we'll go."

"I got to think about this," she said.

Keith glanced over his shoulder at Rod, who looked nervous. "This isn't really an optional arrangement, Lu," Rod said. "Your services have been purchased."

That got her back up a little, but Keith squeezed a little harder on her nipple, sending a fiery sensation through her chest that made her grit her teeth, so she nodded quickly. She knew enough not to buck guys like this head on. But she wasn't able to pick up the Owens stone as they marched her out, and she would lose her last connection.

Dear Diary,

Little did I expect when I made my leavetaking from Owens that I would have gentlemen fighting over my favors. This new suitor looks a little like Kid Rock & he said that I was a grand lady & I was very surprised that he took such a liking to me. He easily defeated Rod with the power of his personality and strength & swept me away to the aura of his protection.

When we were alone he seemed to like me for what I am & not just looking at the surface. In his dashing sports car he said that he would find me work that was worthy of my station in life. Little by little he seems to come to care more about me & he took me to an unbelievable beach house just like the movies. I cannot believe my good fortune. They say fortune always smiles on the deserving. Well.

There was something a little wrong with the lemonade that the heavy woman served them out of a big plastic pitcher; maybe it had been oversweetened with a sugar substitute, but he did his best to drink it and so did Gloria. He kept shifting, trying to find a comfortable position on the homemade Adirondack chair with all its odd angles. The women sat in white plastic bucket chairs. A section of baked dirt served as a patio, and it had a magnificent view of the far Sierras over the near edge of the town about a half mile away. The peaks were still snowy and sharp as razors. The sky was a uniform blue, the color of a baby blanket.

"I ain't got her note. I think Clyde took it." Nellie Emm was rounder than she was tall, with her hair in long stiff braids. She was wearing a print dress that had been washed so many times its color was ambiguous. She spoke with that skewed intonation that identified a Native American who was speaking English as a second language.

"Was she acting any different in the last few days before she left?" Gloria asked.

"No, no. Not that I notice. She keep to herself."

It wasn't actually a house, but a beat-up trailer with the decaying remains of a trellis covering where the wheels had once been. The rusting hulk didn't look like it could ever be moved again. The surroundings weren't bad, though. A serviceable fence out by the road penned in a roan picturesquely nibbling the desert greenery in the yard. Jack Liffey saw around them a few mature trees, a big cottonwood as gnarled and beautiful as an oak, a desert shade tree with tiny feathery leaves, and what he recognized as a catalpa with its long dangling seed pods. The trees all looked healthy so whatever branch of government decided such things had ceded the Indians an area where the water table was close enough to the surface so the taproots of the big trees could drink their fill.

"You didn't have any arguments with her?"

"No. She a good girl, really. You remember."

The other habitations along the rancheria roads just southeast of town varied from old shacks to modulars to owner-built cinder-blocks. The pastoral charm of goats and horse-trailers and chicken coops compensated somewhat for the shabbiness and for the con-centrations here and there of abandoned machinery and cars, what Gloria told him Latino families referred to as *yonkes*. It probably derived from the English word junk though he preferred thinking of them as Yankees, piles of creaky old shortstops and pitchers, tossed out to pasture.

"Was Clyde ever alone with her?"

"I guess." She actually shrank back a little as she admitted this, and Jack Liffey guessed she knew a lot that she wasn't saying.

Gloria seemed clear who Clyde was, but Jack Liffey had no idea. Was he a husband, a neighbor, a teacher, a live-in uncle? "Could you tell me who Clyde is?" he interrupted.

"He's my old man, but he got his own place in town. Because of his job. Janitor, nights, at the high school."

"How long have you been together?"

"Almost two year, since he stop seeing my cousin Berta."

"Is he a Paiute, too?"

"No, Clyde's a pale guy. Got leg braces," she added, as if that explained something. "He was one of the really last hard-luck guys that got polio as a kid. But his arms are *real* strong."

"Can we talk to him?"

Gloria took the address and phone number. It was fascinating to watch a pro at work, Jack Liffey thought, finding out without seeming to press. Not all cops were so smooth. But her aunt had a definite blind spot when it came to Clyde.

"When Lu gets upset, she always just talk about going off and doing dirty movies or taking off her clothes in the highway to give me worries." She crossed her heavy arms, and her elbows were dimples, the points of the bone sucked deep into fatty tissue. "She wants to make me feel bad I got so big nobody but Clyde wants to see my body. She been throwing up at night to stay skinny. She don't know I know that."

Out on the plain, a trail of dust showed where somebody was

buzzing along on one of those desert motorbike contraptions. Gloria got out of her the name and address of a close friend of Luisa's from high school, Barbara Thigpen. Then her aunt went into the trailer to hunt down a photo.

"Like one of your usual cases?" Gloria asked him softly.

"More or less. The very first girl I ever tracked down was a runaway who'd been rank-amateur hooking on Hollywood Boulevard until she got swept up by a crooked minister who put her to work in a slave shop making leather jackets. I don't know which was the worse trap."

"Nobody's safe in this world, Jack. Believe me."

"Don't I know it. I've got a wounded daughter."

"Whatever you're thinking, I just don't want you to turn down Nellie's retainer. She's got a share of casino money from the Red Feather up north."

"That makes it easier. I don't usually get thousand-dollar checks from people with their fridges on the porch."

Nellie Emm waddled out painfully and down the three steps with a four-by-five photo of a girl's head, a really striking chiseled face with dark braids and a smile like a flame that shot straight to your heart.

"She's beautiful," Jack Liffey offered.

"That been her curse." Nellie shook her head sadly.

"Qué pues, ése?"

Grinning, Chuy Perez stuck his head in the open French window in the old detached garage where Thumb Estrada had been exiled by his mother.

"Chingao! Man, you gave me a scare."

Thumb was lying on his stomach on a cot, reading a big fat text-book on the floor, which he slapped shut.

"I got some brews." Chuy came in through the window with two big Colt 45s. The only other entrance was the roll-open car door which was permanently locked down now. Thumb had been banished from the house for gangbanging and getting kicked out of school for the third and last time, and he had made the room his own by throwing up untaped wallboard and painting the walls with fancy placas and random images: spiderwebs, a plumed Aztec warrior, guns shooting out dots of bullets, and the smiling-frowning masks: Laugh now, cry later. Most prominent was his *clica's placa*: Bluff Boyz in florid old English letters.

"Trade you some weed."

"You always got lousy *yesca,* man. What you reading?"

He grinned. "Beto's helping me with history after I had to leave Continuation. There's good stuff to know, man. Gimme that beer." He actually seemed excited about what he'd read, flipping some pages back and forth. "You know they really fucked over the niggers, even after slave time. They made this secret deal to pull all the *soldados* out of the South and then the *vatos* down there put on sheets and scared the niggers to death to stop them voting."

"*Ese,* sounds like that Florida thing."

"You don't know your history, you doomed to have it done to you. That's what Beto says."

"Beto's a pussy."

"No, *ese.* Just 'cause he don't bang don't mean he ain't down. He showing me how to get a GED so I can go on up to City. Maybe I could learn computers."

"Computers is great, *simon.* Chente spends half his life on his thing looking at guys getting blown. He showed me some *güera* with a horse."

Thumb laughed and gave his two thumbs-up-and-out gesture. He was double-jointed and had made a little salute of the gesture, pushing the thumbs out from his T-mustache where they just fit. "*Ese,* I can't look at that bad shit. I'm still sick from all the jailhouse *maldad,* guys so horny they wanted to fuck the little wild *ratons.*"

"You wanna go hang at Lugo's?"

"Nah, man. It's too close to Greenwood, they see your *carrucha.*"

"I got new plates."

Thumb shrugged. "I don' like that barrio. They're all stuck up. Bluff forever. Insane respect, man."

They high fived, and Chuy chugged down his malt liquor and left. Thumb tried to read some more, but his heart wasn't in it. He got to thinking about that strange morning in Greenwood territory, driving up to that Anglo guy in the yard. It was something of a blank, a teasing aggravating blank. He knew there was something there to be understood. He hadn't meant to cap at him, hadn't really been feeling angry or rivalrous at all. It was like the events had had a will of their own, each moment summoning the next. He had an idea about it, almost had an idea, thought he had an idea. He sensed there was a reason. This reason was like an animal waiting to be coaxed forward.

But in the end there was no room for it inside him and it would not come out of the shadows.

"How many of the kids you take home, you think stay there?" she asked. She was driving out a dirt two-track toward a ranch south of town where Clyde Hinman supposedly had day work shoveling out a stable.

"I don't take them home if I don't think they'll stay. I'm not on the job to create repeat business, like some dentist offering the kids lollipops."

"It must tick the parents off if you tell them the kid won't come back."

He shrugged. "I think they pretty much know when a kid is past the point of no return. It's not always a bad thing. But it's always different, too. Sometimes, I can get them to come home on their own. Allow a little more time. Force a little family communication 'til all that emotion pours out. Sometimes, you just have to let the rebellion play itself out. Easy to say when it's not your kid. Mostly, you've got to find out what went wrong for the kid, look close at the home life. Nobody runs away from heaven."

"They say Satan did."

"You believe in that?"

"No, but all those old stories have got some kind of psychological truth."

"I don't believe in evil, Glor. Just sickness and sick needs in people. There's no Satan in any kid I've seen, even the sociopaths. Calling something evil is just a way of not looking at it. Religious people love not looking at things."

She slowed on the dirt road to let a family of quail scurry ahead and then dive abruptly out of her path. The last baby quail looked back, almost as if grinning at its successful challenge to fate.

"I don't know, Jack. In my job I've seen some pretty bad kids, kids who really like to hurt people, and sometimes their parents seem pretty much normal when you meet them."

"Humans move in mysterious ways. I don't know. Maybe families are always a lot more screwed up than they look. This is all too general for me, Glor. I'm used to thinking in particulars."

"Like Ken Steelyard." This was her former partner who had tried to eat his gun several times and had finally pulled a reverse on the legendary suicide-by-cop ploy of so many barricaded sad sacks. He had committed suicide by bad guy, a former Green Beret. Steelyard had been a childhood friend of Jack Liffey's, who'd done everything he could to talk him down.

"We both did our best for him," he said. "What part of that tangled mess would you like to call evil?"

"Maybe just something behind the scenes, pulling strings."

"Nah. Ken's misery was born of everything that happened to him from age three on. There's no horned red devil in the bushes. In a way, I failed him, and you too. We failed him by not figuring out what he needed, but maybe that kind of failure is inevitable. We tried. He wouldn't take antidepressants because he was afraid it would get around the office and kill his reputation as a tough guy. How can you ever know enough about someone?"

"I can't figure out whether you're profound or just naïve."

He laughed. "If one of those alternatives makes you upset, or pisses you off, I'm the other one. That must be the ranch."

It was easy to see where the horseshit was being shoveled. A small trailer rested at the wide entry to a stable, and now and then a mass of mucky dirt and hay hovered just in sight before dropping smokily into the trailer bed. Gloria parked to one side, and they slammed the doors hard enough to announce themselves.

In the dimness, a huge bare-chested man coughed once and took a break, leaning on a large flat-bladed spade, his face and shoulders covered with sweat. He had no hair at all and looked like a cartoon wrestler from the waist up, though he had to prop his skinny braced legs against the stall walls.

Jack Liffey felt himself back on the track of a missing child. He knew what he was doing now, and there was always a returning grace in that.

"Clyde Hinman?" Jack Liffey asked.

"Who wants to know?" There was an over-the-top belligerence in his voice.

They introduced themselves as a relative of Nellie's and a friend, looking for Luisa. It was fairly easy to see him stiffen at the name Luisa.

"I didn't do nothing."

"We're not vice cops, Mr. Hinman. If she came to your bed, it's none of our business."

"Screw you, city boy."

"We don't mean you any harm, sir. We just want to ask you a few questions about her."

Abruptly, the big man swung his spade hard at Jack Liffey's head. He ducked, which threw the man off balance, and he staggered a few steps in his braces. Magically, Gloria Ramirez had her pistol out, the black Glock. He wasn't even aware she'd had it under her jacket all this time, but he remembered it was L.A.P.D. policy to have its sworn personnel armed at all times.

"*Freeze.* Now."

"Jeezus!" He dropped the spade as he caught his balance and staggered back a step. Jack Liffey noticed he was wearing what looked like a whole embalmed garlic bulb on a leather thong around his neck. He wondered if there was a vampire problem in the valley.

"Mr. Hinman," Gloria said evenly, "would you like to spend the next thirty days locked away for assault?"

He didn't say a word, but his eyes bored into her, seeking an opening.

"I suggest you sit, right there on that mound of horseshit. Now. I'm a cop, and I can drop you where you stand, and no one will ever question it."

There was a degree of authority in her voice that amazed Jack Liffey. He'd seen her toughen up before but never quite like this. The big man looked unhappy but did as ordered. He tried to cushion himself with his arms but sank into the mound of horseshit.

"Tell us about Luisa," she said.

"Friggin' little bitch." He glared back at her.

While she was questioning him, Jack Liffey noticed something in a corner of the stable and went to look. It was a paper bag that was all greasy inside, containing a spray can of PAM. No wonder he was so belligerent, he thought. That stuff ate brain cells. He'd thought only gang wannabes, junior high delinquents and such did spray. Then he remembered the banana oil smell of Testor's Model Airplane Dope when he was a kid, and he could still feel a faint afterglow of that feeling that said all was right with the world, and he wondered if that was why he'd liked making model airplanes so much. He took out the can and sprayed it empty into the air; the big man looked over angrily. Gloria Ramirez still looked like she was about to shoot, and Jack Liffey wandered back.

"Did you ever get yourself so sprayed up you tried to give the girl a poke?" Jack Liffey asked.

The man gave him the finger, wiggled it, then sucked on it.

"Let's go," Jack Liffey said. "This guy hasn't got enough brain left to remember."

"I'll remember your sorry ass, city boy. You and the fat bitch here. I'll get you some dark night."

"She's not fat. Hell, just shoot him," Jack Liffey asserted.

The other two both looked a little shocked, but she got it first. "Good idea," she said.

"I'll say he attacked you."

"*Hey*—you can't do that."

"What'll we say? He got all sniffed up, tried to kill me with a shovel. You saved my life. Go on, shoot him."

Clyde Hinman turned impudently to face her. "Okay, fuckin' shoot me, bitch."

"I wouldn't dirty my bullets." She lowered the pistol and began walking back to the car, but she didn't holster it.

"One thing," Jack Liffey said. "What's the garlic for?"

The shirtless man looked down at the pendant as if seeing it for the first time. "The bad smell keeps off flies," he said.

"How can they tell?" Jack Liffey said.

FIVE

Wuthering Heights

Somebody had left a poster of a huge frog's face with bug eyes and a pink tongue on the side of the cubicle, just out of sight of the little camera on top of the monitor.

"The clock will kick in right here when you hit the button to take a customer." His finger rapped the spot on the screen where it said **00:00:00**. "After a minute, you got to make them come up with a credit card number somehow. At first, you let on it's just to verify their age, but after three minutes you tell them about the charges. Actually, the charges start at a minute and a half. They'll never know the difference. The clock turns yellow when the money's rolling. Lovey-Dove, Inc., don't get squat, and *you* don't get squat before you see that turn yellow. So hook 'em in or you're just wasting your breath. Show a little skin, show your bra, write what the skeezes want to hear."

Luisa settled back in the steno chair wearing the weird peekaboo nightgown and black underwear Keith's friend Donna had given her. She was feeling very strange and out of sorts, but somehow not frightened. Possibly, because there was a whole row of similar cubicles where a wall had been taken down between two bedrooms,

43

and other girls were sitting in front of other monitors in an eery kind of silence, punctuated by the chipmunk chittering of keyboards, coughs, and sighs.

She knew how to type, so they started her here, but Keith said if she did good he might have them move her up to an audio booth—she had the voice for it. He kept disavowing any personal financial stake in the business. He said he was only functioning as her business manager, to keep her away from the kinds of things Rod had her doing. He pointed to the words **Hi, My name is Ginger. Do you want to see more of me?** on a section of the screen.

"All you got to do is click on the words and they move into your outgoing screen here. Saves you time. There's dozens of scripts in here for all sorts of guys who want you to take it off, or show your breasts or use the aids there." A row of pink and black and silver penises waited like good soldiers on a shelf. "Click on one of the keywords, and you get a different script."

A little menu of keywords down the side said:

credit card
credit card insist
show you
talk dirty
be my friend
you do something
my tits
my pussy
my ass
dick size
toys
up the ass
sucking
licking
biting
toes
mommy
sister

boys
my fantasy
pleasure words

"Get the skeeze writing back to you. Find out his name. You can add it to your answer before you send. Makes it personal. The longer you keep the guy online the bigger your percentage. A good prick-tease can make fifty bucks an hour, maybe more. Why don't you peek over the curtain and watch how some of the other girls work it for a while. I'll come back to get you later. Don't worry about anything. I need to see a man about a plan."

The instant he closed the door behind him, there was a wave of hisses, rude noises, and other sounds rippling through the cubicles.

"Kiss my ass, Keithie," said a throaty woman's voice nearby. "I got a good fart coming."

"Oh, the goose walk fine, the monkey drank wine," somebody warbled.

"Tease *this*, you big twerp."

"Welcome to Lovey-Dove, hon," said a calmer voice, right next door, and Luisa could tell it was meant for her. "What's your name?"

She stared at the **My name is Ginger** still up on the screen. "Luisa."

"Welcome, Luisa. Next one of us on a break will—" The woman's voice broke off abruptly, then came back a few seconds later. "—take care of you. These cameras snap you every 20 seconds, and you got to get used to getting back into a pose quick, like you're in the mood. Guys don't want to catch you picking your nose."

There were several laughs.

"This guy would eat my snot, that's for sure."

"Don't think I haven't had guys ask to eat snot."

"How much can the camera see?" Luisa asked.

"You'll see. Ooops!" Pause. "When you key on, you'll see the camera shot of yourself in a window at the bottom. A little red light gives you two seconds to get ready for the snap."

"Don't go spending that fifty bucks an hour right away," another woman called out, which was greeted with guffaws. "Twenty-five, a good hour, that's tops. Hello, you stupid little momma's boy creep, you like seeing these?"

"Stay away from Dangerous Games, kid," someone called, with real concern in her voice. "Whatever else some prickhead pimp like that offers, say no to DG."

"What's that?"

"Just stay away, believe me."

There was a roar of laughter all at once from the far end of the line of cubicles. "I got a guy wants me to call him needle-dick."

"The first honest skeeze today."

The girl had agreed to meet them out at Frog Rock after sundown. She told them to head out County Road toward the hills and they'd know.

They speculated on why she wanted to meet them at such an obscure place, and not until evening, but Clyde's maniacal shovel assault might have had something to do with it. They passed a pokey little county campground, with spindly year-old trees and RV spaces laid out bumper to bumper. There was only one RV visible, a truck-mounted camper, and a man and boy had long ropes lashed to the top of it and were rocking it as if trying to pull the whole vehicle over.

"Man, let's give that one a miss," Jack Liffey said. "It's not your precinct."

"L.A. doesn't have precincts. We have divisions."

"You know what I mean. Anyway, what do you think Clyde's problem is?" he asked.

She shook her head. "You do enough police work, you see Clydes. Some of the guys call them F-DODAs. It stands for fatal dose of dumb-ass. There's no knowing what they'll do. These are the guys who're permanently pissed off and so crazy they can't even get it together to take it out on the wife. They shoot their own toes off. I had one once took a bet he'd put a pistol in his ear and pull the trigger. He won, but he'll never collect. It's a little worse among the poor because it's all that much closer to the surface when you're out of money. I think some of the projects, we'd be best off sending a crop duster over Friday nights and spray them with thorazine, calm everybody down."

Jack Liffey thought for a moment. "I've seen my share of anger. But there's usually a logic somewhere."

"Trust me, Jack. There's a large segment of the population that doesn't live in your world."

"Maybe like the guy who shot Maeve." His lips tightened.

"Sure. Maybe that banger didn't like your looks. Maybe he just got a new pistol with a hair-trigger. Maybe he didn't know how to use it. We'll get him, but it doesn't mean we'll find out why."

"I really would like to know. I realize it's a possibility we'll never find out, but it makes me nervous to think things might be utterly random."

"There," she said, nodding. There was no way to miss Frog Rock. It had probably looked a lot like one to begin with, but someone had got at it with green and black paint to make sure you got the joke.

"Jesus, that's ugly." The rock was embayed in a recess in the weathered range of low hills, as if left behind after a parade had passed by. A fire-red 1956 Thunderbird, the model with the little porthole, was parked on the dirt just beyond the frog. It even had whitewall tires.

"That's her dad's, for sure," Jack Liffey said. "No kid would value that car enough for the headaches."

"Don't be hasty," Gloria suggested. "Kids do funny things." She parked beside the T-bird and they got out and introduced themselves to Barbara Thigpen, who was sitting on the fender of the car. The black girl would have been quite pretty with about fifty fewer pounds, but she was wearing a mini-skirt that left nothing about her thighs to the imagination. Still, that was her business, he thought. She wasn't much heftier than Gloria.

"How come you wanted to meet us out here?" Gloria asked.

"Have you seen Clyde yet?" the girl asked.

Jack Liffey grinned. "Two minutes after we met him he tried to kill me."

She nodded. "Then you know. The man is a wacko. Plus I can smoke out here without some busybody telling me it's going to give me cancer." She shook out a Marlboro.

"It's going to give you cancer—and emphysema," Gloria Ramirez said. Jack Liffey frowned at her, afraid they might start off on the wrong foot, but Barbara just ignored it and lit up.

"I'm immortal. Everybody my age is. And the deal is, yes, we're the only black family in town, and, no, I don't like it all that much. My dad works for the L.A. Water Department, and he was transferred here, from a nice safe black community in Pacoima, out to the one place where L.A. stole all the local water, the whole river, so we're not very popular here on that account either. Segregated twice, you might say. But me and Lu were great friends."

"Tell us about her," Jack Liffey said.

"The only problem I had with her was an almost total lack of a sense of humor. She was sweet as could be and soo earnest, and I was lonely in this super white town. She had a secret Paiute name that she eventually told me, and other stuff."

"What is it?" Jack Liffey asked.

"Sorry, that's what makes it a secret. She had a thing about books and wanted me to read the same books as her so we could talk about them, and I suggested some books about princesses and Victorian girls. She tried, but she preferred simpler stuff. She had a little trouble with the language, unfamiliar words and stuff."

A car came slowly up the road, an interloper, its headlights washing tentatively through the craggy canyon. It almost stopped, but then it passed on up toward Mt. Whitney, its engine noise gradually dying away. Maybe teens looking for a good spot to neck, he thought. They had all watched the car pass as if fearing something.

"Was Luisa good in school?"

Barbara Thigpen made a face as if she smelled something that had gone rotten. "There's all kinds of smart. I don't think anybody at school ever said to her, 'Luisa, you're just a dumb Indian,' but it was kind of designed that way, you know—home ec and catch-up math, where all the Indians were. The high school is too small to have AP classes, but there's an AP study group, and we get credit if we pass the tests, so some of us can get into good colleges. She wasn't invited, or it just never came up, I don't know how it worked. Most of the Indians drop out when they can. I said she wasn't dumb. Our AP group read *Wuthering Heights,* and I had her read it, too, and it blew her away. She struggled with the language, but she really loved it."

She ran out of steam for a moment, watching the glow of her cigarette tip. Gloria started to say something just as a harsh wind gust off the Sierras made them turn their heads away from the fine grit blowing into their faces.

She wiped her eyes and started again. "Do you think Clyde tried to molest her?" Gloria asked.

"More than 'tried,'" the girl snapped angrily, and then the wind stopped as abruptly as it had come. She shook her head slowly as if clearing off the dust. "I wish somebody would bitchslap that dip-shit good."

"We're not really here to do anything about Clyde, but I'm not saying it can't be put on the agenda," Jack Liffey said. "First, though, we need to find Luisa. She seems to have threatened to run away a lot, and she'd say she was going to go into porn. Do you know where *that* came from?"

Barbara Thigpen snorted. "That damn legend of Little Deer!"

"Pardon?"

"You never heard of Little Deer?"

Jack Liffey shook his head and glanced at Gloria out of the corner of his eye. She looked just as baffled.

"You don't watch a lot of triple-X, do you?"

"I guess not."

"Holy shit, we even get it up here. Little Deer came off one of those big Sioux reservations in the Dakotas back in the late nineties, I think it was Pine Ridge. In L.A. she was an instant hit in the porn business. She made so much money she funded some scholarships and things. I'll bet most Indians everywhere know about her if you asked. I've seen some of her films. She was really slim and beautiful, plus the boob implants of course, and she had that great thick Indian hair. Anyway, she was the only role model Luisa probably had for a way to run away."

"Shit," Jack Liffey said. "Whatever happened to waitressing?"

"Pissy men and lousy tips. Would you like to try minimum wage?"

"As opposed to screwing a bunch of guys, at least one of them almost certainly HIV-positive? Yes, I would."

"That's just your puritan objections masquerading as medical."

"I don't figure it matters what I think, Miss Thigpen. I just want to find Luisa before she gets herself in trouble, and L.A.'s the place where trouble finds you first. I promise I won't bring her back here if she doesn't want to come."

"Do you have any idea where to start looking for her?" Gloria put in.

"You could look up Little Deer, if she's still around. Lu might just try to find her for help."

"How about an Indian name that Luisa might use?"

Barbara smiled gently. "The secret name." She lit another cigarette immediately. "Lu was funny. Every time she finished a book, she wrote down the date in the back of it and the secret name, Taboots. I think it means rabbit in Paiute, though I never heard her ask anybody to use it." She thought for a moment. "Whenever we went someplace, she always left a smooth rock in some corner, she carried a pocketful of them. It was like she was trying to mark a trail through her life."

They heard it first, and then they saw the wash of light from the car coming back down the road. As it passed Frog Rock, there was a derisive yodel and a beer can sailed out and skittered along the ground.

"Dorks," the girl said. "You know. I bet there's one of Lu's rocks right around here somewhere."

"Maybe she's hoping one day to find her way back to the place where things started to go wrong," Jack Liffey suggested.

The girl raised an eyebrow. "Whoa! Pro-found. But with Lu it might be a whole lot more daydreamy than that. Maybe she's leaving a track for her guardian angel to follow."

"Was she religious?"

"Not in any ordinary sense. I just mean that as . . . I don't know. Wherever her head was at."

"The way *you* leave a trail of cigarette butts."

"Hmm. Dad won't let me smoke inside the T-bird, and, boy, can he tell if I do."

"I don't blame him."

"He says he'll give it to me if I get into Stanford this fall."

"If you take that to Stanford, you'll be the most popular girl in the whole West Bay."

"I could stand a little popularity. The only action I get here is brainless jocks with the mistaken notion that all black chicks are just dying to have sex with athletes."

"I have a feeling you'll do fine," Jack Liffey offered. "You seem to be able to poke fun at yourself."

"Thanks. First, though, I gotta get myself to some place where they appreciate that." She glanced over to Gloria, who'd been quiet for a while. "You two are an item, right?" Barbara asked. "Are there some more like him?"

"I don't know. I haven't figured him out yet."

"He seems like a keeper to me."

"How can you tell we're not married?" Jack Liffey asked.

"No rings. I always check it out. And a kind of carefulness you've got, like you're walking on eggs."

Gloria laughed softly. "Jack's right, you'll do okay."

"I can tell you more. I bet *he's* the one pushing for a commitment, and you've been putting him off." The girl wagged a finger to emphasize her guess.

"That's enough," Gloria said. "I'm a cop, and marrying a cop is a hard road."

"Ten-ninety-eight," Jack Liffey said. It meant, in the LAPD ten-codes, assignment complete, getting back on patrol.

"You keep him," Barbara Thigpen insisted. "If the other stuff is working out."

"That's none of your business, young lady."

"Guy just took her away from me, man," Rod Whipple complained as he plopped down on the bed. "Just walked in and took her. Said he'd pay me for her later in whatever I wanted, grass or speed or work. Serves me right, I guess, for getting mixed up with him."

"You said it. I thought you'd've learned after those Italian fuckers wigged on us."

Kenyon Styles' room in the two-bedroom apartment they shared in Mar Vista was tricked up with a big Mac G5, two twenty-inch monitors and the rest of the editing equipment for a small cutting station. A tableload of computer equipment, a switcher, an effects box, and a fancy software program could now replace several million dollars worth of professional editing gear. *Dangerous Games II* was going to look pretty good for an indie production— better, for sure, than the first one—and now they'd figure out how to market it themselves on the Web. The two Sopranos in silk suits who'd forced them to sell the first one outright for $50,000 were going to make millions out of it. It had been just like something out of *Goodfellas,* a lot of solemn dick waving and glaring and that stupid New Jersey accent. *Ya sign da release or ya get a long nap in da foundation of some new fuckin mall.*

"Yeah, sure, I'm a loser. I left my Superman suit home."

Kenyon opened a Yoo-hoo and made a face as he swallowed. He said it soothed his burning gut. Rod tried to tell him they had cures for all that stuff now, but Kenyon hated doctors ever since high school when they'd shoved a long black tube all the way up his ass without anesthetic, him screaming the whole time. Never again, no doctors, he'd sworn.

Kenyon had two images up on his monitors—the same woman from two angles—and was trying to fuss with the color so her skin tone looked the same on both. Every time he got her skin out of the green, the dress turned purple. The one problem they still hadn't licked, given the fact that they were shooting on the fly with two different cameras, was getting a good white balance. Cutting from one to the other would look jarring and amateurish.

"Look at this." Kenyon tapped the keyboard, and they both watched a piece of his latest rough cut. Two old men bobbed and feinted, squirting tins of Zippo lighter fluid at one another in an alley, with a lit Bic in the other hand, like gladiators with dagger

and flail. They waved and thrust the lighters at each other. The duel
went on for a while until there was a whoosh of flame on the sleeve
of a flannel shirt, smothered rapidly, then another charge with the
Bic and a ripple of fire took a shirttail with a triumphant cry. Neither man seemed in much danger, since they were so drunk they
were not connecting with much of the naphtha.

"You zoom too much, dude."

"Eat me."

"I can cut most of it out. Just slam the lens to closeup, okay? Or
slam back to full." Kenyon was the better technician, and they both
knew it.

"Sure, fine."

One of the bums on the screen suddenly rushed off into the
night, screaming, his long greasy hair afire. Then the editing console burped and froze, a wavery flag of flame emanating from the
old man's head.

Kenyon frowned. "I've got some kind of hit there. Goes full lock."

He fidgeted his fingers rapidly over the keyboard without luck
and then hit the reset so that both monitors went black to start the
annoying reboot process.

"The girl was great, too. Lovely. We could have used her
somehow. I just can't hold onto things." Before moving to Jersey,
Rod Whipple had grown up in south Chicago, amongst fairly conventional Polish working-class parents with a nice conventional
Polish name. He'd always wanted to be a filmmaker but was gradually getting depressed about the amount of time he was putting in
at the squalid end of the film food chain. Though his metalworking,
duct-forming, union-loyal father was dead now, his spirit continued
to hover disapprovingly. Luisa had cheered him up for a while, and
now she was gone.

"We don't need a girl."

"I thought we could throw in a little obligatory T and A, like
those babes in wrestling who hold up the round cards, prancing
around with breasts like Winnebagos. We could've put her in a
bikini, or even topless, and had her hold up title cards: *Gladiators
of Fire.*"

Kenyon made a face. "People can get tits anywhere. We'll never compete with that. Violence is the new porn."

"Risk and danger. Uh-huh."

"Cruelty," Kenyon added

"Straight-up brutality."

"Trans-gression." They traded a soft high five.

"Man, if we can make our ownselves sick with this stuff, we *know* we're onto something," Rod concluded.

In the last scene of *Dangerous Games I* they had filled a small bathroom floor wall-to-wall with yellow baby chicks and hired girls in stiletto heels to walk around on them as Kenyon filmed the scene down at heel level. Rod and both girls had eventually thrown up into the bathtub. Kenyon had had a second Yoo-hoo and all the upchucking had just given him a new idea for a vomiting sequence—finding somebody who could barf on command and setting him loose on municipal buses, movie theaters, jazz bars.

On the dark drive back to town, Jack Liffey watched the chaparral slide past and mused about what it would be like growing up in that isolated little town and how circumscribed your life and ideas might become, knowing only TV and maybe books. He'd met enough people in the big city, though, who couldn't have found North America on a big world map so he wondered if it mattered all that much where you grew up. Maybe any life, lived anywhere— even Clyde's—was as complex in its own way as some symphony, with an expert conductor hammering away at your soul with his baton.

"You pick up anything I missed?" he asked as she drove.

"How would I know what you missed?" she replied.

"Don't get philosophical on me. I'm too tired."

"Barbara was trying to understand Luisa in terms of her own loneliness and longings," Gloria Ramirez said. "That business about leaving a trail through life may have nothing to do with Luisa."

"You're a suspicious woman, aren't you?"

"What do you mean?"

"That was one opening the girl gave us that had possibilities, and you're ready to reject it out of hand."

"Yes, Jack. I'm a party pooper. I've seen too many girls chase too many rainbows. We've got some hard facts to work with. Little Deer, if such a person exists. The name Taboots. And the porn industry, which is mostly within a five mile radius of one alley in Van Nuys."

They approached the Mojave airfield where more than hundred airliners had been mothballed ever since the downturn in air travel after September 11—747s, MD-11s, L-1011s, 737s, even some odd ones he didn't know, probably European Airbuses. Most of their logos and company colors had been painted out—avoiding bad advertising, he guessed—and big plastic plugs covered their engine nacelles like coffee can lids. All in all it was a bizarre sight, like a toy store for giants.

"You seem pretty up on the porn biz," he said.

"Cops know these things. My first post out of the Academy I worked in the North Hollywood Division. That's got about three-quarters of the porn merchants in the known universe."

"I don't even know what I really think about pornography," Jack Liffey said. "I've never bothered with it except as it sucked in a runaway I was after. But in a way, it's just pictures of people loving each other. I suppose it reminds lonely people what it's like. What's really wrong with that?"

She shook her head. "You can say that, but that's the end product. I see girls being exploited, exploiting themselves, if you like—treated like random receptacles for men. That girl mentioned the gangbang thing. A few years ago there was a trend for gangbanging—some girl taking on over a hundred men. Think of the risk."

"Yeah, okay. But don't they make some films just about couples making love?"

"Jesus, Jack, I don't know. I was three months in Vice, and I know there were biker rape films, and animal fuck films, and pretend snuff films and every kind of degradation you can imagine. I never made a study of it, but all I wanted was out of Vice."

He was willing to grant her all that, though it seemed terribly defensive somehow, so he fell silent. This was a question that put into play some of the real differences between men and women, he thought.

Just then they came around the dogleg turn of Highway 14, past the airfield again, and he noticed another difference between men and women. They were passing the last mothballed jets on the immense airfield, and she hadn't even glanced at them. No man on earth could drive past over a hundred immobilized airplanes without a hint of curiosity or wonder.

"Okay, I thought I was the hardnose," Jack Liffey said, trying to make peace.

"I'm hardnose about girls being used and hurt. I always will be. I never had much of a childhood, and I think every kid should have one."

"Jesus, you think I want to imagine Maeve getting caught up in some racket like that? I just want perspective on it. Sexual urges are pretty deep in us. Maybe some of the women in the industry can deal with it, make their money and get out, without their psyches going ballistic."

"Hundreds of guys at a go?"

He winced. "Okay, but there's excess everywhere. How many cops did it take to subdue Rodney King?"

"Let's not get started on that. You think one way because you're a civilian, but those of us on the job are always going to feel a little different about the King thing. We've had too many big guys stagger back to their feet and pull out a knife."

He held up the flat of his hand. It wasn't something he wanted to argue.

"Being a cop has its trials, Jack. I can't walk into a party and get introduced without some jerkoff jumping to his feet and shouting, 'I didn't do it!' And everybody you approach, absolutely everybody, starts lying to you."

"Including me?"

She looked hard at him. "You will."

All of a sudden, he felt as lonely as Barbara Thigpen—sitting beside this woman he lived with and didn't seem to know very well.

A chill took his spine. Maybe this one wouldn't work out either, he thought—a sudden uneasiness that extinguished a lot of the relief he'd been feeling for several months. He was abruptly, and against his will, very angry at her and had to rein in an urge to turn spiteful.

It wasn't that he hadn't ever lied in his life, or wouldn't again, but she sounded like she'd never be willing to give him a break, never let him relax from some model of perfection she carried around with her. It was the gold standard or nothing. It's no wonder, he thought unkindly, that she'd been alone when they met.

They drove in silence for a while, and eventually she reached over and rested a hand on his thigh. "It shouldn't really eat at you so bad, Jack. It's just the way we're forced to be on the job. I thought you were tough enough to put up with me."

It wasn't quite enough for him to feel forgiving. "So did I," he said.

They rode a while longer, and for several miles he thought of Maeve. Then something dark lifted from his spirit for no reason that he could discern. "Oh, damn, here I've gone and sulked through half the alphabet streets. I can't challenge you to play Maeve's name game." They had just shot by K Street on the Antelope Valley Freeway.

"What's the game?"

"The next letter street. You have to name a tree or a flower beginning with that letter. Or an actress, a city in Europe. Whatever."

"We're coming up to L," she said. "Let's name felonies."

He laughed. "How about just character flaws? That'll give me a chance to play." He wasn't sure she saw the taunt in it.

"Okay. Come on."

"I've got one. We both say ours when we hit the L overpass."

They reached the overpass, a forlorn bridge with no connecting roads on either end. The whole alphabet of mile-apart overpasses had been a conceit of the days when L.A. was planning to build a giant regional airport out here, 80 miles from LAX, but it had never happened.

"Lying was too easy," she said. "Lethargy."

"Lacerating wit," he said.

She frowned but gave it to him. By the time the letter streets petered out at S—with spite and sanctimoniousness—they seemed to be friends again.

"Tell me about *Wuthering Heights,* Jack. I've never read it, and it might be important if Luisa reacted so much to it."

"Do you mind a little run-up?"

"Of course not. I could stop for a late bite, too."

"There's a nice restaurant and saloon at the top of the grade. Not far, I'll tell you." He thought about it for a while and decided he really was over his snit. "When I was in the radar trailer in Thailand, there wasn't much to do, so I decided to perfect my education. They would chopper in damn near anything you wanted, so, methodically, I went through at least one book by every great nineteenth-century writer. Every culture . . . Well, the major cultures. I didn't read any Bulgarians.

"I started with the French and pretty soon discovered that they all wrote the same book. It was astonishing, really. *Père Goriot, The Red and the Black, Nana.* A callow youth comes to Paris from the provinces looking for money and social position and sex. And he gets it all. It's a subject that's just inconceivable in Victorian England. The English novels were much more polite and prudish. They were mostly about disappointments and misalliances or about kids being oppressed, Dickens. Stiff upper lip. All but one of them. There was this blinding flash, like a meteor across the whole of English literature. The passion in *Wuthering Heights* just burned to the ground any book you put next to it. Intensity—betrayal and longing and revenge and love turning to hatred. It's not what they call a guy book, but even a jaded techie draftee was shaken a bit by it, after all those books about good manners."

"So what would it do to a provincial Indian girl?"

"A girl who has no reliable resources for even puppy love . . . " He made a face, as if he'd smelled something bad. "Don't blame literature. This kid is already primed to shoot herself straight through the heart. Unless she's tougher than we think. Some kids are amazingly resilient."

"I'd rather not count on it."

"Then let's find her before *Wuthering Heights* strikes."

Dear Diary,

Keith has been making me feel safe. He said last night that he respected me too much to sleep with me until we was united in a bond of blood so this morning we both cut our hands & signed our names on a piece of paper in our own blood & then we put the note in a wine bottle & launched it afloat into the ocean near the beach house where we stayed all night for a party I didnt like too much. He said that this moment marked the precious time that we will always remember at the beginning of our new relationship.

But Keith can be moody too & after breakfast at a little place on the coast he got cold and angry all at once & looked at me hard. I thought about that moment all day & could not figure out what I had done unless it was when I mentioned how I didn't really like the kinds of jobs I had to do for Rod. I was wondering if I would ever have as happy a morning ever again in my life or if it was all over but then his mood changed & he was sweet again.

SIX

Our Relationship Is Teething

"Can I help you, Maevie?" Her mother's voice came softly through the flimsy door.

"No, I'll do it myself." She had locked herself into the upstairs bathroom and was on her knees beside the toilet with her jeans down and her shirt off. The illustrated instructions they'd given her were taped on the wall in front of her. The transparent bag that dangled from her side was almost full and pretty much the color she expected, somewhere between light brown and gray, the color, in fact, of liquid shit.

You can get used to anything, she told herself. There was a clip on the bottom of the bag which she slid off gingerly and let the contents drain noisily into the toilet. That's an interesting smell, she thought, wrinkling her nose. It was more like cowshit than human for some reason. She reclipped the bag and could have left off there, but she wanted to see everything.

Making a face, both at the general tenderness she felt and the idea of what she was doing, she peeled the bag gently off and saw her new stoma for the first time. After cleaning it up with a wet rag and being surprised that there was almost no sensation in the thing—it looked like a big wrinkly nipple that had drifted preposterously across her body to the wrong place. There was a kind of medical gasket around it, where she would reattach the bag.

"Jesus," she said. "All right, if you and I are going to be together for a while, you need a name. *Squirt* popped into her head, but it was too cute, and she dropped it immediately. She thought of an old boyfriend who was snubbing her, but Dick wasn't a very good idea either. She'd just read *The Tin Drum* and decided Oskar would be perfect. "Okay, Oskar, you and me are going to get along. You can refuse to talk and you can beat your little drum whenever you see something you don't like."

Oskar chose that moment to fart loudly, and a foul smell emanated through the bathroom.

Maeve shut her eyes, counted to ten, and began doing up the bag again.

"Hey, Beto."

"*Qué hubo,* Thumb?"

Beto Alvarez was in his messy office in the *Centro,* his feet up on the beat-up old steel desk, reading a book, with all the kids out front playing ping-pong or caroms or chess. The clatter and roar of so much play was audible even down the long corridor. Thumb sat down on a rickety folding chair.

"*Aquí nomás.* I'm reading that textbook, like you said, I got up to the Hayes-something deal, in the South."

"Tilden."

"Yeah, that's it. Where they fucked over the niggers, huh?"

Beto brought his feet to the floor and sat up straight in that earnest way he always had.

"Do me a favor, Thumb. Say blacks. You may not be thinking beyond the *barrio* right now, but if all of us people of color stay off in our own *vecinos* and dis each other all the time—you know, it's always niggers and gooks and japs and *we're* greasers or spics, that's us, *esse*—we gonna stay weak. Those Bushes and their friends gonna do a Hayes-Tilden on us all over again."

"Seems like they doin' it to us already, *carnal.*"

Beto got that crafty look in his eye. "So tell me how they're doin' it, Thumb. How are the rich *gabachos* screwing you right now?"

"I don't know—they send the big blue gang to beat on us. They keep all the good stuff and the good jobs for theirself."

"You all ready to take a job programming computers? Maybe put on a white coat and cure somebody's disease?"

"Man."

"Do you remember Chairman Mao?"

"He was that fat Chinese Communist guy."

"*Simón,* good. I'm not saying he was the greatest. Dude had a lot of problems, but he said some good things. One was, 'No investigation, no right to speak.' When you're ready to tell a bunch of those angry kids out there *exactly* what they need to do to change things, then you're ready. Knowledge is power, my friend. You can't have too much knowledge."

"*Chingao,* I'll keep reading on that book, and you keep ranking on me, just like this, and if I don't beat you to death first or shoot you in the *cojones,* we get over."

Beto looked like he wanted to laugh but decided against it. He just fastened his eyes on Thumb, keeping his gaze fixed in a benign deadpan.

Finally Thumb grinned. "I got a favor to ask," he said softly.

"Uh-huh."

Thumb produced a small box, the size of a book, wrapped round and round with silver duct tape. "Don't ask me no questions and keep this for me."

Beto examined it skeptically. "Promise me this isn't *yesca* or *coca. No drogas.*"

"I swear on *mi madre. Absolutamente no es drogas.*"

Beto reached out and took it, weighing it for a moment in his hand. "It's heavy, man."

"*Carnal,* if you're going to X-ray it or shit, just give it back. It's a favor to see if you really trust me and I can trust you."

"*Qué pues.* I probably shouldn't do this, but you've got a lot of potentials. Okay. Consider it our secret."

"*Viva la raza.*"

"*Si,* man. *Viva el pueblo.*"

"We don't hire a lot of *guys* here, not unless you can really hold your wood."

Jack Liffey knew exactly what he meant, but why give him the satisfaction? "Oak or mahogany?"

"Very funny."

Jack Liffey wasn't sure what he'd expected—probably a fat old man in suspenders smoking a cigar—but it was practically a kid sitting at the little card table in an inner room. He had a bad complexion with lumps everywhere, a spot band-aid over what was probably a recently popped zit on the side of his nose. A long sideboard made up of industrial shelving beside him held cardboard banker's boxes and upright magazine files full of papers plus a very old computer with a small greenish monitor. It looked like the whole business could be cleared out in about five minutes, or just abandoned if it came to that.

"Hell, at my age I'm lucky when I get it up at all," Jack Liffey said. He set his business card down in front of the kid. The card was becoming embarrassing. An old girlfriend who'd run a print shop had made a thousand up for him years ago and not only did it have a big eyeball on it, like something in the movies, he had to write in his new phone number by hand. "I'm looking for a runaway girl. If you'd be kind enough to look in your files."

The office of Intercontinental Talent was up a metal staircase only a little fancier than a fire escape, on a short dead-end street in an industrial area of Van Nuys. Still, the sign on the door had looked respectable enough. There had been no receptionist in the empty waiting room, just a few bus station benches and a big sign: *Models: First fill out the form, THEN "ring" the bell and wait.* He could identify no particular reason that irony should attach to the verb, which referred to an ordinary pushbutton like a doorbell— and he assumed it was just another instance of the indiscriminate proliferation of quotation marks like "fresh" fish and "gourmet" salads that had crept onto menus everywhere.

The only wall art facing the plastic benches was a fairly demure poster of a large-breasted woman in a cocktail gown receiving a statuette. It wasn't one of the awards he knew—the Oscar or the Golden Globes. Maybe something the porn industry had invented to mimic the mainstream awards. The Randy or the Roger.

"What's this lost girl's name?" the kid at the card table asked him.

"Luisa Wilson. She's a Native American about eighteen. She'd have been in here in the last two weeks."

"*About* eighteen, like, doesn't cut it in this biz, bro. Sticky, the underage thing. Remember the whole Traci Lords thing."

"She's eighteen, no worries. Long dark hair. Very striking."

He shook his head. "Nah. They're *all* striking, believe me, but that one ain't been in."

"Could you just check your records, as a favor to me."

"Whoa, dude. No strongarm, okay. I tell you, I ain't seen her, I ain't seen her."

"You do sign up women for sex films?"

"We prefer to call it the adult entertainment business. And we usually say girls, you know? No dis intended."

"Son, I don't care what you call it. This girl has a mother who's worried about her, and I just want to talk to her. I'm not here to make trouble for her or anyone else in the sex business. No dis intended."

The boy frowned and got his back up a bit. "Hell, man, I'm proud of our business. You take your regular Hollywood movies, now—they put a girl who's sexually active in the story, even a little bit, they got to find a way to kill her off in the first reel or make her pay for it somehow. She doesn't get the desirable guy or the good job or the happy life. She's got to be punished for liking dick. Our girls like it right out in the open, and they get to live all the way through the show."

Jack Liffey laughed. "I never thought about it that way. As long as they don't get AIDS."

Clouds crossed the boy's brow. "We're real responsible about that. They get monthly tests and a lot of shoots use rubbers now."

"I don't need a deposition. Let's say Luisa Wilson didn't come here. Where else would she go in town looking to get into the adult business?" Adult business: he could give the kid that much.

"There's really only four agencies that serve the professional producers, but there's plenty of amateurs, too, these days. Everybody thinks it only takes an old VHS camera and a couple kids willing to screw to make some hot movie and make a million bucks. But the product usually looks like shit, and they always get beat trying to distribute. That end's all sewed up. Still, they keep on trying, like swarms of bees trying to get into the honey tree. There's wannabe adult business all over the place. But if your girl got smart, she only came to us or one of the other places."

He gave Jack Liffey a flyer with the addresses of three more modeling agencies along with some general advice on AIDS and staying out of trouble on the streets and how to find a place to bed down for those just off the bus. It looked like something they'd hire winos to hand out to lost-looking kids on Hollywood Boulevard. He found himself folding the flyer a couple of times before putting it into his pocket, as if it might soil his shirt.

"Do you know the name Little Deer?"

He whistled. "Jeez, do I? She was the real thing. Like a Marilyn Monroe or something. She's retired now, far as I know."

"Do you know how I'd find her?"

"Naw, but I think she directed a few times at the end of her career. The smart ones do. You might try the Liberty of Speech Coalition." The effort of being helpful was starting to show.

"What's that?"

"Some of the old-timers financed a lobbying and legal group to look after their interests. Every redneck that gets elected D.A. anywhere in America tries to beat up on the biz to score points with his local Talibans."

The bell buzzed, and the boy perked up.

"You ever performed?" Jack Liffey asked him.

"Aw, man, take a good look at me. All I could be is a stunt dick, and I'm no woodsman." He winked. "But I get a little on the side now and then, so don't worry."

Jack Liffey just wanted to get away from that office and take a long shower to wash off anything that might have stuck to him.

"Thanks." He reclaimed his card. For some superstitious reason, he didn't want his name hanging around that office. In the waiting room now there was a very insecure-looking girl in a falling-off bright blue sundress. She had obviously augmented breasts, and clutched a clipboard that held the information form. She smiled hopefully at him as he came out.

"I'm nobody at all, hon."

He almost turned back at the door to suggest she go home to Iowa, but it wouldn't help and there were probably a hundred like her arriving every day.

"Jack! Long time no see!" Babs leaned out the kitchen window, looking a bit less like Veronica Lake after the two kids in quick succession. She still had the long silver hair, though.

"Hi, Babs. Is Chris here?"

"He's out in the back. He's tending the computers and kids."

They had made the detached garage of the little Lakewood house into their computer room. It was quite a retrenchment from the glory days when Chris had lived in a huge place in the Hollywood Hills and co-owned a computer game company called Propeller-Heads. The big shakeout in the game industry had killed all that. He knocked beside the open door.

"Jack, good to see you. Come on, come on."

The former garage was half filled with a profusion of old computers wired together, and Chris Johnson carried a baby in his arms, while a two-year-old puttered with some toy trucks on the floor. Jack Liffey noticed that the reset buttons of all the computers had been removed or covered over.

"The online nursery business died?"

"Just about all online business died. Except porn, of course. I set up Web sites for folks now, and host them. Babs is studying architecture."

The boy on the floor started making thut-thut-thut machinegun noises.

"How would you like a jackliffey.com?" he suggested.

"I don't think so, Chris. I don't have a computer. I don't even have a cell phone. It's good to see you and Babs are still together."

Babs had been in a lesbian relationship when Jack Liffey had first dragged her into helping with one of his jobs, and he had introduced the two of them, without any ulterior motives whatever. He had to admit Chris Johnson was a pretty charming character—he had the sort of buoyant energy and confidence that always attracted dogs and children—and he wasn't bad looking in the bargain. He was so blond he was almost transparent, and he still had the football body he'd once worked at in order to play wide receiver for a college team. Babs had startled Jack Liffey back then by latching onto Chris almost immediately, abandoning in the process a long-time girlfriend. Jack Liffey had been afraid he'd get in dutch with the whole lesbian world, but nobody seemed to object.

The baby started to wail, and Chris tested the diaper, then offered a bottle. That did the trick.

"I've learned to type one-handed." He sat and demonstrated at the keyboard of what must have been his primary computer. It was amazing, the blur of his right hand, while the left cradled and fed the baby. "Multitasking," he said. "I can even tuck a phone in my ear at the same time. I hear you're shacked up with a cop out in East Los. How's that working out?"

"It's interesting. At our age, we've both had enough disappointments in life that we're still a bit cautious."

"You mean she's about to kick you out."

Jack Liffey laughed. "I wouldn't say that. Our relationship is just teething." He thought of mentioning Maeve's drive-by shooting, but he just didn't want to go into it. "I like Gloria a lot. Trusting takes time."

"You never went all that long in between women, my man."

"Maybe that was my problem. What about you? At the time, I didn't bet an awful lot on you and Babs hanging in there."

"These little guys make a big difference." The boy with the trucks was now making airplane swooping sounds. "But they're worth every worry line. They make you look at life fresh."

He didn't want to get sidetracked into the glories of fatherhood. He had Maeve, and she would do fine. "I have a favor to ask."

"Of course. You never show up unexpectedly to play handball."

Jack Liffey pulled up an old ladderback chair. "I went to a sporting goods store one time looking for a handball, and, you know, the guy there said they stopped carrying them because they were the number one theft item. Isn't that a great concept? Eventually they'll eliminate the number two and number three, and then the store will have nothing worth stealing at all, and maybe all sports will die."

"I forgot you were an anti-fan."

"It's not important." Jack Liffey handed him the flyer—explaining who he was looking for. "I visited that first talent agency on the list, and already I want to run myself through a sheepdip full of disinfectant. Can you hack into their databases and look for her name for me, or anyone else who sounds like an American Indian and signed up in the last two weeks?"

"Child's play. I'll check out some other sources, too, and call you this evening."

"Thanks, Chris." Jack Liffey squatted down by the little boy and picked up a plastic airplane he hadn't noticed. It was a P-40, with very slight indentations in the gray plastic to suggest the toothy Flying Tiger grin. If there had been a decal, it was long gone. It was strange how seductively beautiful the old prop warplanes could be. "This is great."

"From my own youth."

"The last time we were on the same side as the Chinese."

"Yeah, but they make all our consumer products now. We don't dare piss them off. We'd have to start over at the Stone Age."

Jack Liffey flew the fighter around a bit and tried out his own thut-thut-thut. Little Vance Johnson won the dogfight with brute force, crashing a dump truck into him.

"I hear you did good today," Keith hollered over the windrush in the Miata as he drove her over Topanga and down to the Malibu beach house. "You're a quick learner."

She was back in comfortable clothes, jeans, and an old pearl-snap cowboy shirt she liked, with her B-4 bag in her new room. She saw no reason to shout back to him, especially as he wasn't asking anything much, and she just felt like settling in with the flow of everything, him, the drive, the job. She loved the yellow chaparral along the road, broken up by sumacs, tree tobacco, a few coast oaks—multimillion dollar homes set way up on their own roads.

She stared at one of those homes for a moment, and though sums of money in the tens of millions didn't mean very much to her, she decided that, put together, all the homes she'd ever known in Owens wouldn't trade for one fancy six-car garage like the ones they were passing.

Ten million here and ten million there and, pretty soon, you're talking real money. She grinned. One of the girls had said that at break.

"I got the beach house from surplus inventory of this company I used to work with, picking up failed savings and loans. It didn't cost me a penny, and, technically, it's invisible to the tax people. Life is all about deals, kid. You gotta get unblinkered about stuff."

He seemed too young to be talking like that, but they came down a hill and turned onto the coast highway. It was a really breathtaking moment for an inland girl, the water blue as a robin's egg, choppy with a handful of sailboats as the sun was about to go into red couds, and the breakers rolling up and crashing right against the edge of the road. Seeing the Pacific always made her feel an outsider but more so like when it was getting dark, like the other night at the party.

"If the Levine boys are waiting, don't say a word."

She didn't know who the Levine boys were, but it didn't matter. She wouldn't be inclined to say much to anybody. Soon they came to a row of beach houses right up against the road, only the garages visible, the houses trapped between asphalt and surf. A Porsche was parked diagonally in front of their garage, and two lanky men with no hair at all glared at the Miata as they approached. One of the men looked Asian but tall for an Oriental. Keith did a funny whoop-whoop with the accelerator and came to a stop as the men sauntered over.

"Hey, *thong miao*," the Asian guy said.

"Fuck you, too," Keith said evenly.

"You better be stone cool, you welching cunt," the other one said.

Luisa had never heard a man called a cunt before. It seemed weird. The Asian man pulled back a cowboy vest to show that he had a big black automatic pistol in his waist. Looking at the pistol made Luisa feel sleepy.

"I can get plenty of guns, dipshit," Keith said.

"If this place had deer," the other said languidly, looking over the beach houses, "they'd put out a cocaine saltlick."

"We get deer off the hills. I got your money right here." He tossed them a fat roll of bills held by a rubber band and waited while they flipped through it.

"You're my absolute picture of a big time operator, Tweak," Keith said, "just the cat's hairball. Next time leave the muscle home, or you can do business with my whole crew of angry spades."

"Next time, be on time, jerkoff. Levine waits for no man." They got into their Porsche, started it noisily and zipped away without looking back into traffic, causing a pickup truck on the highway to fishtail and honk.

He took her inside and told her to hang out or fix herself some food or whatever, while he did some work in the back of the house. There was a deck over the water that was just stupendous, and she opened the rolling glass window and went out to watch the waves for a long time. They made her feel good, as if in time they might just wear away everything she didn't like about the world. The rising and falling roar was immensely soothing. The sun finally went down into a line of cloud over the water, with lights coming on in a few tall buildings down along the curved coastline, probably Santa Monica.

After a while, he opened the sliding door to say he had to go out, and he'd be gone until late. When it got too cold to stay outside looking at the lights, she came in and watched a huge flat screen TV for a while. But there was nothing on she liked, and the videos lying around were all porn and chop-socki, which didn't interest her, so she went into her nest and went back to reading.

She was asleep on the white leather sofa when he came back. He was on something, his eyes flitting around restlessly, but he took her hand and hauled her back to a huge bed in the back room. She undressed and let him do what he wanted to her because that was the way it worked, and she may as well not have been there while he bonked away. Just before he came, he broke a little glass tube under his nose and sniffed something and cried out. Then he rolled off and sighed.

"Kid, wake me up with your mouth at nine." And then he was snoring like a cartoon.

> Dear Diary,
> It's so hard to have a love affair with one of these hell-bent types. I had such longings & hopes for this man & me but he did me wrong almost at once. I slept & wanted to be taken off to some magical place where everybody was nice but even in my dream the men were mean & asked for things from me all the time. They would make fun of me when I got lost in this big city & I didnt know the words they used. I think Keith was one of them.
> My crime was I didn't wake Keith up early enough for him, as he said to, & he was very mad & as punishment he tore my book in two that I was reading & threw both halfs off the porch onto the sand. It didn't matter that I had set out a bowl & the cereal for him & made coffee. He wasnt nice to me one minute until he needed me to get in the car. My heart is cracked & I feel so dejected & alone again. Help me, Diary.

SEVEN

A Little Hotbed of Tranquility

The rear fender of the bicycle had fins hacked off an old Cadillac, bullet taillights and all, and they were lashed on crudely with wire and sticking out diagonally. The little trailer platform behind rode low between what looked like blue plastic hot wheels, and on the trailer stood the object that his eye had lit upon before all the rest—a brightly painted five- foot tall Virgin of Guadalupe, complete with her full body golden aura. The old Latino in charge was pedaling his mistress hard up the slight incline. It seemed a lot of weight to be hauling around, physically and metaphysically.

"*Buenas días, Virgen,*" Jack Liffey offered out his car window as the statue's fixed eyes passed fleetingly over him. There were probably far more appropriate salutations, but he hadn't learned them yet.

A radio hung off the handlebars playing loud *rancheras,* some sad complaint about lost love, the Latino equivalent of country and western.

He could practically have walked to the police substation from home, but he wanted to go on to the Valley to make another stab at finding Little Deer. He was there because Sgt. Padilla had left him a phone message that morning to come in and look at some mug shots.

Padilla himself wasn't visible as Jack Liffey entered, but a younger uniformed officer stood at a table dropping an assortment of items into plastic baggies and storing them in a carton—a watch, lidless mustard jar, a hearing aid, a glass globe with a snowman in it. He gave the snowglobe a good joggle to watch it snow before storing it away.

"Is Sgt. Padilla around?" Jack Liffey asked.

The officer nodded over his shoulder. He had taken the snowglobe back out of its baggie and was shaking it again. Undoubtedly, he had never seen *Citizen Kane.*

"Liffey! Back here."

Padilla was in a barren interrogation room, tidying up what looked like several pages out of a family photo album. The sleeves were stiff and opaque brown with cut-out windows that showed only faces, presumably to cover any captions and conceal names.

"Have a seat. I'll be ready for you in a minute. How are you and our Gloria getting along?"

Now that he was publicly living with a cop, Jack Liffey recognized that maybe they all thought of him as part of the extended cop family. Perhaps it would be appropriate to be a trifle friendlier to all lawmen than he usually was, but in this particular case he was still having trouble figuring out the man's attitude. Anyway, he knew Gloria's and his relationship was their own business.

"Just great," he answered.

"No you're not. Nobody gets along great with Ramirez."

He remembered the way he'd put it to Chris Johnson the day before and decided to try it again. "Our relationship is teething. We'll be okay."

The cop brought his eyes up to look at him without moving his head. "Suit yourself. How's your Spanish? I hear you're doing a course at City."

Jack Liffey was a little disturbed to be under so much observation. It was as if the entire LAPD and their loved ones made up a small gossipy town. "Mi espagnol es *muy* shitty. Can you believe I wasted my time taking Latin in high school? So now I can talk to very old priests and pharmacists."

Sgt. Padilla scowled. "Why the hell did you do that?"

"All the college prep kids did back then. I don't know, it was a survival of the old classical education days, Greek and Latin, or maybe we were afraid to go into the Spanish classes and compete with all those native speakers." Racism might have had a bit to do with it too, he thought, but he wasn't about to mention that.

"You'd have found out a lot of those kids named Sanchez didn't speak Spanish so good. They could talk about going to *el churcho* in their *carro,* but that was about it. Some of these *cholos* get a real shock when they do down to TJ and get laughed at."

"Es una lingua hermosa," Jack Liffey said diplomatically. "I'm only doing three hours a week, so it's slow. I guess I know just enough to get myself in trouble."

"Well, here's a phrase for you. *Estirar la pata.* Literally, it means stretch the paw. It's about the same as saying kick the bucket. That's where you're gonna end up if you're not careful with these guys."

He tossed three sleeves across the table, each with about a dozen mug shots.

"I eliminated a lot of unlikely bangers, guys who live in Compton or Riverside. But these fit your description."

Jack Liffey saw him immediately, on the first sheet, but didn't let on. Padilla had obviously chosen all the ones with unusual mustaches, droopy Pancho Villas, pointy imperials, bushy shrubs hanging over the lip, mustaches with goatees, and several other T-mustaches like his man.

He kept on talking to Padilla aimlessly while he looked the photos over, as if scrutinizing closely. "Did you choose to work in this division?"

"I grew up in San Antonio, but I like this part of L.A. It's got history. You know, the White Fence gang has been here since 1920?"

"You didn't have gangs in Texas?"

"Oh, sure, but it wasn't the same. L.A. is the gang capital of the universe, and we're exporting to every country in Latin America now. The blacks are colonizing Kansas and Ohio with little sets of Bloods and Crips, and Mara Salvatrucha controls El Salvador."

"It's drugs."

"Sure it is. But you tell me the secret to stopping drugs."

"Jobs would help." He tried to push the sleeve up against the photo a bit to see if there was a name or address associated with the photo, but the stiff cardboard wouldn't budge. "I've narrowed it to five. Can you arrange a lineup so I could see them in person?"

"Point them out."

He choose all the T-mustaches, and one that was almost the same with a blunt imperial. Padilla put Post-its on the photos he pointed to.

"I'll see what I can do. We'll have to do it over at Hollenbeck. They have a lineup room with a one-way."

"Thanks."

"How's your kid doing?"

"She'll make it. She's tough, but she has to wear a shit-bag on her side for a while, and no one her age is going to like that."

"Beats *estirar la pata,* man."

"You said it."

He realized he hadn't heard from Chris Johnson for some reason, so he stopped to call from a pay phone at a gas station on the edge of Boyle Heights. Functioning pay phones were getting harder and harder to find, but he couldn't really afford a cell.

"Dude, is that really a pay phone?"

"Sure."

"Hold on."

Jack Liffey heard a little symphony of electronic sounds, and then the noise broke off abruptly as his three quarters chimed down into the coin return slot.

"I don't think I want to know how you did that."

"You don't. I left a message a while ago on your home machine. It took me longer than I thought because one of those nude model outfits actually turns their computers off most of the time. You can't beat that for a firewall. I'm afraid there's no record on your kid or anybody like her in the last two weeks, I'm sorry."

A huge high SUV, with tire wells like bomb shelters, pulled

alongside the phone and throbbed away as the driver gave him the evil eye. Probably waiting for a drug call.

"Could you do another hunt? Don't tax yourself, but there was a porn star a few years back called Little Deer. I think she was a Sioux."

"Yeah, a real beauty. She did some high quality stuff at the tail end of that era when they still shot on film."

"You heard of her?"

"You probably don't even know who Bettie Page is, do you?"

"Nope, but Betty Boop and I used to hang out."

The driver in the tall SUV looked at his watch ostentatiously, gave Jack Liffey the finger, and then abruptly gusted away.

"Tsk, tsk. A guy in your position should keep up on the popular culture."

"That's why I've got people like you and Mike Lewis to keep me briefed. I can concentrate on Derrida and Baudrillard instead of P. Diddy."

"Okay, okay. You want an address for Little Deer, if she's still in town?"

"That's the idea."

"Consider it done. Hey, Jack. What's the only mammal in all creation that can't jump, can't ever lift itself off the surface of the earth?"

"A roadkill possum."

"Very funny. The elephant. I saw it in one of the kids' books. They just don't have the muscle to boost all that weight."

"Bye, Chris."

He brought the Miata to a screeching stop in front of the Lovey-Dove building at about 10:30 and reached across her to push the door open. "Don't get too used to this job, kid. You're destined for bigger things. If you ever feel the need to strap up and tuck a nice ladysize piece in that little purse, protect yourself, let me know." Now Keith seemed to be being nice to her again.

"No thanks."

"Never know what creeps hang around this biz. Here." He stuck a yellow Dilaudid tablet in her hand. "Takes the edge off and gets you happied up for work. See you this evening. Don't believe everything those cunts in there tell you. Half of them are going downhill fast."

She got out, and he switched his attention away instantly, speed-dialing a cell call as he drove out of the lot. She'd always been sensitive to the way a man behaved in those moments when he left her. She wanted her boyfriends to look back once, wave, acknowledge her somehow. But with all Keith's other deficiencies, this tiny offense hardly mattered.

It was an old stucco house with blacked-out windows right next to a mini-mall that contained a dry cleaners, a tattoo parlor, and a doughnut shop. She had a few dollars and thought of going over for coffee and a doughnut in peace and quiet, but she remembered there was free coffee inside. Then she thought of just walking off, taking a bus as far as her money would carry her, and looking for work again. Her dreams about Keith had been rudely disspelled, as she had told her diary that morning. But she didn't even have a change of clothes, which were all back at his beach house.

Funny how much easier it usually was just to go along with guys, she thought. She wondered if she ran into some guy about to shoot her in the head if she'd just smile and let him do it. Time to be a grownup, Taboots honey, and take a little charge of your life.

The plastic plaque on the door said *Lovey-Dove: Authorized Access Only.* She stepped in and immediately heard the sound of the keyboards and a soft-voiced cursing from the back. She turned left towards the kitchen. One of the girls, a light-skinned black girl, overweight and over made-up, was refilling a coffee mug that had a cross on it with little rays coming out and said *In Case of Rapture, Catch this Cup.*

"Hi," Luisa said.

"You sure got yo'self banker's hours, hon."

She shrugged. "I got no car. Keith's in charge. For now."

"You best get that transmogrified soon as you can. First he be turning you out for Jap business fairs and a little throw-in fucking and then he'sa want you on the danger games thing. Don't be doing that, if you know what's good fo you. I gotta get back."

"Thanks." The woman left and Luisa sniffed the pot, stale and without chicory, so she gave up on the coffee. She hid the Dilaudid tab in the cupboard behind a big bottle of generic aspirin. Then she found her black skimpies from yesterday in the changing room, but it took a lot of staring at them before she decided to put them on.

It was a nondescript office building in Northridge, and the hand-lettered sign on the door might have been an allusion to the big earthquake of 1994. But then again it might not: *If this room's a-rockin', don't come knockin'.*

There was an official nameplate, too, like something cut out with a woodburner kit by a kid, that said *Adult Entertainment Coalition* and *Emergency Committee for Free Speech.* Jack Liffey knocked once and went straight in. Here there was a receptionist, with more blond hair than a Swedish circus and a scoop-cut frilly blouse that hinted at breasts bigger than his head. She had a few piercings, but mostly in the normal places—ears and the side of a nostril—at least as far as he could see. He thought involuntarily of other places he'd found studs and rings and bars. *What you don't see can't hurt you,* he decided, *as long as you keep not seeing it.* Thank God Gloria stayed with the earlobes.

He decided to go for broke. "My name is Jack Liffey. I'm a detective." He showed her the phony badge and wallet he'd got through the mail from the World Wisdom College of East Orange, New Jersey. "I'd like to speak to whoever's in charge."

"That'd be Mr. Wingfoot Peace. Could I inform him of the nature of your business?"

"Not unless you're clairvoyant."

She wrinkled up her brow but seemed to decide to let it remain a mystery. She depressed an old-fashioned intercom lever. "Mr. Peace, I believe there's a detective here to see you."

There was a grunt and a grudged burst of static. A tiny voice seemed to say; "Don't tip over the outhouse."

"He means, wait a sec," she explained. She winked. "He might have been asleep just a wee. He's got to put his nose on."

She didn't explain this, and he didn't ask. "Have you been working here long?"

"About a month. They promised I can move on to the Vegas office where they run the awards show."

"I saw a picture of that award the other day. What do they call it?"

"The Eros. It's got a little boy with a little pee-pee on him."

"But all in good taste."

"I should think so." She winked again. She'd do fine in Vegas, he thought, a city where subtlety was not highly valued. She had a kind of radiance, though, that made up for a lot, and she seemed quite content with who she was.

Jack Liffey was about to sit when the door opened and a tall man in a powder blue cowboy suit peered out. Jack Liffey noticed immediately that something was wrong with his nose, too pink and rather artificial in some way, though not as bad as the silver nose Lee Marvin's ostensible twin had worn in *Cat Ballou*. He tried to imagine how someone could completely lose a nose.

"Come in, sir. Drop down, cool out."

Jack Liffey followed him inside. There were yellow lateral files everywhere, as if storing a century's worth of bank records, and it was all very tidy. The photo blow-ups on the walls were fairly discreet, mostly award presentations to smiling women and cinematographers at work behind cameras with their subjects off shot.

"Welcome to our little hotbed of tranquility, Mr. . . . ."

"Jack Liffey." He held out his hand.

"Wingfoot *De*-vote Peace." They shook hands.

"That's quite a mouthful," Jack Liffey said.

"Southerners do tend to overwind the watch. My best friend in primary school was Aloycious Pitston Autolycus Merrick, I don't know what his ma was *thinkin'*. But our manners do get us through the winter."

"Indeed they do, Mr. Peace." They sat on opposite sides of an ornate desk. "I'm looking for a young woman who's gone missing from home. She alarmed her mother with her intentions that she would go into the adult film industry." This was the mildest euphemism he was prepared to offer. "Her name's Luisa Wilson. I just want to talk to her and make sure she's okay and doesn't want to return home. I'm not interested in issues of age or legality. Because she's Native American heritage, I have reason to believe she might have contacted a woman named Little Deer."

His eyes lit up. "Now there's a woman who was mighty well liked in the business, sir. Real kindly and country-smart, a real lady. Plus truly ornamental, of course." He got up and went straight to a file cabinet. It screeched a bit as it came open, and Peace winced, as if carefully held territory had been breached. He handed a manila folder to Jack Liffey. "Just have a peek."

They were mainly eight-by-ten publicity stills, done by a glamour photographer. Little Deer's name was burned onto a blank spot at the bottom of each one. He stopped at one with a big toothy smile that radiated confidence. In quite a few of the prints she wore jet black braids and little else. He wasn't surprised by the near-hallucinatory exaggeration of her body since he figured much of that was surgical, but it was still pretty spectacular. In one photo, wearing a buckskin dress straight out of Paramount's prop department, her hair was unbraided, a glossy black spray that fell well below her waist. But he figured that too could be rigged.

One of the photos was date-stamped, and he worked out that she'd be in her early fifties now. "I take it she's retired?"

"Some time back." Something dark flitted for an instant behind the man's benevolent demeanor, but maybe it was just Jack Liffey's imagination.

"Was there some sort of trouble about her career?"

"No, sir. Not that I am aware. She made a passel of money and won respect from all, and then she directed features for a time and waved good-bye, holding onto a pot of money."

Yet that wasn't the whole story, not according to his body English. In a kind of nervous fidget, the man poked around his problematic nose with both hands, as if trying to make sure the glue was holding, but realizing, too, that all the fussing was only drawing attention. Jack Liffey wanted to lean forward and give the too-pink schnozz a tweak to see if it actually was fake.

"Names like this give me a problem," Jack Liffey confided,

studying a photo that showed her in one of those subliminally servile porn poses, body squared up for display. "Tell me—if I meet her, should I call her Little, or Miss Deer?"

Wingfoot Peace chuckled and seemed to rediscover his confidence. The question had been mainly intended to get his mind off his nose. His hands came down to rest on the desk in front of him, and he looked at them as if they were separate willful animals. "Yes, I always wondered if I ran into the guitarist of U-2, if I should call him *The* or Mr. Edge. But I have no right complaining about names, not with my house-of-wonders sockdolager."

"Perhaps I could meet Miss Deer and find out the proper etiquette."

"Ah," the man said nervously. "I'm afraid you just pulled the wrong sow by the ear, Mr. Liffey, so to speak, that is. I can't rightly give out anybody's phone numbers or addresses."

For a moment Jack Liffey thought the whole nose business would start up again, but the man subsided.

"You can understand how some of our clients and members might come to be harassed by the general public. Or worse. Ever since Rebecca Schaeffer got herself killed by that stalker, even the DMV won't give out addresses. I don't mean to turn you down cold-footed, sir, and what I can and will do for you is accept a letter from your hands and send it on to Little Deer. If the Lord's willing and the clothesline don't fall, she'll see her way to getting in touch back. More'n that I cannot do."

Jack Liffey wondered what the clothesline might have to do with it, but Peace's offer was probably as much as he was going to get. "If she's that hard to reach, maybe the girl I'm looking for won't have found her either."

"Adult entertainment is a small community, Mr. Liffey. If she tried hard and batted her eyes some, there's folks might not be as discreet as present company."

Wingfoot Peace made a Xerox of Luisa's photograph, in case she showed up, and Jack Liffey left him the dubious business card with a note on the back to please call him. He didn't put a lot of faith in any of it.

"Come the 26th of July, Mr. Liffey, wet or dry, always sow your turnips. And along in September they'll be five or six inches round and good to eat raw. That's what Harry Truman always said."

He wasn't quite sure whether there was some veiled message embedded in the Trumanism. "Harry S Truman, with no period because the S didn't stand for anything," Jack Liffey offered. "Everybody's forgotten that these days, even our major newspapers."

"Indeed, sir. Maybe it's best forgot. Harry was always a close chewer and a tight spitter."

If he didn't get out of there fast, he'd be suspecting oblique messages in every item of Peace's peculiar phraseology.

He snapped the Panasonic onto a monopod to help steady it and planted it on the sidewalk across Fifth Street from the three blue plastic port-a-potties the mission had put up for the homeless. Kenyon Styles was at the end of the block, looking out for cops who might drift onto the scene in the full daylight. He seemed to note something and sauntered over.

"There's a patrol car, but it'll move off. They're just giving the winos around the corner the once-over."

Rod Whipple relaxed and leaned against the wall.

"You really grew up in Jersey?" Kenyon asked.

"After Chicago. Bradley Beach."

"No shit. You don't have much of an accent. Do you know the Oxeye dance hall?"

Rod Whipple had practically lived there in high school—rather Radoslaw Wojak had, when his widowed father had shipped him off to live with an aunt on the Jersey Shore. He'd had his first drink out of a paper bag behind the big brick monstrosity at the beach, heard legends of Springsteen doing a surprise performance there one night before it shut for good in the late 1980s, even spent a half hour in the parking lot with his hand in Mary Lou Nowak's pants not getting any more then wet pussy before she passed out from drink. The Oxeye.

"Never heard of it." Since then, he had spent most of his life trying to get back to Chicago, or at least as far away as geographically possible from the Oxeye.

"I heard Springsteen play there. That great 'Born to Run' set."

"Oh, bullshit. That's just a story for the rubes."

"Have it your way." Kenyon Styles wandered back to the corner.

How did he end up making a disreputable video on the nickel in L.A—Fifth Street, one of the sorriest skid rows in the world? He'd come west with an armload of reels to show, real underground quality stuff with East Village actors like Dino Hurt and Eddie Marcantonio, but all it had got him was entry to expensive extension classes on directing and editing. AFI never answered, and the universities wouldn't touch him because he'd dropped out of CUNY with bad grades. Extension was about as effective a career path, he knew, as running a Xerox machine at Universal.

But he knew they could make a fortune with this stupid idea of Kenyon's, and his share of the fortune would finance the film that was working itself out in his head, a sensitive portrait of a screenwriter so lost in Hollywood hell that he sells his soul to the Devil, who happens to look just like——————. Any name he could entice into doing a cameo.

He heard Kenyon's characteristic two-finger whistle and powered up by instinct. The Beanpole clapped once and pointed at a group of shabbily dressed winos smoking in a group across Fifth. They waved to the camera and entered the three port-a-potties. He caught them clearly in the daylight and stayed wide, leading a little to the right of frame to leave room for what was coming.

There was another whistle, and he heard the big SUV's engine roar as it headed their way. All of a sudden the giant beast hove into view, and its fat bumper sent the first shitter flying back against the brick building, then the second popped straight up and crumpled, before being dragged into the third one to give it a glancing blow that sent it spinning away. The SUV yanked back off the curb and sped away, and Rod let the zoom drift in slowly on the wreckage. The first wino now appeared out his sprung door and waved gamely, blood streaming down his forehead. The third one appeared, too, flapping open his door and crawling a few feet with what might have been a fractured leg. But there was no stir from the collapsed crapper number two.

Rod started to worry, imagining himself standing before a

hanging judge who was glowering down at him and bellowing something about voluntary manslaughter. He zoomed farther in on the mangled and dragged outhouse, where there was still no motion.

The first wino went to tug at the crazily crushed door and finally got it open. He reached inside and helped a dazed man climb out. This man, with long tangled dreadlocks, sank down onto the sidewalk. Bleeding from his chin, he looked up and grinned to show off a total lack of teeth. Whooping like a coyote, he accepted a high-five from his friend.

It was extraordinary. Maeve had never seen a bird just die like that. She was on her knees on her mom's window seat, looking out, and the sleek raven had abruptly fallen out of the big ash tree like a stuffed specimen. It was the tree that made so much mess, little winged seeds choking the lawn, the one that Bradley, her mom's new husband, wanted to have cut down. The bird hit the sparse lawn, and then beat one wing toward her as if tossing something—as if making one last desperate hurl of some precious keepsake to those who would carry on. Then it just froze.

Its legs were stiffly side by side now, like pictures of Cock Robin. She supposed hunters saw birds die a lot, but she was thinking that for all the billions of them you saw in the air, you almost never saw them lying dead. Where did they go? she wondered. Maybe predators got them within minutes. She wondered if the raven had died of natural causes, and then she smiled to herself, speculating about a tiny ostomy bag under one wing that might have prolonged its life a few months.

Oskar, under her own bag, immediately gave his scoffing opinion in the form of a wet Bronx raspberry that she felt against her side as much as heard. It was an embarrassment over which she had no control.

The seven-year-old twins, her exasperating little half brothers, Bradley's kids who her mother occasionally forced her to babysit, had already begun poking fun at her uncontrollable farting and the liquidy shitting noises, and she was trying to work up a pose of casual indifference about the damn bag. Then her eyes went wide and she felt the clammy damp against her thigh.

She tried to ignore it. It seemed disrespectful to the poor raven, to the great mystery of life itself, to spring a leak while she was still contemplating the bird's mortality. Her dad had told her that he got cold sweats sometimes thinking about his own death—the thought now taking on a reality for her that it never used to have.

She couldn't pretend to ignore the chill on her thigh any longer. She mustn't have fastened the clip properly. She swore softly at Oskar and headed for the bathroom before things could get any worse. The instant she locked the door behind her, she tugged her loose jeans down and felt her thigh, but there was no dampness. She lifted the shirt and the bag showed no evidence of a leak. Puzzled, she hoisted and wriggled the jeans back into place and then she began to laugh.

Amazing what tricks the mind will play on itself, anticipating the worst. She could feel right away that she had a whole pocket full of quarters, and it was only a metal chill she'd felt through the cloth of the pocket.

> **Dear Diary,**
> I am really sure now that this job is not for me. The typing makes me nervous tho I am pretty good at it & switching back to clicking things on the screen confuses me. And little did I realize that it would make me bashful to think a man is looking at me in this little round eye on top of the screen. Oh really I just dont like stringing men along & pretending their not on a timer yet when they are already. The other girls are nice & helpful to me but I just keep imagining dancing in the forest in a white robe & my buckskin coat with an eagle feather. I felt so good those days with Tuu-ee the deer watching before Bobby & Jo ran off together & left me.

EIGHT

Little Deer

The viewing room at Hollenbeck was shabbier than the one he'd been in over on the Westside, but so was everything else on the Eastside that depended on public funds. Looking for a runaway kid once, he'd had a quick tour of all-Latino Roosevelt High near Gloria's house, and by the time he got to the graffiti'd bathroom with the toilet-stall doors ripped off, he'd decided that a suburban white PTA would have lynched any administrator who allowed this to happen to their kids' school. But the alienation of children was such an intractable problem, he thought—showing up as graffiti, random vandalism, litter, and good old daily hostility. Poke it down here, and it popped up there.

"Stand by, Liffey, it's the usual," Sgt. Padilla said. "When they march in, the suspects won't be able to see you through the one-way here."

For some reason the back bench of the viewing bleachers was filled with a half dozen cheerleaders in tiny purple skirts, chewing gum and giggling. They looked junior high age, all Latinas except one girl who looked Chinese, and he did his best not to look up their microskirts.

"Are they here to root for their favorite suspect?" Jack Liffey asked.

Padilla barely smiled. "They're here for the next show. You can put up with it, right?"

"Hell, yes."

"Come right up to the glass and get a good look."

Jack Liffey came down front, and Padilla looked him over like an unusual species of rodent, not necessarily repellent, but not something you wanted around. "You didn't by any chance connect yourself to the Maravillas, did you? I mean, so the gangbangers would think so."

"Huh?"

Padilla shrugged. "I suppose not. You see, the Maras are evergreen on the street."

"Could you say some of that in English?"

"They don't pay street tax to the Eme so the O.G.s have declared them open season. No special reward. It's just okay to hit them any time you want."

He got some of that: The Eme was the Mexican Mafia, at least the Southern California form of it, and O.G.s were Old Gangsters—the seniors and leaders. "Christ on a crutch. Did I make some gang sign accidentally?"

"Relax, it's not like a Cub Scout salute. You got to go out of your way. Let's look at the bangers." He hit a button on an old squawk box on the wall beside a torn grille. "Dori, send in the heavy boys. No butt-pinching on the way."

"Dean, how dare you! I'm too wore out for such jokes."

"We happen to know you like those tight teenie butts, that's all."

There was only a feedback squall, making Padilla wince and switch it off. Six young Latinos sloped in and faced front under the big numbers as if they were familiar with the drill. Most did their best to put on a stony face. They all wore some variation of the uniform: baggy Chinos and checkered wool shirts or plain white T-shirts, and all had either the odd T-mustache or a mustache plus some form of lower-lip beard. It was the second one, and Jack Liffey recognized him once again, just as he had in the photograph.

He was muscular, a little shorter than the others, impassive, closed off from his surroundings as if living completely in his head.

"See anyone?"

"I don't know." Jack Liffey settled on another one with a T-mustache. "Could you have number five come forward a little?"

The sergeant switched over the intercom and ordered number five to take two steps forward and then turn to show his profile. The boy flashed a hand sign with splayed fingers as he came forward, probably his gang sign.

"I didn't say show us your brains, *Chato,*" Padilla bawled.

One of the other youths broke up and had to bite his lips as Number five glared back at him.

"Nah. Sorry. Too tall." Jack Liffey had the definite sense that Padilla was watching him with much more interest than the boys.

"He was in a car, how can you tell how tall he was?"

"Tall people broadcast it."

"Let's try the short one then. Number five, step back. Number two." The shooter took a breath and came forward without making a fuss. "*Cabrón,*" Padilla announced, "I want you to look straight at the mirror and challenge me. Say, 'Where you from?'"

The boy mumbled a little, looking straight ahead.

"You can do better than that."

"Where are you from?" the boy said, leaving too much space between the words as if he were translating from some other language.

"Doesn't sound like him," Jack Liffey said.

"You sure?" Padilla seemed to know something.

"I had a good look at the guy. He's not there."

Padilla went on a bit longer, calling boys forward, but Jack Liffey shook his head and shrugged them all off.

"Okay, *latas,* beat it. All of you, out."

The cop turned on Jack Liffey again. "You're not running some game on me, are you, Liffey?"

"What would that be?"

"I think it's called Get My Own Revenge."

He shrugged. "My daughter's doing a lot better today, and I've calmed down. The guy wasn't there."

"Sure, sure. Just don't let me find one of those kids beat to a pulp some night and your knuckles all scraped up. I'll remember."

"You got it. Thanks for trying."

Jack Liffey slipped away as fast as he could—as Padilla was dealing with the cheerleaders—and he hurried down the musty yellow corridor past tired propaganda posters about fighting crime and stopping graffiti. It was as ugly and dispiriting a space as any in creation, and he almost sprinted to his VW in the Official Police Business lot. He started up and pulled out to wait in the alley behind the station as a black-and-white accelerated out past him in a big hurry, then turned on its siren briefly as it sped onto the next street. Two of the boys came out and got into a beat-up Hyundai, not an especially common car in Boyle Heights. Another came out and strutted away angrily. Finally, his guy stepped out the back door of the station. He sauntered across the lot, still lost in his own head, and unlocked a big American-style bicycle that was chained to a substantial pepper tree in the parkway of Chicago Street.

Jack Liffey let the car drift along the alley and then turned to follow up a residential street as his guy pedaled hard, and he stayed a block or so back. The bicycle was going fast enough so it didn't feel terribly unnatural to drive so slowly. It was a balloon-tire, coaster-brake Schwinn, just like his first bike back in San Pedro. He didn't know they were still around—probably a retro fad.

He had to brake the car for a moment as three boys ran a small ice cream pushcart fast out of an alleyway. Behind them, an old Latino in baggy whites, probably a recent immigrant, was just zipping up after wetting down a bush when he noticed his cart was missing. The boys were already digging into the chest and hurling Eskimo pies and Fudgesicles into yards left and right. A wisp of dry ice vapors trailed out of the cart's open hatch, like some ghostly emanation.

Jack Liffey had no time to deal with popsicle theft. He kept his eye on the bicycle pulling ahead and accelerated past the scene. In a few moments, he was only a block behind it again. There was one worrisome period when he had to idle, double parked, as his quarry parked and popped into a mini-mart that had an Aztec warrior painted on the front wall. He came back out rapping a pack of cigarettes and headed on.

There was another nervous moment after a red light caught him at Chavez with the bicycle dwindling north ahead of him. This was the business heart of Boyle Heights, once known as Brooklyn Avenue, and the streets were busy enough here that it would have been easy to lose the kid. But he wasn't far back when he saw the bike turn up an alley. This was a problem, since the alleyway was only a car wide and his old VW would sound like a taxiing 747 in the space. Jack Liffey waited at the alley entrance, the road surface as cracked and weedy as a mud flat, assuming the boy was almost home.

Fortunately, he was right. The kid stopped and leaned over to open a gate in a low wooden fence and then yanked the front wheel into the air and dexterously pedaled unicycle-style through the gate and into the yard. The gate shut behind him, but Jack Liffey could see one side of the big swing-open windows on the detached garage open momentarily.

He drove up the alley as quietly as he could. What he saw of the old clapboard garage was covered with muralwork and fancy graffiti. It sat behind a small cottage, the back yard full of bougainvillea and geraniums and a pile of used lumber. I've got you, you bastard, Jack Liffey thought.

He paused in the alley when a graffito came into view that he felt he could translate:

Siempre quise ser alguien
Ahorra soy yo.

It wasn't that hard even though the writer had misspelled a word and left off all the proper accents. *I always wanted to be somebody: Now I'm me.*

Jack Liffey drove on around the block and down the street in front to get the address. Sleep tight, fuckhead. Stay yourself a while longer.

She was taking a break in the old kitchen, sitting at the Formica table with a cup of coffee that she'd finally broken down and poured, listening to a girl named Debbie, who came from Beatty, Nevada, maybe one hundred miles by fast untraveled and unpatrolled two-lane highway from where she'd grown up in the Lone Pine Rez.

"I hate that effing desert," Debbie said. "I really do. It dries your skin like a furnace, and it's full of crotchety old farts who never give a soft word to nobody. My pa used to say, all the Okies who came out west and couldn't make it on the Coast bounced back to the desert."

Debbie was in her forties and would have been good looking but her mouth seemed to have caved in as if her jawbones had been extracted and new ones substituted, two sizes too small. When she opened her mouth, Luisa could see that her teeth were yellow and crooked. For break, she had thrown on an immense T-shirt with stylized flames and a slogan that said: *My old man went to hell and all he got me was this damn T-shirt.*

"That's not my case," Luisa said. "My people been there forever. I heard grandma say they used to send the sheriffs up into the hills to drag us down in chains and make us work on the white ranches."

"Aw, that's awful. We had us Injuns in Beatty, too, but they seemed to me even meaner than the whites."

"Maybe they had a reason."

"I'm not criticizing, Lou. I just like people to be gentle and kind." She sipped at a glass of something bright red like Kool-Aid. "I had a guy this morning kept talking about my package. Wanted to see my *package.*" She laughed. "I thought I ought to stick a big bow in my undies, see what he said."

"Most of these guys are so sad," Luisa said. "I mean they're kind of like those high school boys who get rowdy and pull your hair when they really want to just say they *like* you. It's so stupid. What do they get out of watching me play with a vibrator?"

"I don't know, hon. For a lot of guys, I think they just like to be reminded there's sex someplace in the universe. And maybe the more stupid we look, the better for them."

The front door slammed and they fell silent, wondering if it was

Joe, the fat man who ran the adult magazine and video store down the block and came in once an hour to make sure everybody was behaving.

"Hey, girls. Crapping out on my time, I see?" It wasn't Joe. It was Keith, and Luisa could see he was really fucked up. She could read him now by his eyes, and his eyes were all over the place, squirrelly and going flat.

"This is our break time," Debbie said.

"Did I ask you?" He grabbed Debbie's hair and yanked her head back. "Did I ask you?"

"I don't work for you, man." Her voice squeaked a little over the pain.

"You still better respect me, bitch. Are you really from hell?" he said, noticing the T-shirt.

"You think you're a cop?"

"I asked you a question, bitch."

"Stop it, Keith," Luisa demanded.

Without looking, he backhanded her, and his hardened hand knocked her off the chair to the floor. She thought about biting a chunk out of his leg, right through the fancy slacks, but remembered the wonderful advice her grandfather had given her once— Never kick a bear unless you can kill it.

"Are you from hell, bitch?" he repeated.

"Yeah, you bet."

"You bet what? Say it, say I'm from hell."

"I'm from hell."

"I can't *hear* you, bitch."

"I'm from goddamn hell, *sir.*"

He let go of her hair with a showy flourish. "See how easy that was? Now the only thing left between us is respect."

"Sure thing."

He helped Luisa up. "I got another job for you. You're destined for better than this shit-hole. Put this on." He took a minuscule knit bathing suit out of the pocket of his jacket. She could see that it wouldn't cover much. "Are you smart?" he asked her.

"Why?"

"*I* ask, you answer. You're always reading books. You got to be smart enough to memorize." Debbie was glaring at him, sipping at her red drink, as if very near hurling it at him.

"I guess so."

He handed her a four-by-five card solid with printed text. It seemed to be about a video game called *Robo-Tanks Invade*.

"Just so it's not Danger Games," Debbie said, and Luisa remembered she'd been warned about that.

"You want some more, Miss Hell?" He held a finger an inch from her eye.

"No, sir."

"You're graduating today to spokesmodel," Keith told Louisa. "You get to stand around looking sexy in front of a big TV screen and talk whatever shit, while a bunch of businessmen and fifteen-year-old boys try to get a look at your tits. How hard is that? Just memorize that shit. Let's go."

"What about this job?"

"That's all squared. Forget it. It's history. I'm going to take you places."

"Call me," Debbie bleated, and Keith glared at her as he grasped Luisa's upper arm with his hand and hauled her out of the kitchen.

"Forget her," he told Luisa. "Trailer trash like that will only drag you back. You're on your way to being a star."

She wondered how she was supposed to change from a frilly negligee to a bathing suit in the little open Miata, but when they got outside, he had a big white van instead, and he trundled the door open to reveal a half dozen other young women in skimpy bathing suits, sitting on their haunches on the bare interior. Their eyes all came up at the sound of the door, and they fell silent, near alarm at the sight of Keith.

"Girls, this is Luisa. Somebody share a little nose or something with her to charge her up, and we're off for the Convention Center."

As usual Chris had cadged an address for him out of the system, he wasn't even sure he wanted to know how. If it was still current,

Little Deer lived in Woodland Hills on the north flank of the Hollywood Hills looking out over the San Fernando Valley. Not a bad address, something on Sorrento, not far off Old Topanga Road. Italian names often added a little class in Southern California, though he doubted that would work in Connecticut.

On his way into the hills, he had to pull to the side suddenly to avoid a conga line of kids on blade skates who were steering right down the middle of the road, three boys and two girls. They were coming very fast, and each of them wore a plastic globe with rabbit-ear antennas, like a space helmet from some fifties sci-fi movie. But what really grabbed his attention was the fact that the space helmets were all they were wearing, not even knee pads, on their pasty white flesh. He waved cheerfully as the snakeline of naked kids rattled past, like scalded animals, but they were intent on maintaining their course. It suggested one of the new humiliation TV shows, but he didn't see any cameras.

He entered an older neighborhood and found the house. It was pseudo-Norman, with thick stucco walls, a steep pitched roof to throw off all the snow and a big parabolic window in front. It had the look of being lovingly tended over the years. A cobblestone driveway appeared to have been added lately and a magnificent bed of roses, though none of this was necessarily Little Deer's work, he realized. With the turnover in Southern California, you were always inheriting somebody else's sweat and dreams.

He knocked. There was a little old-fashioned eyehole, a metal grid the size of a postage stamp with a tiny swing-open door inside. He had his phony badge ready and noticed that he was starting to lose some of the silvering off the plastic. He'd have to get something better.

"Speak," said a raspy voice as the eye-door came open.

He held up the badge. "I've been sent by the Adult Entertainment Coalition to talk to Miss Little Deer. About her trust." That was ambiguous enough, he thought.

"They should have called."

He nodded. "They should have called," he agreed. It was lunchtime at the one-man office so it wouldn't do her much good if she tried to phone for verification now.

He heard the unsnapping and sliding of a half dozen bolts, and the big heavy planked door came open a few feet. Jack Liffey rotated his chest a little to give himself just enough space to slide into the tiled entryway, but he wasn't prepared for the person he saw there. A wizened old crone, shrunk as a raisin, rested her weight on two aluminum arm crutches, her head wrapped in the kind of turban women use when they're going through chemo. There were bright pink blotches the size of silver dollars on her sunken cheeks, and she couldn't have weighed more than 90 pounds under the baggy sweatpants and T-shirt. He had a terrible premonition but did not want to make a misstep.

"My name is Jack Liffey," he said, hoping for reciprocation.

"And you want?" she rasped. She hadn't budged, and he could not get any further into the house unless he kicked out one of her splayed crutches and elbowed her aside.

"Are you Little Deer?" he asked, as neutrally as he could.

She stared for a while. "That name is no longer in use," she declared. The weird impersonality puzzled him, as if Little Deer had fled the place, taking the name and all the cash, and leaving this shadow behind.

"What name is in use?"

"Talutah Sunkawakang." Her voice was becoming weaker, losing force, as if strained through a wad of cottonwool. "A medicine man told my parents that name was suited to my birthpath. It has an English translation, but I have never liked the idea of using English words in this context. Little Deer was invented by a pimp."

So this was what was left of Little Deer, he thought. He couldn't help comparing the wraith before him with the vibrant woman in the photos he had recently seen. It wasn't difficult to guess what had happened.

"Even the name Sioux is a corruption of a French word for our language group. We call ourselves the Dakota, the Lakota and the Nakota. I'm Dakota, or Santee." She seemed to be running down and breathed heavily as if she'd just run a dash.

"Would you like to sit?" he suggested. "It's HIV, isn't it?"

"Full-blown AIDS. But you won't catch anything, Mr. Liffey, unless you fuck me or drink my blood."

"I know that, ma'am. What you see in my face is not fear. It's meant to be sympathy." On purpose he touched her arm, and offered her his to help her inside. "Let's sit down."

She let the half-crutch dangle from its wristlet and took his arm. "Thank you. I have a month or two to live. This visit isn't about the Adult Actor's Trust, is it?"

"Well, not trust in the sense of a monetary fund. But, trust, yes."

The living room to the right was down three steps, and she took them extremely slowly, planting both feet on each stair before feeling for the next one down. Leather sofas and chairs faced a wonderful view of the Valley out the picture window, the way other living rooms faced a TV. There was no television set, he noticed, at least not here.

"I was in the wrong business at the wrong time. But for a while—a profitable while—it seemed like the right business and it let me help several other people. I was good at it, very good, and very beautiful."

He saw that she had a taste for plain speaking. Maybe the approach of death did that, he thought, or maybe it was just her former profession. He lowered her gently into what was apparently her preferred chair. She sat, ignoring him, lost in her own thoughts.

Her self-absorption interested him. She herself seemed uninterested in the purpose of his visit. But it was understandable in her position, he thought. He didn't know how he would take looming mortality. Even a random nighttime insomniac premonition of death left him covered with sweat.

She stared out the big window at the air that was beginning to yellow up around the high rises on the valley floor. But still she said nothing.

Jack Liffey took out Luisa's photograph and studied it a moment before leaning across from the sofa to hand it to her. "Could you tell me if you've seen this young woman?"

She looked at it and didn't reply. But something suggested to him that she had seen Luisa. "Who are you?" she asked finally.

"My name is Jack Liffey. I find missing children and take them home if they want to go. If they don't, I do my best to make sure they're not in trouble."

The dying woman thought about this for a moment. Then she spoke softly: "I saw this girl a few weeks ago. She came to my door just as you did. I don't know how she found me."

Jack Liffey started to say something but she held up her hand.

"She was horrified when she saw me, of course, and I tried to use that to get her to go home. But she wouldn't listen to me. She had an idea that had gotten her this far, and she was determined. She thought she was good at sex and wanted to earn her living that way. There was nothing more I could do to discourage her, and as soon as she politely could, she left."

She began to cough, and Jack Liffey, who'd seen a pitcher on a table, went over and poured a glass of water. Handing it to her, he asked, "Do you have any idea where she went?"

"I'd heard of a young man who called himself Rod Whipple. An old colleague mentioned he might be better than most of them—or, then again, he might not. But I gave her his name, and if she was as determined to find him as she had been to meet me, well, then, he's your next visit, I think."

Jack Liffey thanked her politely and left, seeing himself out. As he started the car he realized he was out of breath, as if he'd run a long, long way.

NINE

Salvage

The blaring commotion was almost unendurable—mindless infuri-
ating noise. A TV screen the size of a bus just behind her bathed her
in ever-shifting flicker, and there must have been huge loudspeakers
behind the screen, pouring out the *blurps* and *fizzes* of laser
combat. *Robo-Tanks Invade* had to compete noisewise with similar
games throughout the huge hall, and she was meant to find the
dead moments here and there to bark out the phrases she had memorized, "A new generation of complex surface rendering! Four gig
data transfer! Do the math."

Only one made any sense to her: "Renegade machines on the
rampage against America." She was also supposed to switch from
foot to foot and shift her pose around three points of the compass,
to make everyone aware of the banner just below her chest that said
"Robo-Tanks Invade, by Intuity." Maintaining the cheerful smile
was the hardest part, but obligatory. The muscles in her cheeks
burned with the pain.

None of the girls she'd come with were within her restricted sight
range but several other models were, including a trio in identical
feather boas who were go-going like mad on a platform suspended

over the front half of a life-size jet fighter. This one seemed to be called "Kill, Jet, Kill!" and every once in a while holes in the jet's nose burped a little smoke and red lights inside flashed.

"Hey, you, yeah you, you got great nipples!"

She knew her nipples showed through the loose knitting of the unlined bra and she didn't like it, but there was nothing she could do but smile idiotically at this acne-plagued boy. "Brave American teens rise up to stop the tanks!" she bawled out as something bright red went off behind her head, bathing the boy in firelight.

The crowd was a mix of teens, geekish guys who were mostly taking notes on clipboards and men in business suits talking to one another gravely or shouting into cell phones. There were almost no women, except the bikini girls and a few skinny intense types hanging out with the geeks.

Luckily, she had a good view of a digital clock on the far wall, and since it was approaching nine she expected it all to start winding down pretty soon. It had been a longer and harder day than she'd expected. She was bone weary of posing, and her throat was sore from a genuine attempt to make her outbursts of information heard. One of the girls had given her a little speed late in the afternoon, but that had worn off long ago; now she was ready to sit back down in the van, her back against the metal ribs, and be driven home, potholes and all. She was almost through *Treasure Chest Ranch* and wanted to get back to find out how it was going to end.

Keith came into view around a kiosk that had done nothing all day but flash images of race cars. With him he had a Japanese man in a three-piece banker's suit and several of his other girls in tow. He waggled his hand to summon her off the little platform. As she climbed down wearily, the Japanese guy actually made a small bow to her.

"The night is young, Lu," Keith said. She didn't like the sound of that at all.

"What's this?" she whispered to one of the girls.

"Hostess time," a redhead said with distaste. "For Intuity's international sales force." Another one added, "They smell like old butter except they all use something stinky like Russian Leather. If you're lucky, you can get yours to pass out drunk."

Keith's tiny parade left the Convention Center, making its way across the nearly empty street to a fancy hotel with a lobby like a Spanish mission. Intuity seemed to have reserved a large suite on the top floor, and as they came in they saw a half dozen other Japanese men in suits scattered around the room.

"Look," the redhead whispered breathlessly. "That one's about to light a Virginia Slim." It was true, one of the Japanese businessmen on the end of the leather sofa held a lighter to a long pale pink cigarette. "His dick is going to fall off."

The other women giggled, and Keith turned fast to point at them. "There's later," he warned. He handed each of the women a bottle of Chivas out of a cardboard carton and then divied his crew out to the men. Luisa drew the tallest of them, who rose and bowed to her just like the other one. She didn't know what to do but bow awkwardly back.

"Do you rike great music?" he said to her in a voice so heavily accented it was difficult to make out the words. She thought at first he was asking about someone named Greta Musicker.

"The symphonies by Mr. Baya-do-ven?" he amplified.

"I like books," she said.

"Very good," he said. "I also like your literature. We will discuss Mr. Hema-winga-way and Mr. Fawa-ka-ner." And he led her back out to the hall and then to the room that had apparently been assigned to them.

Kenyon Styles had just chewed him out ferociously for obsessing about the risk, and he was in a bad mood because of it. He'd never been able to handle anger well. If Rod allowed his partner to get the upper hand, Kenyon would just keep for himself the whole payoff they were working for. But this new stunt really was too out-there and even just thinking about it chilled his spine.

"This is completely batshit, Ken," was almost the last thing that he had, in fact, said, a minute earlier. "You're going to kill somebody. I mean—fuckin' A!"

He waited at the bottom of the long curving staircase of the Water Steps that meandered down past several fancy restaurants and shops on the flank of Bunker Hill in downtown L.A. At one side was the rocky rivulet, gurgling away in its chest-high channel, the *water* that gave the place its name, and on the other side was a handrail that might just keep things under control, with a little luck. It was after one A.M., and that irked him, too, because Kenyon knew he had to get home and get some sleep because he was A.D.ing on an early shoot way out at the other end of the Valley in Chatsworth. It lifted his mood only slightly when the horrible irony occurred to him for the first time: his *day* job was porn. Like some girl from Kansas who was only acting in *Hamlet* until the waitressing job opened up.

A single sharp whistle skirled down the staircase, and he brought the camera up, hit start and then put it on pause. Let them live through this, he prayed. At least Kenyon had bought them cheap Styrofoam helmets.

Two whistles, and he brought the camera up to his eye. Just before all hell broke loose, he noticed the flashing dot in the viewer and hastily switched out of pause. He heard it before he saw it, a rattling like a skateboard coming to pieces. The shopping cart was still erect when it came into sight around the bend in the staircase. Two terrified winos in white helmets were strapped inside, clinging to one another and howling as the cart bounded down the steps. The top-heavy vehicle slammed hard into the handrail, ricocheted off with a clang like a hammer on steel and started to list crazily as it continued on. One of the winos screeched and threw up his arms like a teenager on a roller-coaster.

The shopping cart was still well above him when it went over and hit hard on its side, one of the winos yowling frightfully as his arm was caught beneath. The other man hit face first on one of the steps and went quiet and limp. Somehow, the cart spun half around on its side and slid a few steps more before catching an edge so that its prodigious momentum kicked it upward, toppling end over end. Both the riders had gone silent by the time it hit bottom and came to rest against a light pole. Rod ran forward, his video camera still rolling.

He tried to keep shooting as he felt for a pulse in the neck of the bloody mess on top. The beat was strong, thank god, as was the other pulse on the man beneath. Perhaps they'd been so liquored up and limp they'd actually made it down alive.

"Back away!" Kenyon shouted as he hurried down the steps, his camera still rolling. His lens prowled the scene and then Rod saw him dialing 911 on a cell phone. He often liked to get an ambulance arriving to punctuate a stunt.

"What the fuck are you doing?" he hissed. "Get *back*."

"I was afraid we'd killed them."

"What do we care? We got releases."

He stood in the dark alley, watching a police helicopter circle noisily overhead like a huge buzzard. The big searchlight wasn't on, at least not yet, and it was doing what the cops called "orbiting" to make itself a harder target for a random sniper, sweeping a pattern of big circles rather than hovering in place. The focus seemed a block or two west.

He was pretty sure it wasn't there for him, but not for the first time he sensed himself on the far side of a particular divide, one that meant the police presence was the opposite of reassuring. He'd retrieved his old .45 from the hollowed out *Oxford Companion to American Literature* where he kept it in his office at Gloria's house, and he was carrying the bulky pistol in the small of his back. Now would not be a good time for that superbright light to come on while a squad car wailed up to roust him.

He'd seen his quarry climb into his graffiti-covered garage a few minutes ago, carrying an oversized beer bottle and, of all things, a big textbook. Maybe it was a doorstop, he thought. Who knows, maybe the kid was actually studying something. He really wanted to know what had gone on in the kid's head, and he was doing his best not to pigeonhole him automatically as a sociopathic gang-banger. This, even though the enraged portion of his psyche felt he was overdoing the liberalism a bit. The fury Maeve's wounding had aroused in him was no longer quite as intense as it had been, but it was still there, simmering near flashpoint.

Jack Liffey had killed a man once, and though he didn't much like violence, what better reason was there than to avenge an innocent and vulnerable daughter? His thought processes weren't whirring away very efficiently, he could tell that. Mainly, he was wallowing around in what was left of his anger and desire for retribution. There was enough of it to do the trick. He now intended, as he always had, to put the kid down at first sight and walk away into the Boyle Heights night.

A radio was playing *cumbias* somewhere, and another was giving out a *Norteño* ballad as he walked slowly across the alley, opened the low gate as quietly as he could and went to the swing windows on the side of the garage. They had been inserted into the side wall fairly recently, surrounded by patches of rough off-color plasterwork like a bad Bondo job from the body shop. There were no curtains, and the young man inside lay on his stomach on a cot, with his head sticking over the edge to read the open textbook lying on the floor. With two-column pages and small insert lithographs, it was unmistakably a history text—some bizarrely impassive portion of Jack Liffey's mind was noting details while the rest seethed.

He watched for a moment more, and then he took the .45 out of his belt and yanked the unlatched window open.

"*Que pues?*"

The young man craned his neck around without alarm, but when he saw it wasn't a friend, he swiveled around on the cot to come to his feet.

"Just sit tight," Jack Liffey said. He wasn't aiming the pistol as much as displaying it for effect. "Yeah, you know who I am, don't you?"

"Well, fuck you," the kid said.

"No, fuck you," Jack Liffey said.

"Fuck you first."

Jack Liffey actually found himself laughing. "Look at that. We just had a meaningful exchange of views."

"Fuck you," the young man said again, not even changing the tone, as if nothing had gone before.

"What's your name?"

"*Chinga tu madre.*"

"You don't want to spend your last five minutes on earth cursing."

The youth glowered at him so hard that a vein on his temple popped out.

"I guess that means you're trying to look scary, but it needs work. It just looks like you're trying to take a dump and having trouble with it." Within reach was an old chrome and vinyl dining room chair, patched up with black electrician's tape, and Jack Liffey pulled it around to sit facing the young man. "My daughter is going to live, no thanks to you, but she's hurt pretty bad. I just want to know why you shot at me."

A trace of human expression finally flitted across the young man's face. The helicopter came around above the garage, and they both gave subtle evidence that they were aware of it. The boy seemed to be suppressing an urge to speak but finally gave in. "I don' know."

"You don't *know*? Man, have you got a sister or somebody you love? Maybe your mother. How would you feel if I busted a cap in her direction for no reason and I was such a lousy shot I actually hit her?"

He shrugged, for just an instant looking a little chagrined.

"Not so much fun on that side of the gun, is it? Give me one good reason why I shouldn't shoot you where you sit."

"I didn' mean nothin'."

"Well, that's a hell of a reason." Jack Liffey felt himself gliding into a very strange space, an emotional state in some marginal place he had never before been, as far as he could tell. He was disturbed and restless, fidgety, but he wasn't actually angry. The boy seemed so clueless and so much a natural part of his environment—the graffiti on the walls, the shabby furniture, the unwashed dishes on the floor beside the cot—it would have been like getting angry at the weather or a telephone pole. But his eyes never strayed from the boy for long.

"You paint this place?"

"You was at the cop lineup, wasn't you? How come you didn't tell them it was me?"

"So I could shoot you myself, and that's the truth. Nobody hurts my daughter. What's your name?"

This time he gave in a little. "Tino Estrada. They call me Thumb."

"Thumb?"

He held up his double-jointed thumbs, then gave a strange little salute, the thumbs tucked into his T mustache and beard and then pushed away like some fraternal-order secret greeting.

Jack Liffey held up his left thumb, which bent back as far as the boy's. His right thumb wouldn't bend back at all, and anyway, the right hand was busy with the .45. Jack Liffey was having trouble deciding what was going on inside himself, what this weird razor-balanced calm was and where it was taking him. Was it, in fact, the prelude to a cold-blooded shooting? He knew he had complete control over the situation as long as he held the gun. For years, he had survived on this sense of control—plus an occasional whiff of conscience—but this evening was one of those times when nothing seemed to be functioning normally, nothing seemed to be in its accustomed psychic space.

When dealt unpleasantness, he had always been able to steel himself to face it, to squeeze his fear or scruples down into an isolated blank space deep inside so he could do what had to be done, but this situation wasn't operating like that at all. Nothing about the evening seemed all that unpleasant, even shooting this boy wouldn't be a chore. He felt spacy, as if the boy's presence gave off some intoxicating fumes.

"My name is Jack. They call me Jack. The girl you shot is named Maeve. It's an Irish name. She's missing a foot of her intestines now. She's sixteen and has to shit into a plastic bag attached to her body because of you."

"I'm sorry, man. I didn't mean it."

"Yeah, you told me that. What *did* you mean?"

"There was just this thing, this thing . . . I don't know. You wasn't Mexican, so you wasn't even nothing. I didn't want to shoot you. The *pistola* just went off."

Jack Liffey realized he probably wasn't going to get anything more articulate out of the boy, no matter how much he persisted. There was even a certain honesty that he had to acknowledge in the boy's bewilderment. "It just went off, okay, I got it. Well, what do you think is a . . . *reasonable* punishment for this *pistola* just going off in my front yard? How about if mine just goes off and shoots your mother?"

His eyes went wide. "No! Don't do that, *señor*. You got to shoot somebody, shoot me."

"That's a thought." He was maintaining a façade of control, but he could feel himself freewheeling, entering a sort of anchorless drift. Maybe the boy had defined the game for him. Just let it run itself. Maybe something would happen all on its own—as it had for this sick little killer who'd glared at him like a mortal enemy out the car window.

"Man, shoot me, or don't shoot me. I'm getting tired of this."

"Good. That's *good*. I'm starting to get interested. What are you studying?"

"American history."

"What period?"

"Who gives a fuck?"

"I give a fuck. It belongs to both of us, that history."

"It's yours. I'm Mexican."

"This is Mexico, Thumb. Up to 1850 when a bunch of Gringo pirates and thugs like John C. Fremont seized it. And in case you haven't noticed, Mexicans have been reclaiming the state on foot ever since."

This just seemed to confuse the boy. "I want to get a GED."

"Good for you." Jack Liffey noticed for the first time stacks of *Playboys* and *Hustlers* under the cot. "Those won't help much. What's the textbook?"

The young man reached down and showed him the cover: *America The Brave*—one of the usual revolting titles—with a colorful collage of Indians, pioneers, modern soldiers and women in chemistry labs.

"You into it alone?"

"*Dije?*"

"You got a tutor, a teacher?"

"Beto helps me with some of it, but he ain't as smart as he thinks."

"Tell you what, you come over and mow our front lawn once a week, and I'll teach you how to write an essay." Jack Liffey was utterly astonished at what he'd just said. He'd had no idea he was going to say anything like it. He felt like a rummy waking up all of a sudden in a gutter with people staring at him. What was going on here? The dead weight in his right hand confused him. "Writing's more important than reading. If you can write a passable essay, you can get through any subject."

"I wasn't never any good in English." His eyes had narrowed into suspicion.

"It's just a skill, like welding. Look, I can kill you or I can help you—it's up to you."

"You're *loco*, man."

"Loco's my dog. We've got a kind of standoff between us, you and I. You've probably got lots of gang friends, know right where I live, and they can get me any time. I know where you live, and my girlfriend is in the biggest meanest gang of them all, the LAPD. So we either get to have a full-on war or a truce. You decide."

The boy laughed, but without any humor in it. "You're fucking *chingado*. Complete *zonzo*."

Jack Liffey's energy was running down, making him sleepy and confused, and his trigger-finger was getting worried. "It's your choice, Thumb. Come on by the house about noon on Saturday and mow the lawn. We've got an okay old push mower, and then we'll have a beer and learn about nouns and verbs."

The boy said something, all in Spanish, that had a nasty edge to it.

"*Buenas noches*," Jack Liffey said as he backed guardedly over the window sill. He wondered if he'd get shot before he could get to his car a block away. He wasn't sure what had just happened. In a few minutes, the kid would probably be laughing at the crazy old gringo and calling his pals to plan another assault on his house. But something strange had descended on his spirit in that garage as he watched the boy. It made no sense, but the best his rational mind could suggest was this: Some voice had spoken up inside him to insist that Thumb Estrada was salvageable. He could surely take a little risk to turn a life around.

Gloria was back when he got home, collapsed in the easy chair with her feet up and her eyes closed, a glass of red wine at hand. A *Smithsonian* magazine was tented on her lap. The complicated strap holster she sometimes carried up under her armpit was hanging off the chair, like a spiderweb that had captured quite a prize, the black Glock, and he kept his own .45 out of sight in the small of his back under his jacket. She seemed to be sloughing off the cares of her day, listening to soft Gregorian chants from the cheap boom box.

"Bad day?" he asked.

"I miss Steelyard. He was a goon sometimes, but he was predictable." Ken Steelyard had died six months back, shot by someone Jack Liffey had been trying to help. He wondered if trying to help this kid might boomerang as badly.

"Who's your new partner—Gengis Khan?"

She smiled without opening her eyes and sipped. "Gengis *Cohen.* Joel Lenski, actually. He's a nice enough guy, but he's got no street cred. You know the way you can just assume you've got power over a dog and the dog can't help buying in? A cop's got to have that."

"Doesn't work with Loco."

"I'll show you how to do it some day when I'm rested. Poor Lenski can't get it together when kids get in his face. He's either all bluster, or he freezes up. Then, he starts with the threats, and inevitably he has to back down. I'm his T.O., but how do you teach self-confidence?"

He kissed the top of her head, liking the rich natural aroma of her hair, and rested his hands lightly on the ample top surfaces of her breasts through the cotton. "Don't be teasing if you don't plan to go to home base," she told him.

"You get as many trips all the way around the bags as you can handle," he whispered. She reached up and caught the back of his neck with a strong hand and pulled his head down and kissed him.

But he could tell there was no real sexual intent in the kiss, and she soon let him loose.

"Hold that thought and let me unwind. Did you get any closer to our little Native American runaway?"

"I've got the name of a producer she was sent to." He couldn't even remember the name for the moment—his confrontation with Thumb had fuzzed over everything—but he'd written it down. "I met Little Deer today." He let it sit while he went to the kitchen for a tonic and some cherry juice. He still didn't drink—it had been a part of the trouble that had blown up his first marriage—but he'd been thinking of trying it again. Soon.

He came back and sat facing her. "I saw her photos first at an agency for these porn folks, looking gorgeous if a bit artificially enhanced, like all the porn stars. When I found her in person . . ." How did you describe that kind of shock? "She looked like a blow-up doll that somebody had let all the air out of. She didn't weigh ninety pounds. Poor woman."

"AIDS?"

"Yup." He let his eyes rest on some of the colorful Mexican curios Gloria had spread around, cars and altarpieces and skeletons dancing. They'd been made for tourists, but there was still a sincerity in them that made them heartening somehow.

"That's always hard to deal with," she said.

"She won't have to deal with it much longer." He was putting off mentioning Thumb, but he knew he would have to eventually.

"Let me know if you need my help finding anyone. I can run a license, and we got these wonderful reverse directories, tell you who lives right now in 439, apartment A."

"Thanks. I hired a kid to mow the lawn today."

"I thought you wanted to do it." She opened one eye to peer at him.

"It's free. In exchange I'm going to teach him how to write an essay so he can get a GED."

"What's this all about?"

He was on the edge of telling her that the boy was the shooter, but it would get too complicated, so he moved across the intervening space and buried his face between her thighs. She wriggled and spread her legs a little to him, and then the flat of her hand touched his back.

"Jesus, Jack! What's this gun?"

He'd completely forgot.

Dear Diary,

I am so weary I cannot hardly keep my eyes open. There was this Japanese man who got drunk on Chivas & he talked & talked & I couldnt understand a word. He didnt seem to mind I didnt follow him like he was talking to a dog. Then he was very stubborn about something he wanted me to do & it took me a long time to figure it out. I guess I knew their were men like him but I didn't really believe.

Lucky I was only hert a little but Keith was unhappy with me because I hadnt gone and negotiated a big tip. When we got home he tore up my book again & threw it in the wet garbage. It was a new copy. I am just going to concentrate on thinking of being free & happy.

TEN

Silence is Better than Holiness

She moved to the edge of the big bed. After last night with the Japanese businessman, she didn't feel like being touched, even by accident. She might have dozed an hour or two somewhere in the night, but it hadn't helped her exhaustion. She was beginning to realize that there were a whole lot of things in L.A. that were pretty much unheard of in the Owens Valley. And the adult industry or hostess industry, or whatever, wasn't turning out as easy a career as she'd figured.

She rolled onto her side, so she didn't even have to see Keith where he lay snoring, the sheet tucked up to his cute cleft chin. The curtains were wide open, and the sky was beginning to lighten up out over the restless Malibu ocean when there was a loud crash of glass, like a brick going through a window in the next room. Keith sat up in bed beside her like a jack-in-the-box, his eyes crazy as a cat's, and he took a second to get oriented.

"Was that real?" he asked softly. There was doubt and anxiety in his voice that she'd never heard there before. "*Was* it?"

"I heard it."

He yanked open a bedside table and came out with a big steel pistol with a long barrel, just as the bedroom door slammed open. The tallest Jamaican she'd ever seen came in first. At least she was pretty sure he was Jamaican because of the red-green-black knit cap and the striped yellow trousers—she'd seen a Jamaican movie on TV once and they all dressed like that. He also carried a little gray machine gun. The stocky white man behind him had his head shaved and his ears stuck straight out. He wore a fancy white linen suit like he was from somewhere in the tropics, too.

"Drop dat naow an' tek you hands up, Keity!"

Keith and the Jamaican pointed their weapons at one another for a moment, but neither looked very much like firing, at least she hoped so. She held the sheet up to her neck and prayed to all her ancestors to make her as invisible as Hawk in low morning cloud.

"Keith, don't be such a fucking pain," the bald man said.

"Levine, sorry. I guess I didn't recognize your knock. I hope you're going to pay for the glass." Keith let his pistol droop.

The bald man looked at his empty hands, as if inspecting his manicure, then back at Keith. "Just shut up. You're the guy wanted to graduate to peddling skezag to all your movie pals. Ain't that the truth, Terror?"

"First ting, he don' even be payin' on time for all the coke-a-moke, den he get him forward on the H. Get ready fe tek some blows, K. I-and-I ready." He moved forward menacingly.

The bald man put a palm on the Jamaican's shoulder lightly to steady him. "That may not be necessary, Terr. I believe our man Keith is a paragon of honor, and he has already approached a select circle of responsible people in the fuck-movie world, where King H has been experiencing a small renaissance of late— the randy bunch liking to go all noddy and like, though mostly it's for snorting, I bet. I'm sure he has our money all ready for us. Bundled and counted."

"Today, Levine. I *swear*. There won't be any trouble. By noon."

"To-day." Levine tried the syllables out a couple of times in his mouth, as if the word's meaning might become more evident with unusual emphasis. "Perhaps you'd better explain this to my man Pennycooke here."

"The deal's all set up, honest to God. I just got to deliver the skag and cop the money. Man, look, porn is so marginal there's always money somewhere, but it's sometimes a little slow to eke out."

"*Eke.*" The bald man tried that word on, too. "Where I come from, money doesn't eke, Keithie. Did money *eke* back in Trenchtown, Terror?"

"Money in de han, dat's de onliest money. Man say, money go be slow, I say, dem be wicked, and I-an-I boun fe harm de wicked man."

"Yes, we agree. Who's the cute little cunt?" His eyes had flicked to Luisa, and she cowered, unable to help herself.

"One of my girls. She was a hostess at the game expo last night."

"She's worth something to you then. Collateral, shall we say. I think we'll keep her until that money *ekes* into our hands." He wrenched off the sheet, and Luisa, wearing only a T-shirt, covered herself as well as she could with her hands. The night before, she'd decided against wearing the black lace nightgown, the only sleepwear he'd provided. She hadn't felt like wearing anything even remotely seductive.

"Don't, Levine, please."

With the sheet yanked away, Keith was buck naked, and Levine was looking down at Keith's crotch, at a large uncircumcised penis.

"Rumor had it you were somewhere between a Holmes and a Wahlberg. I'd say a point-seven Holmes." He seemed to note with amusement that Keith was unable to keep the fright from showing in his eyes. "How'd you end up uncircumcised, K? I'm curious."

"I was born in Germany. They don't do it in Europe so much."

The bald man looked thoughtful. "Don't you think it's about time? For the sake of personal hygiene alone. What do you say, Tyrone?"

"I-and-I, me tinkin' dred."

"Yeah, me, too," the bald man said.

The Jamaican drew out an old-fashioned straight razor and flipped it open.

"Man, I'll get your money today, I swear!"

The bald man pointed straight at Luisa. "*You,* stand over there."

She did exactly as he asked, climbing out of the bed and huddling in the corner, forgetting entirely about modesty. She had a horror of that straight razor and the kind of clean cuts it could make deep through your skin. Long ago, she had seen two distant cousins fight with box-cutters and only drunkenness had kept them from killing one another by inches. She tried looking away and noticed that the ocean was sparkly with reflected sun now, and had a light morning chop under a streaky sky.

"No, man, no! *Don't!*"

The bald man knelt on the edge of the bed and placed his big hand hard around Keith's throat, pressing down with all his weight. "Don't thrash, son. You'll make it worse."

Luisa's eyes were drawn irresistibly back as the Jamaican reached out and took Keith's long penis in his fist like the handle of a baseball bat and tested the razor in the air, making little limp-wristed arcing cuts, practicing near the tip of the penis.

"I beg you guys . . ."

"Hush, now."

Then in one swift circling motion, he excised Keith's foreskin, if not a bit more. Keith screamed, a cry of both horror and pain, and he kicked out spasmodically with his legs and slapped the bed with his palms, but it was already over. With the bald man still holding Keith's neck, the Jamaican picked up the detached and blooded foreskin, studied it impassively, and thumbed it into Keith's open bellowing mouth.

The bald man let go, and Keith spit and sputtered and then clutched at his bleeding penis with both hands, still wailing in pain.

"Today, Keith. You eke that money our way. We'll keep your cute little friend until you do. I'm sure you understand."

"Let's go, let's go," the director improbably named Ram Gold chanted. "Time is moolah."

The blonde woman in the two-gun cowgirl outfit, little more than an open vest and denim miniskirt, made a puzzled face.

"We paid a fortune for this standing set, Miss Why-not Earp, and I want one tracking shot to make it all worthwhile. You just hop back to the saloon and flash us from the door again."

A big black man tugged a rubber-tired platform back about fifty feet in the dusty street. A cameraman with a Van Dyke beard sat cross-legged on the wheeled platform with a small video camera in his lap.

Jack Liffey waited for a break, staying out of shot. He had found them on Monogram Village Road, a dirt track not far off the undeveloped part of Mulholland in the Santa Monica Mountains above Malibu. A decaying false-front cowtown had been built there decades ago, in the golden age of the Western, saloon, hotel, jail, etc. But it looked like Hollywood had given up on this particular back lot decades ago and big chunks of plaster were spalling away to show the unlikely framing and chickenwire underneath.

"Roll tape."

"Speed, dude."

"Flash 'em at us good. You're telling us you're the best. Then march down here. Action!"

The big blonde came out the swing doors and tore open her snap-button cowboy vest toward the camera, and then she walked clumsily along the boardwalk toward the steps down. She tripped a little on the bottom step.

"Keep going, keep going, we'll get cover."

She stalked purposefully up the street, with the wheeled platform retreating just ahead of her, pulled along by the burly man.

"Draw and fire."

She fumbled a bit getting the pistols out, but both blanks went off, aimed rather askance.

"Cut. Star it. Okay, we can set up for the reverse. Take a break, Trish. You guys know where Sandy's gonna be."

"Can I smoke?" the cowgirl asked.

"You're not in the next shot. You can go practice *feng shui* for all I care."

He turned and saw Jack Liffey approaching, taking note of him with a kind of relief and pleasure, like acknowledging a grown-up entering a playroom of unruly infants. "Temperament, the last refuge of the brain whacked. But you watch my guys move. A feature crew would take an hour and a half to relight and move the reflectors. And *then* they'd still be re-laying the dolly tracks . . ."

He threw up his hands in a gesture somewhere between exultation and despair.

Jack Liffey could tell the director was freewheeling on something, and he realized he'd been mistaken for somebody important, a producer or someone connected with the backlot. Maybe somebody connected with the financing. "So we use the doorway dolly. Some guys use a wheelchair, but that's really down the chickenshit end of things."

"Luisa Wilson," Jack Liffey said, holding up a photograph. "Somebody was supposed to call about her."

"Okay." He wound down a bit, and took the photo to look at it. "Uh-huh. She was here, all right, a week ago."

Jack Liffey waited. There was obviously more to come.

"This girl was right off the farm, all soap and water. Rod, my AD, brought her in. She did a day's work on the set and then our extracurricular courier Keith took her away from Rod, nothing he could do, he said. If you wait around, Keith will roll in here like the roach coach in a few minutes, ready to service every appetite."

"Where's Rod?" Jack Liffey asked.

The director shrugged. "Off on his own Games project too much. I had to fire him. It's Keith you want."

Somebody whistled, and he looked around.

"Danny," he yelled, "get Dyke Clanton. It's shot 30A."

A skinny man in a tie-dyed shirt waved and trotted off and soon came back with another woman in cowboy attire, even larger breasted than the first one, if that was possible. He turned her shoulders against the sun, and a young man with a baseball cap that said *Baseball Cap* squatted down nearby and untwisted a big gold reflector and moved it around until he found where it washed the sunlight over her.

The director turned back on Jack Liffey abruptly. "Look, she was a good kid, and I tried to give her a hand. You can fall a lot lower than sex films in this town. Some days, I think our work is even holy. Some days, I'm the last juvenile delinquent. Okay, I admit to a certain level of bad faith in the air." The man's head was speeding somewhere, on something.

He turned away suddenly and began framing things with a rectangle made of his fingers. "Maybe I can do some good in a bad place," he said and Jack Liffey wasn't sure who he was talking to. "My guru told me that we never get to fight any of the big battles on a field of purity, but only where things are already debased."

"That's the worst rationalization I've ever heard," Jack Liffey said.

Ram Gold laughed. "Which proves that silence is usually better than holiness. Where's Jimmie now?" he bellowed. "Where's makeup? Will people please *stop* wandering away!"

But Keith didn't show up on schedule with their nose candy, and he wasn't answering his pager either. Jack Liffey didn't particularly want to hang around the set any longer. Obviously neither Rod nor Keith was coming.

"You think he'll be in tomorrow?"

"Wherever there are still human needs to fill."

Jack Liffey could either go down the hill to Malibu and then along PCH or over the top to the Valley and 101, and it was just about as fast back to East L.A. either way, but going by the ocean he got to see the water for a while. It was too cold for anybody but surfers in wetsuits and a few hardy sunbathers. It was probably not too bad, though, lying down out of the wind, he guessed. A small plane towed an advertising banner along the beach, but the number of bathers on the strand didn't seem to make the effort worthwhile.

Slowly the plane caught up with his car on PCH, and he chanced a long look over his shoulder on the twists and sweeping curves. They were individual letters, wired together, floating along behind the small plane: TRISH IS A BUTTHEAD.

There was a second plane far back, towing another banner. He wondered if it rhymed but he'd forgotten all about it by the time he'd passed the Incline and come into Santa Monica.

Nobody he tried at the Adult Entertainment Coalition knew anything about a Keith who sometimes provided financing. He guessed the police could come up with Keith's address if he wanted to go

that route. Thinking of the police reminded him that Thumb
Estrada was due to show up to mow his lawn at noon. He got the
old push mower out and sharpened the blade with a hand stone,
but the more he thought about it, the more he realized a voluntary
appearance by the boy was pretty unlikely.

"Your friend a no-show?" Gloria leaned out the door, waggling
a glass of lemonade at him.

"It's beginning to look like it." He still hadn't told her who
Thumb Estrada was. He was afraid she'd be obliged as a cop to
turn the boy in, and though he didn't have a clue why he'd spared
him, he'd made his decision to drag the boy kicking and screaming
into a civil world, and he meant to stick to it, even if he had to go
round him up bodily to start the process.

"You made this off the tree in back, didn't you? We ought to set
up a little booth out here and sell it in the neighborhood for a nickel
a glass," he mused.

"That was *your* ideal childhood that never happened, Mr. Anglo
Middle Class. My ideal childhood that never happened was a
quinceañera gown all in white and big hair and a sea of white
roses."

He put an arm around her. "You never got your gown?"

"My fosters couldn't afford it, not on the $300 a month the
county gave them. The whole point of their scam was living off the
kids. The cheaper the upkeep, the more to keep."

"Ah, shit. Was it really bad?"

She stared at him. "It was worse. Let it go. Do you think this
thing still works?" A cheap old Polaroid camera dangled from its
lanyard off her left wrist, clunky as a toaster.

"They've been pretty well wiped out by digitals, but I think you
can still get the film. What do you want to shoot?"

"You," she said.

"Why?"

"I want to make a collection of the different kinds of shit-eating
grins you get on your face when you're lying to me."

ELEVEN

Notching up the Reality

"I guess you really are a detective."

"I really am a detective. I'm nobody's tame Mexican spitfire, Jack."

"There's only one thing I haven't leveled with you about, and I did it to keep from putting you in an uncomfortable position."

She thought about that, then grabbed his lemonade back and drank it herself, as if to punish him. "I knew I should have insisted right then when I saw you come home with that gun in your pants like some *cholo* punk. You can put things over on me, or you can fuck me. You can't have both, Jack. I never let a man do that."

He was reminded once again how sensitive and angry she was deep inside—at her foster parents, at being given a Chicano childhood for her Indio genes, at a lot of other slights and indignities, and, oh yes, at men. It gave him a funny feeling, like being flattened out to some two-dimensional character in a soap opera and then being forced to defend the ideological territory that came with it.

He opted for honesty. It wasn't always the best policy, even considering his half-assed perpetual thrashing around in search of integrity—what Maeve called his *portable ethics*—but it was generally the simplest course of action once you'd been caught out, that was for sure.

"Okay, I'll tell you, but then I'm going to have to kill you," he said. That didn't help, and he put down the sharpening stone and righted the lawnmower. "Please hear me out. I know you're a sworn officer of the law, and you have some kind of duty to report crimes and criminals wherever life takes you. I was trying to keep you clear with your sense of duty. And with your supervisor, too."

She glared at him and turned the lemonade glass upside down to spill away the last spoonful.

"I mean, isn't it true—if you know something, you have to report it?"

She thought about this for a moment. "Not necessarily. I might be protecting a snitch, or what I think I know might be hearsay. I could name other situations. You get to use a lot of judgment on the street. It's called HBO—handled by officer."

"Now we're getting somewhere."

She went back into the house and refilled the glass, then offered it again. This time he took it from her and gulped. It needed more sugar, and it burned down like acid. Just what he deserved, he supposed.

"Okay, I found the kid who shot Maeve. He lives in a converted garage over on Clarence. I went to see him. I don't know what I was thinking about. Maybe I just took the pistol along to protect myself and make him listen to me."

"Make him listen?"

He shrugged. "Well, he'd shot at me once. I liked him a lot better sitting still and paying attention. You know, I don't think he even knows why he did it. He says it kind of just happened. I think I can see that. He's the usual fucked-up mess, but sometimes kids like that make the best adults of all when they straighten out."

"I see. It's a reclamation project."

"You're always high on Father Boyle and his unconditional love for the gangbangers. I don't think my temperament is quite that forgiving. Hell, I know it isn't. I was actually thinking of killing the kid for a while, and, for some reason, the god of mercy just reached out and whacked me, just like that, and I decided to try something else.

I don't understand it any more than he understands why he tried to cap me. Though I think he was probably just trying to scare me. To wring some respect out of an Anglo. I'd like to help him. Maybe it'd even up some big scoreboard somewhere." He eyed her warily. "Are you going to report this to Padilla?"

She let her head hang for a moment, as if a sudden upsurge of thoughts had created ideas within her cranium far too heavy for her neck to support. "Jesus Christ, Jack. It does put me in a tough place. Sit with me."

There was an old wooden glide on the little porch that had frozen up long ago. He loved sitting on it because it was such an image of neighborly life, and here in East L.A. there were actual neighborly things to see from it, women bent over in flower gardens, children pedaling big-wheel tractors along the sidewalks, teens drinking beer under the open hoods of their jalopies. At the moment, there was only a tiny girl in a pink dress and way too much makeup and an earring, staring straight at them through the chain-link gate.

"*¿Qué pues?* You gonna fight?" she asked them.

Gloria smiled tightly and gave Jack Liffey a one-arm hug. "*No, querida, ya estuvo.* We love each other very much."

"That's good to know," Jack Liffey said softly. "Zing went the strings of my heart."

"Is Maeve home?" the little girl insisted.

"Maeve is away right now," Jack Liffey told her. "She's staying with her mother for a while. It's *muy lejos,* way across town, *cerca la playa.*"

"Oh." She seemed very disappointed. "Maeve plays cards with me."

"That's nice," Gloria said. "We'll tell her you asked for her. Run along now, *ranita.*"

The girl waved and skipped down the road.

"*Ranita,* that's a pretty name," he said.

"It's not her name. It means little frog."

"Sorry, I'm trying."

"That's okay, Jack." She squeezed his knee. "I forget sometimes you're a pretty good man, all in all. I'm sorry I went off on you there, but you got to keep me in the picture, especially if you wander off into deep water and get over your head. Out here in my part of town. *Peligro, esse.* It's a hard rain in the *barrio.*"

They both watched the quiet scene for a moment. It was a beautiful neighborhood, if a bit beat up, full of flowers and much-loved front gardens offered up as a gift to the street. There was just a certain insinuation of protection in the fences that surrounded every front yard, so unlike white L.A., suggesting an undertow of prudence and apprehension.

"Whatever happened to that nice world we were supposed to have where kids played kids' games and grew up slowly?" Jack Liffey asked. "Then they learned a trade and got their own house and had their own families? Most Latinos I know are a lot better at families than my people."

"That world is right out there, *querido,* it's just not the whole picture. A little more respect from the world, a few more jobs, a little less need for macho—maybe it could be the whole thing."

"You still have bad dreams?"

"Let's not talk about that."

"It leaks in, sweet," he said. "You thrash around a lot."

"You can always leave for quieter parts and all the blondes with the good dreams and the Volvos."

"That's not what I mean." He entwined his fingers with hers.

She squeezed his hand back, and he felt the roughness of her skin. "Tell me more about this dumb thing you're doing."

"I'd like to believe everybody's just an inch from okay," Jack Liffey said. "As you say. A little less this, a little more that. Look at this punk who potshotted me. Thumb is his street name." He shook his head sadly. "He dresses like a gangster, he acts menacing at the drop of a hat, and he mad-dogs you. Back in the car, he even held the damn gun horizontally the way all the gangbangers do it in the movies these days. I mean, where do kids like that get off complaining that people take them for gangsters?" He waved a palm in the air as if erasing his argument. "Okay, I'm just frustrated. I *do* understand a lot of it. You fail in school, your dad drinks himself into a stupor and beats your mom, your only heroes are urban warriors, etc., etc. *That's* why I want to give this guy a break. My little Pygmalion."

"Pygmalion? What's that?"

"Better known as *My Fair Lady.* You're the one that loves Greg Boyle and his theories about saving all these kids. You going to turn me in or let me try to do this?"

"Thumb didn't show up to mow the lawn," she said, as if that settled it.

"So, he didn't turn his life around on the first try. Is that all he gets?"

An ice cream pushcart came down the road, tinkling its bell. East L.A. was full of them, unlike the white suburbs, like emblems of the world everybody really wished it was.

"I won't tell Padilla right now, but you got to let me back you up. You don't even speak the language, Jack."

"I try. It notches up the reality a bit. I'm gonna go find Thumb."

"I said you have to let me get your back. I mean it."

"Stop wriggling, young man, or I can't stitch it."

"Who said anything about stitches?" Keith howled and clutched himself again. With his feet tangled in his hastily downed pants, he almost rolled off the stirrup table in the back office. The first doctor's office he'd come to in his panicky drive into Santa Monica had been an OB/GYN and he'd left the Porsche out on the sidewalk, door open and engine running, and blown straight through the reception with a pistol in his hand demanding immediate help. The doctor had sensed some big money to be made and kept his nurse from calling the police.

"You want to be obliged to pee around corners? It's up to you."

"Oh, shit. Then gimme some Mister Blue. Or at least some Hillbilly Heroin. I mean it."

"What on earth is Hillbilly Heroin?" Dr. Steinmetz had been practicing on a very rich, north-of-Montana clientele for years now—often abortions reported as D-and-Cs—and he found the wild boy a refreshing change. None of his Brentwood matrons had ever asked for Hillbilly Heroin.

"Oxycontin, you dummy. Give me something for the pain, *now.* Oh, *Jesus.*"

"I take it you'd prefer to remain conscious and waving the gun at me."

"Yes, yes. Gimme something local."

With maddening deliberation, the doctor sent his nurse for a syringe and swabbed the mangled tip of the boy's penis with alcohol.

"Owww!"

"I could rebuild it a little bigger if you'd like, but it seems quite large already."

Keith put both fists on the pistol and poked it at the doctor's midsection. "I swear to God, one more dumb joke about my dick, and I'll put yours in the same place."

"Patience, my friend," the doctor said in a firmer voice. "I mainly treat cooze in here, but I'm making an exception for your rough manners out of the goodness of my heart, and the anticipation of a lot of money. Your mistreated member will be blissfully beyond pain in less than a minute. And then we can see about making it just like new."

"Hurry the *fuck* up!"

"What says the gentleman?" Kenyon Styles asked.

The squat brown man in a denim jumper was a Filipino and had very little English, and he did mainly tire changes or brake linings and other simple repairs for the ramshackle garage in Silverlake. The Chicano owner undertook to translate.

"He say you tell him when you want him to start."

"Could we get him to sample it right out of an axle to start?"

"*No problemas.*"

The Chicano owner had been given a finder's fee that was even more than the Filipino was getting, but the Filipino didn't know that. Rod Whipple was feeling grumpy. He'd been fired from a porn shoot and then had an exhausting eighteen-hour industrial shoot the day before and he'd rather be alone right now to unwind, despite an abiding general loneliness. He caught sight of himself in a small cracked mirror under a leggy pinup. The unexamined life, he thought. And then abruptly examined. He was none too proud of what he saw, but turned his attention back to the old Buick going up on the lift.

He had already collected the release, and he had it folded and stuffed into his breast pocket. As the mechanics worked to pull a wheel, he took the paper out and glanced at the name the man had signed and painstakingly printed out on the release: Diosdado Macpagal. He'd expected Jesus or Miguel or something. Diosdado, for Chrissake. Must be God's something or other, he thought. But what god would care about this dumpy old brown man?

"Heads up, Rod."

"I'm ready, man."

"Then roll tape."

I will endure, he thought. Better than this fucked-up guy will. Diosdado Macpagal reached into the opened wheel hub and scooped out two finger's worth of brown axle-grease, wicking up a fine tail like melted cheese. He licked his fingers once and then sucked the whole gooey dark mass of axle-grease off his fingers like peanut butter. Rod's stomach gave an involuntary spasm of disgust. He'd had several sugary doughnuts on the set and a lousy midnight meal of Chinese, and it had all backed up inside him, waiting for something healthier.

He moved slowly sideward to get a better angle as the little man scooped out another gob of the grease and nibbled it coquettishly off his fingers, then broke into a big grin for the camera.

The Chicano owner held out a big opened can of fresh grease with a tablespoon in it, and the Filipino began to eat ravenously right out of the tin. "He like it," the Latino said for the camera mike. "I gotta order extra grease all the time. He make sandwiches."

"Wash it down," Kenyon Styles' voice called out as the man kept spooning out the viscous substance, the texture but definitely not the color of melted butterscotch, taking it into his mouth and chewing ostentatiously with his mouth open.

The Chicano handed him a yellow plastic bottle of 30-weight Pennzoil, and he screwed off the cap and upended it into his mouth like a cold bottle of beer. When he brought it down again, a trickle of gray oil ran down from the corner of his mouth. He wiped his mouth off with his sleeve and grinned broadly. "Mmmmm, *que bueno, hombres.*"

By the skin of her teeth, Luisa had escaped being shoved into the trunk of the Cadillac CTS. She gave them a solemn promise to make no trouble, and now she sat primly in the soft black leather back seat. It was like riding inside an expensive glove. The car wound effortlessly up into the tan hills overlooking the coast. The ocean below was stunning, stretching off toward a few container ships on the horizon. The way the colors interwove, it was a pinto surface of green and deep blue, dotted with the bright sails of yachts that were heeling over on the breeze. She had quickly grown to love the changing look of the ocean and wondered if anyone ever got tired of looking at it.

Getting tired of things was a funny idea, she thought. She wondered if men ever got tired of trying to hammer away at every woman they met to make sure they got their share. So many of them approached the whole thing in a permanent state of rage. If they'd just calm down a little, everybody could try to have some fun.

The bald one called Levine was driving the Caddy, and the Jamaican was bent forward doing something with the big revolver in his lap.

"You're a cute kid. How'd you end up with a douchebag like Keith?" Levine submitted.

"I ran off from home and I did the best I could. People keep telling you how pretty and nice you are and they're going to take care of you, and just when things seem to be maybe okay, some guy with a mean streak grab's you by the hair."

She stopped and thought about what she'd just said and wondered if it would piss them off. She admitted to herself that she bore some responsibility for her plight, too. She'd done a little hopeful fibbing to the diary, but it wasn't like she'd been so attracted to any of these guys of the last week, except maybe Rod, and he was pretty pathetic really. The only thing she could say for sure was they seemed to get bigger and stronger all the time.

"I believe that's a pelican," she said, a little surprised. It was unmistakable, with the big pouchy bill, gliding along parallel to the car as if checking them out, and then peeling away back toward the ocean. She'd never seen a pelican, though seagulls made it as far inland as the Owens Valley all the time.

The Jamaican had looked up. "Him be pemmican, for sure—just a scuffle for he bread in the water. You overstan de beast of nature?"

"I'm an Indian. I know stuff."

"Look hyere, dawta, you mean you Red Indian?"

"Well, I ain't no spot-on-the-forehead Indian. I'm a Paiute."

"I-and-I penatrayit. Dat somefing fine. Your mind born free."

The car came off pavement and jounced along on a well-graded dirt road in the hills.

"Where are you taking me?" A chill of fear had overcome her.

The Jamaican looked over at the driver, as if for permission to let her into the secret.

"We've got a crib up here," the driver said. "You be a good girl, and we'll all get along. Are you really Keith's old lady?"

"I don't belong to nobody, and not especially that creepoid. He just started to think he owned me. He made me work as a model and then a hostess. I didn't like it."

"You mean he turned you out?" the driver said.

"I don't know what that means." The Jamaican was looking over his shoulder, watching her, and he grinned with some private joke as the driver spoke.

"It means he made you fuck guys," the driver said.

"I guess. It started out one way and kept changing and then I was stuck with this Japanese guy doing stuff I didn't like at all. I came to the city to be in movies. Little Deer sent me to some guy, and he seemed okay. Maybe I met the wrong people after that."

"Maybe you've met the right people, now—that is, if you want to get over," the driver said. "I remember Little Deer."

"Oh, man, I seen that Likkle Deer, too. She got the shining of Ras in her ownself."

Luisa thought of the poor dying woman she had met and didn't think it would help matters to tell them about her. "Sometimes I think I ought to just go waitress at Denny's."

"Gwaan, girl, dat just an ordinary ting, and you start dat and you be stuck dere for you life. You wan some herb?"

The fact that he pronounced the H confused her at first, but it wasn't hard to figure out what he meant when he held out the fattest cone-shaped hand-rolled number she'd ever seen, like a small trumpet.

"Good God, is that all *weed?*"

"You ain' never seen a proper spliff?"

"Even Grandpa Russell would choke himself on this."

He had it going already, smoking like a steam engine, and she took a big hit, and tried to hold it in and not to cough. It was raw and harsh, not smooth like the weed that Russell grew up in the Sierra canyons, but she felt the buzz right away. She handed it back.

"You wicked, girl." He grinned and took another long, slow hit.

The car drew up to the most beautiful house Luisa Wilson had ever seen, all glass sides and flat roof and patio. There was another house, a little like it, a hundred yards farther on, and a few others scattered on lower roads, but this one seemed to be on the very top crest of the weedy hills. The driveway slumped down into a sunken three-car garage where the door came open automatically to show the rear of a big wide SUV, like something the army would use.

She finally let the smoke out, a slow blue hiss. "You fellows sure got you a house."

"Dawta, we don settle for no lowdown 'commodation."

"Make yourself comfortable, my dear," Levine said. He even opened the car door for her, and she felt like a princess, all of a sudden. "No one is going to harm you here, I promise. But this is our house, and we've got two rules for you to remember. No crying is allowed here—all crying is blackmail. And, number two, if you got a problem, you come and ask us about it *only* if you want to get it fixed. It's what we do. You just want to whine, that's what your girlfriends are for."

She thought about that for a moment. "I bet you leave the toilet seats up, too."

"You want 'em down, get your own house."

Gloria was already frowning at him as he peered in the French window. The room was well lit, and the boy stood facing the far wall, his left hand rooting in a big bowl of what looked like chicharones on a barstool. With his right, he was using a spraycan to add dimension to a swelling bulbous graffito the size of a bicycle that seemed to be spelling out nothing more adventurous than THUMB.

Jack Liffey watched patiently for a while. The boy had excellent control of the spray pattern. He wouldn't have thought you could get that subtle a shading with an ordinary spray can.

"Jack, this is making me uncomfortable."

They were, of course, plainly visible to anyone who might come along the alley or peer out the kitchen window of the house. She stood a few feet back from the window, her badge on a chain around her neck just in case. She had insisted he leave his pistol at home, but she had hers clipped inside the back of her skirt.

"That's a new one," he said. "An uncomfortable cop. You've got the neon sign that gives you the right to do absolutely anything you want to in this town."

"I know some cops treat the badge like that, but it's not my way."

"Okay, *vamanos,*" he said and rapped on the window twice before pulling it open. He'd already told her this was the only way in.

Thumb Estrada looked around and made a disgusted face when he saw Jack Liffey stepping over the sill.

"Missed you at the lawn mowing today," Jack Liffey announced. "I thought we had a deal." He glanced back to see Gloria standing at the window like a sheep standing patiently at a field gate. "Thumb Estrada, this is my friend Sgt. Ramirez of the LAPD."

"No te doy color," the boy snapped.

"Sorry, I didn't get that," Jack Liffey said. "Something about giving you color?"

A lot of emotions were passing over the young man's face, some angry and some just confused.

"He says, basically, that you don't exist," Gloria explained.

"Ah. That may well be, Thumb, in your world, but I'm lifesize in mine. We had an agreement. In case you've forgot, if you don't mow my lawn, I turn you in. That's pretty simple, really. It's straight as I can make it. We are not sorry for our sins if we are not willing to make amends. I don't think Sgt. Ramirez here agrees with this deal I made with you, but I think she'll let me honor it if we get started pretty quick. The mower's all sharpened up and ready."

"Fock you, man."

"I forgot. I also promised to teach you how to write an essay. Nice mural, by the way."

The boy looked back at his name on the wall, as if longing to add a few touches. He shook the spray can absently, and the ball inside rattled. For some reason, Jack Liffey felt a heavy pressure against his chest, as if a belt were tightening around him. He'd had a collapsed lung not long ago, and he was sensitive to feelings in his chest.

"The wall's not going anywhere."

"Caifás con me lana," Gloria said sharply.

The young man answered in sullen Spanish, and they talked for a while. As near as Jack Liffey could tell, she was seething with suppressed anger, but probably as much of it was directed at him as at the boy. That was where it came from, he realized, this sensation in his chest. The pressure of her anger was like a standing shock wave.

"Okay, I go with you." Thumb's face was rigid as a steel mask.

"Why don't you skip trying to be an outlaw for a while? It takes so much extra energy. I'm offering to be a friend."

Jack Liffey held out his hand, but the boy only glared at it as he stalked past him.

"Well, maybe later," Jack Liffey said brightly.

Dear Diary,
I dont know if this is all going from worse to better or what, strange things happen in this life. I was laid low by everything when these new guys show up & everything is different again. I seem to be starting to get over that boy Keith. My new friends make me laugh and that is what grandfather said always saved the Paiutes from bad times. Ha-ha. I laugh at Keith holding his thing & owwing after Trevor circumscribe him. Way to go Trev or Terror as he is also AKA. I sens that my destiny is now with these two. I guess I'll just have to wait and see.

TWELVE

The Ugly Contest

It's just too difficult to decide who someone is, he was thinking, what he's *really* like, which one of all the contradictory parts is going to step front and center and which one is going to retreat. He could barely work out who he was himself, or Gloria, but there were worlds of bad faith standing between himself and this boy. *Hang on tight,* he told himself.

He had decided it probably wouldn't be a good idea to sit up on the porch like a strawboss while Thumb slaved away at the lawn so Jack Liffey got out the old edger to keep his hand in. He was hacking away along the walk and the driveway but only managed to gum up the dull blade with damp grass so that it was virtually useless.

Thumb was doing a conscientious job, his shirt off to expose the tattoos on his brown torso, mostly blue and blurry and unreadable in Olde Englishe letters, the usual prison or juvie tats. He mowed an up-and-down pattern rather than the shrinking spiral box that Jack Liffey favored, and when he emptied the last bag of cuttings into the rose bed, Gloria brought them both lemonades and the boy, forearming sweat off his brow, took his gratefully.

"*¡Ay, que padre!*" he exulted after a long swallow.

Since his English was perfectly good, Jack Liffey figured Thumb was getting his own back by excluding him from the conversation.

"Do you go to the JC?" Jack Liffey asked him.

The boy just stared at him without speaking.

"I saw the history book," Jack Liffey said neutrally.

"It's for a GED, I told you," he finally allowed. It was as if he'd forgot for a moment that he was supposed to be hostile, and then something hard came into his eyes again and he turned away. *"Pendejo."*

"There's nobody else here so you won't lose face if you're polite. You ever smell rotting meat?" he asked out of the blue. He'd tried this ploy once with a particularly snotty girl, and it had worked like a charm.

The boy's face opened up a little, curious.

"It's that almost sweet repulsive smell that makes you want to throw up. I was near a dead body once in Nam. Imagine stepping on a cat that's been in the gutter for weeks, that's turned soft as jelly with maggots crawling through it." He paused for effect. "Believe it or not, that's what starts to happen to your insides when you disrespect yourself. Act like a cheap hoodlum, and your bones start turning into wet cardboard. Pretty soon you'll smell, and not even your mother will want to be anywhere near you."

Jack Liffey went off on in this vein—crazily, he knew—for a little longer, inventing grosser and grosser details of rot, just to see if Thumb could be made to react. Eventually, the boy shook his head and waved a hand casually, as if flicking something repulsive off it. "You one spacy dude."

"Listen to me," Jack Liffey demanded. "I do this for a living, dealing with kids who think they're tough punks. I've seen a million just like you. You know what, there's always a lonely lost kid inside, under all that bullshit, trying to look hard as nails but crapping himself when the cops show up to take him away. What you really want is respect from the world, just a little respect, It's not much to ask, I know, but you don't have a clue how to get it."

He saw the first flickerings of self-pity expose themselves as he looked evenly at Thumb. The cold reading was a cheap trick, really: every fortune cookie was true of everyone. All it took was enough force of personality to shift someone's perceptions a few inches so that they acknowledged what you pointed out. He saw the boy's eyes flick up to where Gloria had been—but she'd known enough to absent herself. This was a moment between men.

"Why you being like this?" Thumb's voice spiraled down into a drone. "I'm sorry I shot at you. I said I was."

"That's a start. Look, I'm trying to work on my own anger. Why shouldn't you try the same?"

"Huh."

"Let's say I shoot you to get even. If I do, everybody loses. You're dead, and I probably go to jail, my girl has to visit me 400 miles away through bulletproof glass. If I teach you how to write a passable essay, we all win. Most important, my daughter wins. She didn't get shot in vain. You're up to the Civil War, right?"

"Huh."

He was absently rocking the old push-mower back and forth a few inches, and Jack Liffey took it away from him. "The South after the Civil War, Reconstruction."

"*Si, esse.*"

"That means you're well past the Mexican-American War. Write me one page about how the U.S. stole this part of the country from Mexico. If that's too big for you, you can limit it to how the war started. Don't just use that textbook you've got. Look in a couple of books."

"I can't write good."

"You will when we're through, I promise, unless you're afraid to learn. Have it for me tomorrow."

"Tomorrow! *Dame chanza!*" Thumb was indignant.

"Hey, was that 'Give me a break?'"

Thumb nodded. Jack Liffey could see he still hovered on the edge of rebellion.

"I'm learning, too. Let's go do the back yard."

He could tell by his cranky reaction that a little too much was being asked of Thumb at one go. But the boy had taken that first step now, and he seemed resigned to accepting Jack Liffey's authority, which, of course, was the point.

* * *

Thumb was negotiating the mower around the plum tree, and Jack Liffey was building the rudiments of a compost pile inside a chickenwire ring against the cinderblocks at the back corner when Gloria came down the back stoop with the cordless phone. She mouthed "Maeve," and he took it from her. She watched the boy with an unreadable expression for a moment and then went back inside, while Jack Liffey retreated around the side of the house for an extra margin of privacy.

"Hi, hon,"

"Hi, Dad. What's going on there?"

"A kid's helping me mow the lawn." He wondered what sort of reaction she'd have if he told her about Thumb, but he decided that would be stupid. She was so good-hearted she would undoubtedly forgive the boy eventually, probably want to help him herself, but there was no sense pushing it while she was still healing. The ostomy bag was still there as a constant reminder.

"Physical labor getting too much for your advancing age?" she teased.

"I'm always ready to help the underprivileged with some pocket money."

"I miss you, Dad, and I miss Gloria. Mom won't let me come there. Can you visit me?"

"How about tomorrow? We could go for a drive up PCH."

"Wicked." She loved the Pacific Coast Highway, especially where it ran right along the water in Malibu.

"How you doing with your apparatus?" He glanced up at a terrible fingernail-on-chalkboard noise as the boy wrestled the mower over some pavers that stuck up from the crabgrass.

"Apparatus. That's a new euphemism. You mean my shitbag. It actually came in handy last week."

"How's that?"

"We've got some tough girls at Redondo High, believe it or not. They try to corner you and go for your lunch money and stuff. I was in the head to empty the bag and this J.D. girl came in to smoke and started hassling me through the door. When I laughed at something she said, she kicked open the stall door, but all I had to do was turn around and fire Oskie at her. Man, did she run away, gagging and screaming."

Jack Liffey laughed. "Glad he's your friend and protector. I'll see you tomorrow. I love you a lot."

"Met, too, Dad. Bye."

When he rang off, he could feel the heat behind his eyes, he was so proud of her cheerful bravery in the face of the disability. He watched Thumb wrestle the mower with powerful biceps and wondered how brave Thumb would be with an ostomy bag. Maybe— who knew?—given that portrait gallery of the maimed and dead at the police gang substation, one day he'd have a chance to find out.

Luisa stood on the fieldstone patio out back looking at the ocean far below. The way the hills and canyons rumpled away from the patio, she could see only one wide slice of water between the tall windbreaks of eucalyptus trees and the shrubby yellow hillsides. But it was enough. A half dozen other houses were visible on knobs and ridges but none nearer than a quarter mile. She had a good eye for distance, because back home her world was measured in bicycle distance—to school, to Joseph's Bi-Rite market, to the health center and to all her friends' houses. When she got up to a good cruise on her old Schwinn, ass-banging hard because of the packed clay instead of air her grandfather had put into the tires, she could do a mile in three brutal minutes.

"All fruits be ripe here, dawta. You overstan'?"

She smiled privately, looking away from him. Neither of these guys had tried to sleep with her the night before, but she'd grown fond of the colorful up-and-down Jamaican music in this one's voice. It was as unexpected as a kiss and tickle, though she only understood about half of what he said. His confidence affected her, too, and the amazing colors of his wardrobe.

"What a great place," she said. "I can smell salt water on the wind, it's different from creek water. And eucalyptus and sage. Those are easy." She sniffed. "There's hawkweed out there, too, and goosefoot and some others that I only know the Paiute names. Ootoop' and Oos'eev."

"Them some damn strange names. I guess every person, dem got dey words and dey knowledge. Jah rule. Tek de simple concep' ob live wid love for all man and woman. No need for waar and envy. You no see it?"

"Sure. How does kidnapping and cutting people's dicks fit into that?"

He grinned slyly. "Weall, naow, I-an-I got to protect from bad business. I-rie."

Levine came out the sliding glass door with a cold six-pack of Jamaican beer and a Jamaican ginger beer. He offered the ginger beer to Luisa.

"Thanks, I'm already a little woozy from that hit of weed." Remains of those giant joints were lying all over the place, like traffic cones.

Levine grinned. "Be careful. The ginger beer is stronger than the beer."

"You mean stronger with alcohol?"

"The ginger will blow your head off."

She took a sip and the liquid burned its way down her throat like acid. It was as if someone had grated fresh ginger into the drink, but she liked it. Terror took a beer and tipped it up, his Adam's apple bobbing until it was two-thirds gone.

"I-and-I challenge to domino, Mr. Big," he said to Levine.

"I can't stand the way you play, Ter. I'd rather have my ears drilled out with a jackhammer."

There was a table and chairs at the side of the patio, and the Jamaican beckoned to Luisa. "Woman no afraid, you see it? Mr. Big, bwai, you jus' one big damn coward naow. Boo-yah, oh don' be hurtin on me, Mr. Terror, *please* don'. Me sooo skeered, I got me a inferior complex."

Levine burst out laughing and headed back to the house. "Eat me, Tyrone."

Luisa sat down gently opposite the man and helped him turn a worn box of dominoes face down. She watched his long dry-looking fingers work deftly at it. "I think I know how to play. Do you and Levine own this house?"

"When time come, we forward out of hyere. We live on de earth, dawta, in no special place here in Babylon."

"Please call me Luisa."

She wondered who owned the lovely hill house and what had become of them. Maybe the two were house-sitting. She hoped there wasn't some rich couple in a shallow grave just beyond the patio.

"Dis de boneyard, Miss Lou," he said, indicating the pool of face-down dominoes. "You tek seven cards, and don' be fret my talking trash at you, dat's just the way of the game. You some sorry ass likkle lost Indian girl."

Luisa glanced up sharply.

"See, dat what I mean. You got to unnerve de enemy."

"*Enemy?* There's no such thing as a friendly game?"

His forehead wrinkled up in mock perplexity. "Course not."

"You dumb black cocksucker," she said tentatively.

He yowled happily and slapped down the first tile so hard that the table jumped, and they had to pick up a few pieces that had bounced off onto the flagstones. "Dat de idee, Missie! You not so dim, least for a Red Indian whitetrash likkle bitch can't find her own pussy with both hans."

Luisa picked out a tile with a three to match the one he'd laid down and slapped it onto the card table about half as hard as he had. She tried to remember some of the insults she had heard in the break room at Lovey-Dove, Inc. "I hear your mother was so ugly that when she went to the ugly contest they said, 'No professionals allowed.'"

Terror Pennycooke threw back his head and howled.

"I know I've told you about this place, but somehow we never made it here until now," Jack Liffey said to Maeve. "You sure it's okay to walk the best part of a mile?"

"We're out in nature," Maeve said. "I can go off into the bushes if I have to. And I sure don't remember you telling me about a *waterfall*."

Gloria was hiking along with them, dressed in jeans and a tidy safari jacket so clean that it looked like it had just come from Banana Republic. In fact they had used her purple RAV-4 for the trip up PCH, a pleasant enough drive in the fall when the beaches weren't crowded, but Gloria was still prickly and tense. They were just across the L.A. County line into Ventura near Point Dume.

"I'll believe a waterfall when I see it," Gloria said.

"I know two others in Southern California," Jack Liffey bragged. "But this is the nicest one, with a soaking pool at the bottom. Some other time, we can walk way up into the hills here, too. Not today, though." And if they indulged him, on the way back he could check out a beach house where Chris Johnson had found out that the fixer/dealer/procurer known only as Keith was supposedly shacked up. As long as Rod Whipple was out of the picture, Keith was his warmest lead to Luisa Wilson, though he hadn't told either Gloria or Maeve about it.

A few minutes after they set off, Maeve stumbled badly. He was only a few feet away, but he held back and let her catch her balance unaided. After a moment of patting her side to make sure everything was still attached, she glanced at her father. "Thanks for not running for a telephone booth to put your Superman suit on."

"It's been my observation that you're pretty good at taking care of yourself."

"Look at this," Gloria said. She had stopped beside a whole colony of sparse bushes covered with delicate pink cupped flowers the size of dimes.

"That's mallow," Jack Liffey said. "It's native. There's a much more orange variety up in the Sierras. Not many plants flower this late in the year except rabbit brush and stuff most people would call weeds."

"How do you know this?"

"Maeve and I used to take field guides on hikes and learn the native plants, but I still don't know garden stuff. I can't tell a zinnia from an iris. You ask me any of these, though."

"Okay, *that* one."

He grinned. "It's called a big green bush with oval leaves. Sorry, ask me when it's in flower. My memory's not what it used to be."

Maeve bent over and looked closely. "Monkey flower, Dad. And what's that beautiful vine with the red leaves?"

They shared a knowing smile, but Gloria had already moved toward the vine that was growing thickly on the bank of the dried up stream. She was just about to pluck one of the leaves when Jack Liffey snatched her hand away. "Whoa, hon. Your Paiute senses are failing you. That's poison oak. Leaves in three, let it be."

"If I ever had any Paiute senses, they were beaten out of me," she said angrily.

"Sorry," he said.

She looked at him for a moment curiously and then visibly decided to ratchet down her inflamed sensibilities. She took his arm when he offered. "Next time I'll wear moccasins and turquoise and woo-woo if you like."

His heart soared with the easing of her pissed-off state, even the lame joke, and he took her roughened hand where it was clutching his bicep. "We're almost there."

The problem was that the waterfall was largely a bust. In the late fall, the stream was so feeble that water barely dribbled over the mossy fifty-foot cliff to send only a trickle into the pool. Still, the pool at the bottom was full and inviting, maybe three feet deep. "If we had suits we could at least soak," he said.

"It's going to be a while before I'm in a bathing suit, Dad," Maeve reminded him.

"Yeah, sorry. I guess even one of those ruffled Victorian bathing costumes wouldn't do the trick."

"Victorian bathing machines would be better. You know about them?"

"Never heard of 'em." He had, but he knew she loved it when she got to explain something to him.

"We did turn-of-the-century customs in my class on Time and Culture. All the popular beaches in Victorian England had these weird bathing machines. They were little wheeled cabins that were closed on all the shore sides. The women got inside and sat on a bench attached to the wall and changed into their bathing costumes. Then horses backed the bathing machines out into the water so that the women could dabble their feet and stay completely unseen. The ayatollahs would have loved them."

"Why wear anything at all if you're that hidden?"

Gloria squeezed his hand once as prelude to extricating her fingers. "There's no end to the silly stuff men expect us to do so they don't have to control their own emotions."

"I understand completely," he said. "Gloria, you could put on a chador so all I could see is those lovely brown eyes and you'd still drive me nuts."

That earned him a soft punch on the shoulder.

Maeve turned to face them both. Putting on her most earnest look, she stopped dead, arms akimbo. "How come you two are mad at each other? It's like the ghost at the feast."

He waited a few moments, but it didn't seem Gloria was going to say anything. "I was a bad boy," Jack Liffey said. "I've been trying unsuccessfully to negotiate the terms of my surrender ever since. I lied to Gloria."

Maeve's expression took on that panicky look she had sometimes, when life started moving too fast for her. "About *what?* I hope this isn't another one of your world-historic failures at keeping your pants zipped."

He smiled tightly for an instant. "No, hon, and I think you exaggerate that problem a little. Anyway, Gloria is who I want and I'm not on the prowl."

"Well, sometimes the problem is that there's a woman who is." She looked at him pointedly. "What about the Dragon Lady?"

He knew who she meant and wondered if the warmth in his cheeks meant he was blushing. "Hon, there are times I'd prefer not to look at my life in comic terms." He'd been looking for a missing Vietnamese girl at the time, and her employer had come after him hard.

Jack Liffey and Gloria Ramirez now stared at one another, each waiting for the other to blink. He didn't want to tell Maeve that he'd found the boy who'd shot her, but Gloria was giving him no help. "I withheld some information that I thought would put Gloria in an uncomfortable position as a sworn officer of the law. We'll tell you about it a little later, if you can trust us until then."

He yearned for the days, right after Maeve had broken a couple of promises to him, when he could pull rank. But whatever credit you gained that way inevitably trickled away faster than you could make good use of it.

She reached out and took Gloria's hand and then his hand and put them together petulantly until they clasped reluctantly. Maeve was still part child, in willful denial of the world of separation and divorce, of conflicting interests, loss, defeat, and general human breakdown. "Give each other a kiss now."

They pecked, and Maeve sighed. "I guess that's the best I'm going to get. Please don't scare me, guys. I've had too much change already. I like you too much." She put an arm around Gloria and clung.

Apparently, there was a Santa Ana brewing up. A gritty blast of wind erupted down the trail and made them all turn away and cover their eyes, breaking the tension.

"'Whirl is king, having driven out Zeus,'" Jack Liffey said softly. "Unfortunately."

"One of the Greeks?" Maeve asked.

"Aristophanes, I think. We'll do our best to stay together, hon. That's all I can promise."

"I need a tall bush to hide behind," Maeve said in an abrupt change of tone, clutching her side. "And something to dig with."

Gloria hadn't spoken in some time, and her silence had been swelling in his psyche like a lit fuse.

"Sit over there a moment," Gloria said. "Jack and I'll dig you a pit against the cliff."

The ordinary considerate words felt to him like a fever breaking.

Dear Diary,
Lord, this happy Jamaican is built like a big truck & really he really sees me & talks to me. When I'm in bed tonight I hope he comes to me. Black skin dont make no nevermind to me at all. Its so funny we play dominos & just insult each other so much & it makes me so happy to be insult by him Im still laughing. Up here makes down there seem so far away. I feel like a princess in a castle.

THIRTEEN

A Strong Faith System

The wind was so powerful, gusting out of the northeast, that it was hard to keep the tall RAV-4 in lane. They were on an exclusive stretch of the Pacific Coast Highway in Malibu, with overpriced beach getaways on stilts lining the ocean side of the road, shoulder-to-shoulder like a long irregular fence.

"You folks mind if I double-park here a minute?" He pulled off the road, blocking a gray two-car garage door on a nondescript modern house Its only notable feature was a sunburst doodad lamp on the clapboards that really belonged on a sixties apartment building inland.

"The Coastal Commission hired me to make sure there's still beach access." In theory, all of the beach—seaward of the mean high tide—was public, but when celebrities built their beach houses elbow to elbow along the water, cutting off access, they'd pledged to keep open a few stairways. Little by little, of course, the access stairways had been walled off or actually built over, in order to keep out the riff-raff.

"You're kidding," Gloria said.

"I'm kidding. But I have information that your Luisa might have stayed here, even might be here now."

"I see."

"Dad's on the case," Maeve said. "Was that the whole reason for this trip?"

"Of course not, hon. But you know how I like to double up my errands." He actually did. It gave him a primitive kind of satisfaction, this temporal economy. "I knew you wouldn't mind. You guys wait in the car in case some zealous traffic cop shows up to give us a ticket. I'll just pop in and see what's up."

A wooden staircase led down from the shoulder of the road right next to the address that Chris Johnson had unearthed for him. He walked past the house door and continued down to a deck that was still well above the sand. It was chest high, but he boosted himself up and climbed the railing to wait in a corner of the deck against the cedar clapboard wall of the house. Nobody bothered closing curtains here, and there was a young man in a bathrobe sitting cross-legged in the living room talking into a cordless phone. He looked unhappy and kept pressing his hand against his crotch as if easing a pain.

The wind whistled and moaned around the house and down the staircase, but he could still make out the louder moments of the phone conversation.

". . . You think I can't imagine it? Somebody kicks sand in your face and you go home and karate the mirror for days . . . I will come there and use the damn blade if you don't get my money. Today."

The young man stabbed the off button hard. Then he cut a line of coke on a big white ceramic tile beside him and snorted it up with a thin red straw. Jack Liffey saw no evidence of Luisa, but she could have been in back or downstairs.

He slid off the deck and went up the steps to the main door and rang the bell. He heard an awful rendition of the opening bars of *Here Comes the Sun*. He waited a reasonable time and then rapped pretty hard.

"Gas company!" Why not? he thought. "We show a methane buildup here. There's a danger of explosion!"

As far as he knew, there was no methane problem around here,

but who in L.A. could afford to ignore a warning like that? A whole
row of shops across from Farmer's Market, not far from the big
CBS studio, had gone up in an awesome fireball in 1985—putting
an abrupt end to plans to continue the main subway line down
Wilshire Boulevard to the west. He'd just read that the entire
expensive Playa Vista development had been built over a giant
rubber membrane pierced by tall vent pipes to exhaust the gas
buildup. But, methane or not, the young man was ignoring him. He
heard a door close somewhere in the house, then a grinding noise,
and he started to head back to the deck for a peek.

"Jack!"

It was Gloria, sounding urgent. He hurried up the stairs to see
the house's swing-up garage door wedged partially open against the
RAV-4. Maeve was still in the car, her eyes the size of saucers.
Gloria pointed toward Santa Monica, but there was nothing much
to see.

"A young man in sweats and a big revolver rolled out underneath and took off running down the road. I didn't think I had
reason to shoot him."

"You didn't."

"He looked like the hounds of hell were after him. He actually
got up enough speed to jump in the back of a gardener's pickup
truck, a white Toyota. He rapped with the pistol on the window of
the cab and that seemed to keep the driver going. I could only get
the initial 4J off the plate. There can't be more than a hundred
thousand Latino gardeners with Toyota pickups."

"Jesus. It's like when you turn on the light switch and the same
second an earthquake levels the house. That's one spooked kid."

"What did you do down there?"

"Nothing to cause that. I'm going inside for a look around. If
that offends your official sensibility, you can wait here."

"Since the garage is open, it's not technically a 459. Just trespass,
and even that wouldn't stick if you don't do any damage."

"I'll tread softly."

But she did follow him in, ducking under the springs at the side
of the door. Some kind of big square SUV was under a tarp; beside

it was a little red Miata with the top down. The door into the house was shut but not locked, and he called a couple of times, and then Gloria obliged him by yelling out "L.A.P.D.!" They entered a stainless steel and granite kitchen like something out of a design magazine, but cluttered with old pizza boxes and KFC buckets. There was also a baggie of white powder that he saw Gloria eyeing, though there wasn't a damn thing she could do about it since she wasn't in the house legally.

"This is a drugged-up kid camping out in somebody else's house," he said.

"Maybe."

The living room had a lot of white leather furniture and a few bad paintings. He made his way down a hallway to a bedroom with a mattress on the floor. There was a cardboard box with what looked like women's underwear and jeans and blouses. A copy of *Wuthering Heights* was tented open on the floor, with a stack of Harlequin romances beside it.

"I know one thing," Jack Liffey said. "Our guy wasn't reading this." Then he noticed a small rounded stone in the corner and pocketed it. It strengthened his belief that Luisa Wilson had indeed been here.

"Now it's a felony," she said.

"I thought it had to be over $5,000 to be a felony."

"Grand theft is down to $400 now, but if you take anything at *all* you qualify for a 459, burglary."

"Door was open."

"Let's not be lawyers."

"Oh, let's not—not being a lawyer is my life's ambition. I think this is Luisa's stuff. I'll come back some other time."

"It must be nice not to have to follow the law."

"I'll tell the guys in Rampart that," he said. Rampart had been the worst police scandal to hit L.A. since the 1930s—from planting evidence right up to shooting inconvenient witnesses—and you only had to whisper the name of the division to make any L.A. cop wince.

"Okay, okay."

* * *

There are different things in Mexico from here in the United States like language and food that are not the same and houses. There was trouble in Texas and US wanted to grab a big part of land. California to. Mexicans fought hard and kill at the Alamo. Then Mr. Santa Anna got butt-kick. And Rio Grande is the border. Here Tijuana is the border. Texas is the home of President Bush.

The page was illuminated like a parody of a medieval manuscript, the text surrounded by colored pencil drawings of cacti and eagles carrying snakes in their beaks and a couple Virgins of Guadalupe with their golden radiance.

Jack Liffey read the paragraph a second time while Thumb Estrada guzzled a Pepsi across the kitchen table. The essay was bad, but not as bad as he'd feared. There were actual sentences, and even some facts, or near facts, hidden in the garble.

"I don't know why you think you can't write. You can put a perfectly good sentence together. It needs work, but that's not the end of the world."

The boy studiously avoided his eyes. Jack Liffey wrote a big 1 in the corner of the essay and circled it. He intended to take his reluctant pupil through as many drafts as the boy would tolerate.

"Read your first sentence," Jack Liffey said, and slid the paper across. "Just to refresh your memory."

Thumb deigned to look down after a rebellious glare. Moving his lips slightly, he read the sentence to himself.

"I've got two questions for you. What does it have to do with the Mexican-American War? And who do you know in this whole wide world who doesn't know what your saying? You don't really need to say things that everybody knows. In Mexico, they speak Spanish. Mexico has different customs. Mexicans eat tacos. Mexican towns are colorful. *Ay que!*"

The boy looked up at him, with a flat puzzled expression.

"Now look at the second sentence you've got. It's not perfect, but it's where the essay really starts. I want you to take this first try home and rewrite it tonight. Throw out the first sentence. Start with the second. And this time I want you to include at least two dates, two names, and two battles. And I like your art, but you might want to leave it off since you're going to rewrite this over and over until you get it right. Okay?"

The boy frowned but folded the paper and put it into his pocket. "You liked the pictures?"

"I think you've got real talent, but even at art school you're going to have to know how to write."

"Tomorrow, I gotta meet Beto for my GED study."

"Okay, come Tuesday. Is that enough time for you?"

He thought about it but finally nodded and finished off his Pepsi. Jack Liffey asked about his family, but Thumb was still all too aware that the man sitting there was the *gabacho* whose daughter he'd shot. He answered in monosyllables.

"Okay, see you then." Jack Liffey followed him out to the front yard where his bicycle was lashed to the ash tree with a fat chain that would have stopped the Queen Mary in its tracks. Thumb Estrada looked at the old VW Bug parked on the street.

"You got a kill switch in that, man?"

"Who would steal a 1962 Beetle?"

"Man, lots a guys want them vee-dubs, make sand bugs and shit. Even a *ruca* can hot-wire that thing."

"What's a *ruca?*

"A girl. I get you a kill switch." This was a good sign, Jack Liffey thought. Like a cat offering its kill at the back door, but then he felt a bit patronizing for the thought. Until he remembered that Thumb had shot his daughter.

"Thanks. I'll pay you to install it, if you can."

"Course I can, man."

Carne asada under the stars, good buddy" Levine said. He was stoking up a stone barbecue built into a rock extension of the deck, squirting on masses of lighter fuel in a perfect example of the fire-lighting technique Luisa's relatives had called Paleface Napalm. "Gourmet hog heaven, that's what we got."

"Amens," Terror Pennycooke finally said. "You i-sire some fine ganja?" He held another of those giant dirigible-shaped cigarettes out toward Luisa, who shook her head. One small hit of that stuff was more than enough. She turned her attention to the hilly coastal chaparral, different from the inland chaparral that she knew so well. It was lit now by discreet floodlights surrounding the house. Out away from the house, she had already seen a coyote, two jackrabbits, several snakes and lizards, a family of quail, and a young deer. Neither of the men had noticed any of the wildlife, so far as she knew.

The taller and wispier plants were bobbing oceanward in the irregular warm wind, and it was definitely a Santa Ana, warming the air and letting them stay outside after dark in shirtsleeves in the early winter. She was a little worried about sparks from the barbecue, since there was far too much dry brush near the patio, but the fire seemed to be well contained.

"Dat man deah is a saps," Terror Pennycooke said softly, as he took a lingering hit on his joint. "No pay him no mind."

"How come you're in L.A.?" Luisa asked. "It must be a long way from home."

"Tings dred inna J now," he said. "No money, no life. Ai man, I-an-I a-forward hier. Is a good lan' to prize de livin' god for a time. Some ob de Rastas say dis hier is Babylon, for true, just like Englun, but dey is no ting of slavery left hier if you stan' tall. Make any church you wan', prize you own god."

"You're lucky your people still have a god," she said. "My people's gods were all killed or something. A long time ago."

"Haile Selasie, him live forever. Him say, love the fist open," he said, and he rested his hand gently on her shoulder for a moment. "The people of color in de world got to be of one blackheart, you no seeit?"

"My people were slaves, too," Luisa said proudly. "In Owens, they made them work on white farms and if they ran away to the mountains, they sent the sheriffs and the army to bring them back in chains. I was told the only real way they had to fight back was burning down barns in the middle of the night. That happened a lot."

Terror Pennycooke chuckled. "Blood fire fe dem, dawta. De

weapon ob de weak is dred. De likkle kitty sneak behind and bite you arse when you no seeit."

"Who wants pork and who wants beef?" Levine called.

Terror Pennycooke's face took on a savage scorn. "Pork no be ital. *Dat ting!* Pigs is scavengers ob de land."

"All the more for me, Ter. I put on a couple of yams for you, see how much I think of you."

"Ah, cool runnings, man."

"Can I try the yam?" Luisa asked.

He grinned and dangled an arm loosely across her shoulder. "You bonafide, dawta."

"We're losing momentum, man. I can feel it. It's getting like the same old stuff we had in Games I. Mailbox baseball, guys jumping off roofs, guys eating snails and lizards—we'll never beat out the old one like that. We need some *ideas*—we gotta be *stone* outrageous."

Rod Whipple nodded. His partner was right, but Kenyon Styles' definition of outrage included real injury and risk of worse. They'd wind up with manslaughter charges before they were done. They'd already had to edit out a couple of serious injuries, and the current one gave him the willies.

Encouraged by an early heavy snowfall over the Sierras, they had bundled up in parkas and shifted production to the pro snowboard slope at Mammoth, right in front of a red sign that said cryptically *Wall Hits Not*. He wasn't even sure which was the verb or what the Teutonic syntax was proposing, but it made for a nice hint of mystery.

Kenyon pointed to a medium-sized limber pine far down the hill and off to one side, standing out like a glowing skeleton in the moonlight. "Make your way down there. They ought to be going into overdrive by then." He'd talked a couple of snowboarders into braving the expert slope on big uncontrollable plastic trash barrel lids.

The mountain held about eighteen inches of powder, half of it manufactured just to jumpstart the season, plus a thin crust from the daytime melt. Rod could still manage to high-step his way down with care, crunching through the crust in tall waterproof boots. He stayed off to the north edge of the slope where it wasn't quite so steep, but he didn't have a clue how anyone could ski down this run without trending off line a few yards to the other side—which would take you over an escarpment and almost straight down. There was a red flag out, signaling treacherous snow; thus, no one was visible on the slope.

The way the wind was blowing, he couldn't hear anything from the top, but when he got to the tree he braced himself to look back at Kenyon's upraised arm. The daredevils seemed all set to go. The arm swung down.

One of them spun backwards immediately, digging with his palm like an oar trying to straighten himself out. The other caught the rim and tumbled once before somehow righting his craft again.

They were probably fifty feet down the run, still gathering uncontrollable speed, when Rod saw his partner toss something into the snow behind them. In a moment, quite a lot of snow heaved up into the air; a few seconds later the blast caught him like a punch in the chest.

Panic overtook him. He felt suddenly ill. Kenyon had given him no warnings about explosives. A big apron of fresh snow tore loose along a perfect break near the top of the run and puffed up instantly into a wall of white smoke that headed down-hill toward him. He dropped the camera on its lanyard around his neck and scrambled up the young pine, bough to bough. He got up maybe twenty feet, then unbuckled his belt to lash himself to the skinny tree.

Only when he felt he was secure did he pick up the still-running camera, and aim it up at the barrel-lid riders. They were close, riding the forward edge of the avalanche like surfers with a look of tidal-wave terror on their faces. He felt the rumble up through the tree which suddenly seemed much too frail. The powder wave crested well above where he clung.

"You didn't tell Maeve who you're tutoring, did you?" Gloria asked him.

He glanced up from his book. He was in the living room to be sociable, trying to reread an early Robert Stone, but the cop show she was watching was already intruding. She liked to watch them to make fun of the mistakes, both small and large, over police procedure, or so she said. But he could tell that what she really liked, at least as much, was the flattering portrait of lawmen doing their best to maintain a sense of honor in all the gray zones. There were few bad cops on TV, no racists, no brutal misfits, or bribe-demanders, at least none that survived more than an episode. If America had fetishized anything by the early twenty-first century, it was law enforcement.

"Not yet."

The show started up again, and Jack Liffey started to watch a black cop arguing with somebody in a suit outside a courtroom. He could understand the popularity of TV cops. Everybody deep down wanted to be part of a team of like-minded people working together toward a decent goal. It was the same impulse that had finally made *Star Trek* a hit. He wondered if the cop show passion hadn't subtly replaced religion for a lot of the viewers. Or maybe it rechanneled their impulses to social activism or civil rights—at several removes. He was drawn to the cop shows, himself, for exactly the same reasons. Yet he resisted out of his perverse loyalty to the need for some disorder in the world. Cop shows were always about keeping things in line.

"So, what happens when she finds out?"

"Hey. Maybe Thumb will be a better kid by then. Doesn't your universe brook any forgiveness?"

"Jack, Jack. Don't be so gullible. He's a banger. He'll die a banger, probably violently, in a year or two."

"What were you at seventeen? Gandhi? I was a mess. Everybody I knew was a mess. Hormones get us, if nothing else does."

"Were you into turf wars and drive-bys?"

"Those things weren't big in my neighborhood. God knows, I might have been. When I was thirteen, my friends and I got into a stupid rock fight with a group of kids from the next block over. We started lobbing things over a house at each other. We weren't even that pissed off, just bored. I ran out of rocks and grabbed up a piece of a broken bottle. It was as stupid and thoughtless as it gets, but there it is. A few seconds later I saw a little girl come screaming around the house with a bad cut on her forehead. I don't know if I did it, I don't know if it left a permanent scar that changed her life forever—but . . ."

He shrugged. "It happened. You back out of your driveway, and you just happen to be angry about something, and you don't see the kid on the bike. Thumb doesn't even know why he capped off, but it wasn't about Maeve. As the actual target, I ought to get a little say in this."

Gloria shook her head. "I wish I could take you out in the squad car for a few days. You might think differently about second chances."

"Two seems fair," he said.

"It's probably this kid's hundredth."

"I can't know that. I'm having a little trouble liking him, it's true, but off and on he seems to be trying."

"Just remember, I warned you. And keep him away from me. I don't buy into this sainthood you're aspiring to."

Jack Liffey reached out and touched her leg. "You're not mad at me, are you, Glor?"

"I'm furious at you." She took a deep breath. "And the trouble is, I don't know why."

"Jesus."

"It has to do with me, Jack. I know that. I'm really sorry."

"Do you want me out of here for a while?"

"No, *querido*, please. Just think of me right now as PMS on patrol. Ten-24." She almost smiled. "That means, trouble at the station." She slapped herself, roughly over the heart. "The trouble's in me. I'm the station."

"I'm here for you if I can be," he said.

"I've been seeing my rabbi—Donald. My mentor. You know what he says, that we all need a faith system, the stronger the better. Right now, mine isn't working. Pretty wise, for a cop, don't you think?"

"I won't let you down," Jack Liffey said.

"Oh, yeah?"

FOURTEEN

Professional Integrity

Terror Pennycooke had one of the most amazing bodies she had ever seen, all glisten and sheen. Here and there it almost disappeared into the shadows that filled the dark room and then reemerged like something molded of hard rubber, stuffed with muscle, and beaded up with sweat. She liked the casual way his dreadlocks flopped around when they weren't stuffed under the big knit cap.

"Can't I call you Trevor?" she asked. "Terror sounds so violent." He had been nothing but sweet to her, not a terror at all. She'd offered to go down on him, and it was generally so much easier, anyway, but he shook his head and said something about that being for white boys. He had touched her all over with his long dry fingers and then made love to her tenderly, and longer than she had ever experienced. She didn't know she went in that far. He found his way to places she didn't even know she had. She only had to pretend a little at the end.

"Boo-ya," he said into the dark room. "For you, you can call me Fontleroy if you want. Hah. That a joke, you no dare. You got you a special name?"

"Just for you, you could call me Taboots. It means rabbit."

He laughed, easy and warm. "TAH-boots. That nice."

"You seem like a big powerful buffalo to me."

"Ah, buffalo. What you call buffalo?"

"Cooch."

Now he made a face, and grabbed up a handful of sheet to wipe the sweat off his face. "Cooch. Sound like dat place 'tween you legs. Got anything else?"

"How about horse? He's Cabi."

"Cabi, dat's a fine ting. But only you can ride Cabi, Taboots."

She rolled over and kissed him.

"But you got to stop eating the flesh of animals an' dead creeturs," Terror declared. "That no good at all, make you fret, full a science stuff, bad crap. You got to avoid all food in packets and tins, too."

"Okay. I'll do it for you, Cabi."

He ran his finger slowly down her nose. "You step up. Maybe we see about a ting."

"What?"

"Ting dey call Dangerous Game."

"What's that?" she asked, feeling a chill.

"Man, I hear it's a way we make lotsa money fast. Maybe get us out of Babylon, dawta, forward to a fine likkle farm on J."

Rod Whipple found himself at least 500 feet farther down the slope than where he had belayed himself to the tree, without his pants or even his boxers—all of which had vanished into the avalanche along with the top half of the tree. He now lay nearly strangled by the nylon cord that held the Panasonic around his neck. He knew he was fortunate to have ridden the frothy upper layers of the snow wave, and as his panic began to subside, he found his head and one arm in the clear, with the cold crisp air burning his nostrils. As avalanches go, it had probably been small potatoes.

He got the fish eye from the Mammoth Ski Patrol as they dug him out. After all, it was pretty late, and he clearly wasn't fitted out to be on the slopes for any legitimate purpose. They didn't know what was up, but they had heard the dynamite, of which he quite rightfully pleaded ignorance. They gave him an old pair of sweat pants for which he traded a phony name and address.

Kenyon Styles seemed to have evaporated into the moonlit evening, but Rod figured he was just in hiding, waiting for things to simmer down so he could make a discreet return to their old station wagon in the village. He had no idea what had happened to the trash-lid riders, and he hoped they had been able to ride it out alive, but the minute he found Kenyon he was planning to pound him senseless. This time his recklessness had gone way, way over the top.

Gloria had rolled out ahead of him at the crack of dawn, saying she said she had to write up a report, and so he had drifted back to sleep. He wasn't usually a slugabed, a term his ex-wife had favored, especially since he'd stopped drinking, but he'd been feeling tired and slow for quite a while now. It might have been something to do with the collapsed lung that had spontaneously reinflated a while back. The last time he'd seen the psychiatrist who'd been forced on him—so he could collect workman's comp—the man had talked about incipient depression. Jack Liffey had figured life was a lot simpler if he just said he was a bit tired.

"Some juice, Jack?"

She was all uniformed up for some reason—as a detective she normally wore a skirt and blazer—sitting at the kitchen table with a stack of bound notebooks and papers. The first time he'd seen her in blues, he'd found it strangely sexy, but now he was used to it, and it just seemed fussy and a bit absurd.

"I know you're in a rush. I can take care of myself." In fact, he cleared her plate and utensils, and refreshed her coffee before staring hard into the fridge. He'd forgotten why he'd opened the door, and then he remembered and took out the milk. It was taking longer than usual for the cobwebs to clear this morning.

"What's making you so worn down these days?" she asked.

"What've you got?"

It might have been a soft laugh behind him. Now he was stuck trying to choose between two boxes of cereal, his arm frozen in mid-gesture toward the shelf. There was no earthly reason he could discover to choose the raisin bran over the Wheaties, so he just gave it up and poured some coffee instead. He'd converted her to the burnt-tasting French Roast that he loved, and it was great.

"I'm sorry I was such a bitch last night. Sometimes, I don't know what gets at me. It's amazing how things look so much better in the daylight."

"La madrugada," he said. He liked the feel of all those bursting syllables on his palate. He'd missed his Spanish class at city college that week.

He rotated the pile that was *The L.A. Times* with one finger so he could read the headlines. The mayor and the police chief were at odds again, the U.S. was withholding money at the U.N., and a small plane had crashed into a motel in Hawthorne. Nothing of interest above the fold. He'd been a copy boy at the now defunct *News-Pilot* on that busy day Khrushchev had been overthrown and the Chinese had set off their first H-bomb. There had been a third big event that day, too—he couldn't remember what—and the editor of the street edition had been tearing his hair out trying to get all three headlines big enough and all above the fold. That was back when street editions still mattered in L.A. Nobody read the paper in the streetcar now, and nobody much cared. How different that postwar world had been. He'd only had a glimpse of it as a child. Newsboys hollering headlines at the red-car stop. Guys wearing Homburgs. Worrying about A-bomb tests. That world had a soiled feeling, he felt as he contemplated it. Not innocent at all.

The doorbell rang, making Gloria look up sharply. "Who the hell is that?"

"You sound like you're worried some boyfiend might show up before I'm gone."

"It better not be a girlfriend, *mijito*. You get no second chances from me on that."

Jack Liffey opened on plainclothes Sergeant Dean Padilla, already looking a bit rumpled but plainly satisfied with himself. The day behind him was glorious and sunny, the kind that made you wonder how anybody could ever be unhappy in Southern California.

"Sergeant."

"Mr. Liffey. Sgt. Ramirez."

"Come in," Jack Liffey said. "Can I get you some coffee?"

"I wouldn't say no. I don't know why Joe Friday always turned it down."

Padilla sat opposite Gloria, and she closed the report she'd been reading.

"What brings you out so early?" Jack Liffey asked.

"It's one of those mornings. For me, the Santa Anas are a tonic. All the positive ions blowing off the desert and putting everybody on edge to make the assholes turn crazy and challenge us. If attacked, I will wholeheartedly accept the challenge."

"Have they ever taken a statistical look at crimes on Santa Ana days?" Gloria asked.

He shrugged. "I read wife-beating goes way up after Monday Night Football."

"I heard that."

Jack Liffey brought him a cup of strong coffee and an option of milk and sugar.

"Black, thanks." He sipped his coffee and opened a fancy aluminum briefcase, then took out a five-by-seven photograph of Thumb Estrada and slid it across the table.

"He was in the lineup," Jack Liffey said, as the silence grew oppressive.

"*Si, esse,* and this is the very *pendejo* who shot your girl."

"How do you know?"

"We know."

"Can you prove it?" He felt Gloria Ramirez watching him.

"Not without you."

Jack Liffey thought about his words carefully, but he'd already made his decision. "From one glance at a kid in a dark car, I am not going to send him to prison. That one look was not definitive." Of course, closer looks later had been, but strictly speaking, he could pretend he wasn't lying.

Padilla tapped the photo thoughtfully with his finger. "Look harder."

"I'm sorry, man. I can't drop a dime on this guy. Maeve is recovering. I'd like to forget the whole thing."

"What do you think this is, a civil suit over some fucking dog barking after the Leno show, keeping you up? This is a major felony. *We* bring charges. You can't drop it, you got no option that way at all, my friend." He turned to Gloria. "What do you say?"

She took a long draft of her coffee. "I have to get to work. You know I was in the house, Dean. I didn't see the shooting."

"Yeah, but you know what your boyfriend is up to with this shithook. Whose side are you on?"

"I'm blue," she said.

"Don't cut off your nose to spite your face," he insisted.

"What the hell is that supposed to mean?"

He slapped the photo back in his briefcase. "How the hell do I know? Maybe your face can't be made any more presentable."

"That's uncalled for," Jack Liffey said.

Padilla glared at him and stood up slowly. It had been a long time since a cop had got his goat like this, but Jack Liffey stood, too, locking eyes with their visitor.

Gloria sighed. "Let's not have a dick-waving contest here, okay," she said. She stood and got between them, facing Padilla. "He said he can't identify the kid. What do you want him to do, lie?"

Jack Liffey knew there'd be a price for this, but her loyalty to him now was breathtaking. His jaw was still tight with anger, with some guilt mixed in. There had to be a simpler way to make your way through the world, he thought. He was just trying to help a kid who could use as much as he could get and maybe more.

"Tell your man he's lucky I don't arrest him for obstruction. Or shoot him for good measure," Padilla hissed at Gloria.

She grinned suddenly. "Don't waste it. You know it's not a good shooting unless it involves overtime."

Padilla barged out and left the door open. She shut it and turned to Jack Liffey with an unreadable expression.

"I hope that hasn't hurt your professional integrity," he said.

"It did. I used to get along with Dean."

He thought of getting up to kiss her before she went off to work, but actually didn't want to. He knew she was perfectly aware that he was just trying to help the kid—but it struck him all of a sudden how little an understanding like that had to do with the ways of the heart. He'd wager neither one of them was very much in love at that moment.

She needed faith, she'd explained. He guessed he needed a dream. Jack Liffey wasn't used to self-pity, but something like it was dogging him. I seem to want something from life that I'm not getting, he decided.

The grunting and cooing behind him was driving him crazy, making him wish he'd taken the other available seat on the Greyhound, up front beside the violent-looking bearded guy in fatigues with the thousand-yard stare. As Rod Whipple sat down beside the large sleeping black woman, he'd gotten a good look at the girl directly behind him, a blonde with her unbuttoned shirt showing off not just the straps but half the cups of her black bra. The guy in the window seat was only a blur of blue work shirt and mustache.

"My name is Sally, and I'm an ex-Mormon, and I don't give a flying fuck who knows it," she had announced loudly as the bus pulled out. "I do everything those weenies hate and I'm drunk as a skunk."

A hundred miles later, the big woman beside him was pretending to sleep to avoid the noises from the seat behind them. Rod sat cradling the ugly little video camera, cursing Kenyon Styles silently. By the time he'd been released by the ski patrol and made his way back to where they'd parked, Kenyon's station wagon was gone. His own money had vanished with his pants in the avalanche so he had to try various cars around the darkling ski town until he found an unlocked Suburban in a ski lodge lot that he could sleep in. In the morning, he'd made a collect call and had his censorious sister in Grand Rapids very reluctantly wire him some money.

"Ohyesohyesohyes*there*theredoit."

Kenyon Styles had a lot to answer for. Rod's anger welled up. Yet what he really wanted to do was weep with frustration. The worst part was that he knew his own weaknesses and understood that he probably wouldn't do anything. He desperately wanted his share of the money *Dangerous Games II* would bring in. Greed eats the soul, he thought. And this was the first time he really understood how greed worked.

As usual when his sense of purpose was wearing a bit thin, he made a lunch date with his daughter, who had a school holiday. She had recently given him a Jane Smiley novel to read, suggesting he shouldn't think it was a "woman's book," and he suspected it of being a test. Of his sympathy, or his sensibility, or just his ability to shed the toughened skin he sometimes wore.

The wind was still gusty but buffered by the taller buildings around where they sat. They were out front at Houston's, a few miles inland in Manhattan Beach, with all the other prospective lunchers from the high-tech companies waiting all around, carrying the discreet little pagers from the maître d' so nobody had to do anything as uncouth as calling names into the afternoon. He preferred places a little less crowded, but this was Maeve's current favorite restaurant.

"You don't look so good," she told him.

"I'm getting older, Maeve. It happens. We had you late."

"No, you're not. I forbid you to get old. You're fighting with Gloria, aren't you?"

"Not exactly. Basically she's going through some sort of crisis she won't talk about, and it worries me."

"How about your own crisis? That hasn't been over for long."

"Who said it's over? My daughter, the psychiatrist. I should be asking about Oskar." Turning the tables on her was always a good idea.

"He's okay. I'm used to him now, but he still has a few tricks. Let's just pretend I'm normal."

"You are normal, just a lot smarter."

She gave him a half hug with her left arm. "What did you think about the book?"

He pursed his lips. "She can write, but the whole thing's kind of cribbed from *Lear.*"

"Is that so bad?"

"I'm not sure what *King Lear* is supposed to tell me about Midwest America, and I'm also not sure I believe that recovered memory stuff."

A giant black Hummer came past slowly, looking for parking, and he almost expected clowns to come out.

Suddenly, her eyes went wide as saucers.

"What is it, hon?"

"Oskar sometimes gives me a hard time. He bubbles and farts, and I'm afraid of overflowing." Once again, she looked startled, and she clapped a hand to her side, roughly above the bag. "I'll be back," she said, and she scurried inside.

For a few moments he watched the door where she had disappeared, then he realized his own anxieties couldn't help her and might even make things worse. It was all normal, if temporary, he thought. He mustn't make a big deal out of it.

The warm dry wind seemed to have grit in it, even this close to the ocean, and it seemed to carry unease and heartache along with it, too, like a blast of air out of a room where somebody had just died. A party of businessmen trooped out of Houston's talking earnestly. Each of them clutched a cell phone like a prize, a token of the world that they each aspired to unquestioningly.

Then Maeve was back out, waiting for him to stand up. "Is everything okay?"

"Yeah, daddy." Her voice was strange. "It's okay. Oskar's fine after all. They just had the beeper set to vibrate, and it was in my pocket. The Liffeys are up."

In the afternoon Jack drove out again to the Malibu beach house to see if the young man who'd fled had returned. He'd found out the place's renter was listed as Keith Long, which sounded like another *nom de porn*.

Driving past as slowly as he could, he thought the place seemed unchanged. Before leaving, he'd closed the garage door to keep out real burglars. He did a Y-turn across the highway via somebody's driveway and came back to park right where he had been before.

He let the VW drift the last few yards with the engine already off, and got out quietly.

The rote of the surf was light here but insistent, and almost no one was on the beach. Even if it was warm enough, the calendar said it was early winter, and people believed what they read. Jack Liffey walked down to the front door and rang the bell. "Delivery!" he called. "Package." Nobody ever could resist that.

After a while he knocked, then started thinking of breaking in again. Suddenly, the door swept open and there was the young man with his tousled blond hair. What caught his attention, though, was the fact that he was wearing nothing but a shorty muscle shirt and a big diaper. If that wasn't enough, he was holding a long-barreled pistol in Jack Liffey's face.

"Where's the fucking package?" he demanded.

"Don't make a mistake here, I'm your friend," Jack Liffey said.

"Step inside or die," the boy said. His eyes made him seem crazy enough to do anything. "You're looking at my only friend in my hand."

Keith recognized the Cadillac CTS parked on the pad in front of the hilltop house as Levine's. If it hadn't been so shiny, reflecting back the stars, it might have been nearly invisible in the pitch black of the Malibu hills night. A lot of houses up here had motion-activated security lights—his Miata had tripped several of them driving slowly up Highline Road—but this one didn't, and there were no regular streetlights at all. The upper side of the house along the road was blank and windowless.

He'd had a long talk with the man named Jack Liffey but didn't believe his story about hunting for Luisa. He was sure he must work for Levine and Terror, so he had left him securely strapped with gaffer's tape to a chrome kitchen chair.

It had been hell getting pants on over his throbbing penis, but he'd finally managed by wearing the limpest, thinnest trousers he had, a pair of much-washed linens. Still, it took a ludicrous wide-legged waddle to keep even that fabric from bringing pressure and friction to bear. If he took another Vicodin, he'd probably go to sleep right here at the wheel of the Miata so he toughed it out.

They hadn't even bothered to lock up the Caddy. That would make it easier. He worked slowly and quietly, using brief flashes of a penlight to see, removing the five wheel lugs from one of the big seventeen-inch wheels in front. Then, he popped the hood very gently and propped it open. The engine was smothered by so many wires and hoses and tubes that it took a while to find the throttle cable down in the spaghetti. He crimped a lead fishing weight over the cable, just beyond a cable guide.

The first time somebody stepped on the gas it would resist a bit as the weight slid but then the accelerator cable would jam wherever they left it and the over-revved engine would just keep on pulling. He wondered if whoever was driving would have the sense to switch off the engine in time as the runaway car threw off a front wheel and zoomed off Highline Drive.

Dear Diary,
I seem to have become a vegetarian out of love, but it dont matter to me what I eat. This man is so sweet I wood do anything he asks. I got that fuzzy feeling you get in your belly & I just want to be with him all the time and try to see threw his eyes. He sees stuff in funny ways & I like to hear it hes so sure of what he says. Like he says he wont put no cell phone to his ear because it sends rays through your brain & the other one gets angry when he has to make all the calls but he wont budge an inch.

He told me we got to enjoy the scenery in life because you never see it exactly the same twice. I never thought of that. He put a cap from the ginger beer out under a rock & came back & said that cap would always stay there & we could remember it & come back any time to remember this very time we was here.

FIFTEEN

No Humans Involved

The young man stripped the silver gaffer's tape off Jack Liffey's mouth in one yank, but only after establishing with extravagant threats that his prisoner wouldn't try anything funny. He sucked in a breath at the abrupt sting. Gaffer's tape, used in the film business, was a lot stronger and gummier than ordinary duct tape.

"I got to know if Levine sent you to fuck me up."

"I already told you I don't know Levine." Jack Liffey flexed and worked his lips trying to soothe the sting.

Abruptly, a ragged-looking cat raced into the room, did a noisy tour of all four walls like a bike riding up on a velodrome, and raced straight back where it came from. They both watched it.

"Another country heard from," Jack Liffey said. "Yours?"

"I hate cats. An old girlfriend's."

"I hope you feed him."

The kid glanced at Jack Liffey as if he were crazy. "I hope the little fucker dies and goes off to meet God."

"What would God want with a dead cat?"

Something had got the young man riled, probably to do with the diaper that still seemed to be under his drawstring trousers.

"Are you in pain?" Jack Liffey asked.

"I got things on my mind. Like that shit Levine. But I made sure he's gonna be seriously inconvenienced now." He gave his flat smile and walked restlessly, bowlegged, plucking now and then at the loose fabric over his crotch.

"Good for you, I guess."

The young man took a Corona out of the fridge. "I'd give you a beer, man, but you got no hands free."

"I'd rather talk about Luisa Wilson, anyway."

"That Indian chick? She was hanging with me, and I was showing her stuff," Keith boasted. "But Levine and Terror, they took her for what they called collateral, since I'm a little short on an investment."

"Did you say Terror?" That got Jack Liffey's attention.

"Huge Jamaican motherfucker. You know him?"

"Ginger ale," Jack Liffey said. He watched for a reaction. "Terror Pennycooke, if it's him—used to like to persuade people of things by blowing ginger ale up their noses. Ginger beer actually. It's like lighting one of your sinuses on fire."

"Never tried it."

"I thought I sent him home with his tail between his legs."

"You must be one tough guy."

"Everybody's tough when you get the drop first. Look at you."

"Yeah." Keith took the pistol out of his waistband and looked at it before setting it on the counter. "People's karate. No skill needed. You sure you don't know Levine?"

"Come on, kid. Listen up. I do *not* know Levine. I *did* know Terror Tyrone Pennycooke, but it was a long time ago. All I want is to see that Luisa is safe so I can tell her family."

"Well, don't think I abused her. She was ready, willing, and whatever. We even got touched some in our emotionals."

"Could you tell me where Levine and Terror are?"

"I won't talk about that. You'll mess my plans for them. The young man seemed to look at him seriously for the first time.

"Where you in Nam, man? You're about the right age."

"Sure. Mostly I watched a radar screen in an airconditioned trailer and got bored."

"You never killed nobody?"

"Is that so great?"

"It's a test, don't you think? It's got to make you different. Like you've got extra responsibility in the world, you've got to live for the guy who's dead, too."

"Never killed anybody." Jack Liffey had been forced to kill a man, looking him in the eyes while he did, but he wasn't going to tell this unhinged young man about it.

"At least then you know you're not a coward."

"You never know that for sure, young man. There's always worse fear than you think. What happened to you that's got you waddling around like Popeye?"

"Terror cut me. Not even for any purpose, man, just to fuck with me. But I already done something to help even the score."

"Fine. That shows initiative. But I think it's time for you to release me now and let me make a call to stop a police raid on this place. The woman I live with is a cop, and she's been to this house with me. It's the first place she'll think of."

"Right, and I'm the tooth fairy."

"I don't care what you are. Gloria Ramirez is a detective in Harbor Division L.A.P.D. You saw her in the RAV-4 out front when you rolled under the door and hightailed it out of here."

That troubled something behind his captor's eyes.

"I've got nothing against you, Keith." He used the name on purpose. "If you let me go now, I won't press any charges. I believe kidnapping is a capital crime."

"I didn't kidnap you. You came here."

"You moved me at gunpoint, and then tied me up. That'll do the trick in court. Come on, I told you right off I'm your friend. You want to get over, and so do I. SWAT may be on the way as we speak. I'm not fooling around."

That made the young man look to his left, as if there were helmets and flak jackets about to appear at the patio windows.

Finally, they managed a compromise. He would make a call on Keith's cellphone to make sure Gloria wasn't sending an air strike. But Keith got to hold the phone, and if he liked the tone of the call, he'd untie him. It was a risk, but Keith just didn't seem hardass enough to shoot him. He dialed and held the phone to Jack Liffey's face.

"Glor, don't get excited. I'm okay. I'm having a little discussion over in Malibu, and I'll be home soon."

Keith cut off the connection. "You weren't supposed to say where you were," he complained.

"The tape on my arms was your insurance. So that was mine. Now let's clear the bets. Get this shit off me."

The young man thought about it for a while, pacing and opening another beer. He even opened the cylinder of the revolver and checked it, as if some plan of action lay in there. Then he slammed it home again, nearly giving Jack Liffey a heart attack. Eventually the young man started unwrapping the prodigious amount of gaffer's tape he had used.

"Have you ever thought of getting a job you can be proud of?" Jack Liffey suggested, rubbing his arms. "You're still young."

"I'm not good at much."

"What did your dad do?"

Keith laughed. "You want to know my role model. He drove a big vacuum truck around building sites in Ohio and mucked out the port-a-crappers. No matter how many gloves and jackets he wore, he always smelled like the job. I'd die before I'd do that."

The boy jumped clear as Jack Liffey's right hand came free. He brought the pistol out again and held it ready as Jack Liffey set about freeing his left hand himself. "Look at this house, man," Keith said. "I'll bet it's cooler than the one you got. I ain't no loser. I'm my own boss, I get up when I want. I supply girls for trade shows and stuff like that. It's not so bad."

"Pimp is the job title. I'll bet your mom didn't raise a son to be a pimp. Just tell me where Levine and Terror took Luisa."

"No way. Get out of here now, man, and get your woman to leave me alone. I done you right."

"You're so full of shit, Terror."

"No man, blessings, you's the one wrong. You no seeit?"

They'd tried to light a fire in the outside oven, but it kept going out. Now the night was chilly, and it was time to go inside. "There's no big time money in Dangerous Games, trust me, T. It's two slacker college kids exploiting winos for peanuts."

"Dat de ordinary stuff. I know *dat*. Dese guys, dey got movie number two for big stuff. Real stuff. Real money, I knaow it."

Luisa rested her head against his shoulder and let his strong reassuring arm hold her.

"Look, Terr, there *is* a second Dangerous Games, but it's just more of the same cheesy stunts. These guys, I know them, they're seriously pathetic: When they finished cutting the first one, they took it in to Full Flesh Video to distribute, just walked in the door like baby chicks, and the Italians took one look at them, gave them a check for chickenfeed, and said, Don't call us, we'll call you, chumps." He chuckled. "Full Flesh made twelve million on it. It's what happens when the minnows play with the sharks."

Terror Pennycooke shook his head. Luisa could see that he wouldn't let anybody tell him a thing, not even his partner. "Nao, man, is all of it lies. Dese guy, dey know waa gwan inna world. Dey no stupid."

Levine shrugged. "Have it your way, man. Pigs can fly. If you've really gotta have money fast, take some H off Keith and sell it around."

"I-an-I no like that hair-o-wine. It not worthy for a serious man."

Something had ticked Levine off, and he went into the house. A little later, they heard an outside door slam and the Cadillac up on the driveway purred to life. It idled for a while, and they heard it roar out of the drive. Suddenly, there was a dull thump, as if something heavy had been thrown out of the car onto the dirt road—but the engine kept accelerating. Luisa and Terror could barely believe their eyes. The nearly invisible black Cadillac, marked only by its lights, left the road with its engine screaming and arced out over the drop-away canyon at the steepest point.

They sat up in astonishment, just as there was a long cry of wa-hoo-hoo-eee! on the night.

"Jeeze," Luisa said. "Why'd he do that?"

"He on someting!" Terror said.

The car struck the hillside and bounced once, but it didn't explode the way they always did in movies, just tilted sideways and plunged hard to earth again and finally clanged and thudded to a stop well down the canyon.

It was pretty late for a visitor, but maybe Jack had lost his key, she thought as she made her way to the door in her bathrobe. But through the gauze curtain on the little window of the front door she saw Thumb, the kid Jack was so determined to help. She sighed once and opened three inches on the chain.

"It's pretty late for a visit, son," she said.

"Mr. Liffey wanted me to fix my essay today, and I got hung up. *Lo siento, senora.*"

"*No hay de qué. Dame el ensayo.*" She held her hand out near the cracked door for the essay, but then she felt silly for being so cautious. "Oh, wait." She shut the door to slip off the chain and opened it for him. She decided to inspect this kid with her own eyes. "*Pasale.*"

"*Gracias, dama.*"

"My fiancée has nearly got us both into a lot of trouble concerning you," she went on in Spanish.

"Mr. Liffey is not biting his own tongue, I think."

"It is true. He's a straightforward man. Sometimes. Not always. Would you like a Coke? We have no beer in the house. My fiancée does not drink."

The young man looked uncomfortable, but he nodded. "Thank you very much, lady."

His Spanish was not very good, she thought. North American formulations and tenses, mixed with street *Calo*, with all the innate politeness and clarity of the Spanish going haywire. He'd seem like a real rube, talking like this in Mexico, even if he couldn't know it. "Have a seat. I'd like to talk to you," she switched to English.

He hesitated, then sat.

"Not as a cop. As Jack's *novia*. I want to protect my man from your horseshit. If it's going to be necessary." She had started out seething, but the reason now eluded her. Thumb was truculent, sure, but without malice. What he was was a worthless kid who would never escape the barrio tide dragging him down. She could sympathize with that, in a way, but without wanting to go down with him, or letting anyone close to her go down with him. It was what you learned fast on the street: Save your overtime for the one percenters who showed they deserved it.

"Lady, he's making me do this essay thing."

She handed him a Coke and sat opposite him. "Listen, Thumb. I love Jack. I love his daughter. You *shot* his daughter."

"I didn't mean to."

She shook her head. "How can that be enough?"

He started standing up as if to leave. "*Sit!* If you can convince me you're not dangerous to my man, I may let him have his hopeless little game of trying to save your ass from the street. I may not even arrest you. Me, I don't think you can be helped, I don't think you've got the guts to turn around and lead a straight life. Why should I entrust the most important person in my life to you?"

He shrugged.

"Far as I can see, you're nothing but a very bad dream. Hanging out in the land of the losers."

"Maybe you shamed where you come from, *ruca*." He bridled and pulled himself erect. He hadn't touched the Coke.

"That's better. A little spirit. I don't come from where you think, *mijo*. I come from people who used to ride ponies into battle out on the plains and were known as the greatest light cavalry who ever lived." Actually, the California Paiute hadn't ridden horses, but everybody else thought all Indians were the same so she might as well swipe a little prestige from the Comanches and Apaches.

"*Hijole!* You're *norte indio?*"

"*Claro que* yes. What are you proud of in life?"

"I can draw," he said quickly, with his chin jutted out.

"With a spray can or for real?"

Painstakingly he took out his wallet and extracted and unfolded a photograph, much the worse for the folds. It seemed to be a mural on the side of a concrete embankment, probably part of the mile-long Wall of Pride out in the valley or one of the similar mural projects. It was almost worn away, but from what she could see it was a peaceful seventeenth-century hacienda beside a stream. It seemed pretty well done, especially compared to the much cruder bits of other paintings she could see on either side.

"Hmm," she said. "Looks good."

"It's been four years," he said. "It needs to be fixed up from all the weather and shit."

Not too surprising when you paint a mural in a storm drain, she thought.

"Look, Lady." He held out for her inspection one black shoe, highly polished, with a white crucifix painted on the toe. "I loved my grandma, and she died just like that." He snapped his fingers. "The cross is for her. Death comes in a minute. *Así es la vida.*"

Gloria Ramirez took a long swig of his untouched Coke and pushed it into his hand.

"I threw away the gun. I don't know how it happened."

Of course, what he had disposed of was incriminating evidence, and he could well have bought two more by now. But maybe, just maybe, he was doing his best to be part of the one percent.

They watched the busy scene, holding hands, as the ambulance crew and sheriffs' deputies roped Levine up the hillside in a ragged collaboration. He was strapped to a wooden backboard and riding in a metal sled. It was all lit by the headlights from all the vehicles sideways on Highline. A big wrecker was in a turnout just off the road, a beefy-looking operator walking backward downhill unreeling the cable from a big winch.

"I wonder why he took off so fast like that."

"Levine was a big-time saps for pow'ful cars."

People were standing out on the hilltop decks of the other houses scattered around, watching and talking, some with large binoculars. An immensely fat woman in a muumuu chattered away on a cell phone at the nearest house, as if describing what she saw to a friend. The hot wind had picked up again and blew her voice away.

One of the deputies now sauntered purposefully toward Luisa and Terror.

"I'd like a word with you two."

"Yes, sor, officer. Poor Mr. Levine rent dis house hyere. We guests."

"Is he going to be all right?" Luisa asked.

"He'll live, but he'll never play the guitar."

"What you say?"

"His left hand is a holy mess. You say his name is Levine?" He had a small notebook flipped open. "First name?"

"Mister," Terror answered.

The deputy's eyes lifted sleepily to him. "And you, what do you go by?"

"Trevor Whiteside Pennycooke, Esquire. Blessed is the name of the Lord God Jah, Ras Tafari, and blessed is he who comes in the name of Jah, His Imperial Majesty Emperor Haile Selassie the First, and let the name of His glory be blessed."

"Is that all part of your name, Trevor, esquire?"

"No, sor."

"Fifty-one-fifty," the deputy muttered. "No humans involved."

Dear Diary,
Poor Laveen had a bad car accident tonight with Trev & me watching. He will be okay they say. They got the car up & somebody said a wheel came off which is very strange. Its an expensive car. Trev says we must wait here. That is OK with me. I dont miss anything or anyone from before. But I think none of the books prepared me for tru love. Trev is one protector who does the job right. Too bad he couldn't protect Mr. Laveen though. We are both sad about it.

SIXTEEN

A Likkle Respek

"You don't look so good," she said. "You looked better this morning."

It was after midnight. Jack Liffey had spent the rest of his day and evening following up several dead-end leads, searching for Terror Pennycooke. Gloria was still up, hunched forward at the kitchen table nursing her insomnia with a mug of hot chocolate and leafing through Curtis's *The North American Indian*. It was his, but she'd lit up the minute she'd seen it, and she spent hours looking at the old photographs.

She offered him some hot chocolate but he just sat.

"I was tied up for a while," he said. He looked at the photo she had opened to—it was her favorite, called the Cahuilla woman. "She does look a bit like you."

Her eyes lifted. "You were tied up? What does that mean? And what was that all about when we got cut off?"

"It was that kid you saw running out of the house in Malibu. He got the drop on me, but I talked him down after a while."

"You really live on the edge."

"I don't try to. Sometimes, it's just take it or leave it, you know."

"In the department, we try to lower the odds of that stuff. Partners, preparation, backup. You could at least let me know what's up ahead of time."

"Is it me disturbing your sleep?"

She sighed. "I don't know, J. I hope not."

J. was new. She'd never called him that before. She seemed to be in an odd mood, ready to try about anything. "Can I put on Miles?" he asked.

"Softly. It's a bit jangly."

He started up *Birth of the Cool* but kept it faint.

"What can I do for you?" he asked. "You need relaxing. Back rub? Go down on you? Caress you all over?"

She looked at him affectionately. "Nice offers."

He smiled back. Things were looking up.

But then her grin faded, and she said, "The problem is, there's just too much information for one night. Tied up, for god's sake. Sometimes you're so innocent, Jack. But not in a way I can admire. I mean I can, but it's hard sometimes."

He came around behind her and let his hands slide gently around her neck, inside the bathrobe. She shut her eyes and leaned back against him. "That does feel good. Mmm. I've got to protect myself, too. I didn't think anybody could stir me up again so bad as you do."

The problem with her crisis, he thought, was that it filled the whole house and left no room for his. He was little more than a year past what a hack therapist had called a near nervous breakdown—though all he'd really done was shed a few tears without warning a few times. Whatever it had been, he was pretty sure he'd gotten past the critical juncture now. Still, a surge of emotion came back to waylay him unexpectedly and make him feel suddenly fragile and beleaguered. The difference was that these days he was back to the point where he could drag those feelings into that space far inside him where he hid away all the residue that he'd fucked up in his life, or lost, or what just hadn't worked out.

"I don't mean to mix you up, Glor."

"I wish I could pray," she said. "I grew up praying."

"What would you pray for?"

"Maybe to stop needing so much. Needing you, needing respect at work, and needing to know who I am. Needing to be clear."

"What's clear?"

"I don't know. But it's not this horrible empty silence inside me. It's not this sense of exile I carry around."

"Do you really think of living in L.A. as exile?" He wanted to let the question of silence go, since it scared him.

"How could it not be exile, Jack? I'm cut off and cut loose. This is L.A., and it's where my body lives, but my spirit's in Owens. I've known that . . . always. I just didn't know I knew it."

"I think people put too much weight on genes," he said. His hands slid down to rest on her breasts, rubbing softly, and he could feel her nipples swell as he caressed. "If I bought all that, I'd be in some pub in Cork, blarneying and drinking whiskey. You have no idea how little being an Irishman interests me."

She said softly, "Make love to me, Jack. That's what interests me right now."

It wasn't until the morning that he found Thumb's essay on the kitchen counter. Too much had distracted them the night before for her to mention it. He knew what it was immediately and read it twice over his morning coffee.

There was trouble in Texas and Texas was independent away from Mexico in 1836, it started anew. He remembered insisting that Thumb include at least two dates, two names and two battles, and there they all were so he was improving. The grammar and logic still left a lot to be desired, but it was better than draft one. He put a circled 2 up in the corner. Way to go, Thumb, he thought. Maybe you'll get somewhere yet.

After nine, generally a respectable hour in L.A., he drove to see his friend Art Castro, at his office in the Rosewood Detective Agency in the Bradbury Building downtown. It was just a short jaunt from Boyle Heights, across the river and the vast Santa Fe rail yards on one of L.A.'s magnificent viaduct bridges with its deco details and elegant streetlamps.

Halfway across the bridge he had to slow to a crawl for three wizened old Latino men who were crawling across the bridge on their knees, going westward, each dragging a charred piece of wood that might have fit together to make a crucifix. When the oncoming lane was clear, he went around them. In his mirror, he saw they wore guayaberas and straw hats, and the object of their pilgrimage was still a mystery—but he preferred it that way. Too much religious information only cluttered up the space you had available for intangibles.

He took the rattly cage elevator up to the sixth floor. Art Castro's status within Rosewood was, as always, apparent from the size and elevation of his office. A few years back, he had messed up badly—something to do with helping Jack Liffey in fact—-and had ended up in a broom closet annex. Now he was back with the marble flooring and two full windows facing east.

Art actually stood up and forced Jack to do a complicated old sixties handshake, with a lot of tugging and banging fists. "Knowledge is power," Art Castro said.

"Money is power now."

Art chuckled and sat again, put his feet back up on an open drawer. In the corner was a strange hamster run with a double loop of tubing above it, but Jack Liffey ignored it.

"I need to ask you something—why else would I be here?"

"You can ask anything, Jack. It's good to see you. I may not be able to answer, that's all."

"G. Dan Hunt. The old guy the studios used to use as their clean-up man when movie stars barfed on themselves in public, or some reporter was threatening to write that Rock Hudson liked guys. He's the son of the Dan Hunt who was around in the grand old days of Mickey Cohen and Jimmy 'the Weasel' Frattiano."

"I know G. Dan."

"Where is he these days? He isn't in the phone book."

"Retired, where they all go. Some big condo on a golf course in Palm Springs or Rancho Mirage. You sure you want to stir him up? He's not a pleasant guy."

"He used to use a Jamaican for the heavy stuff, and the Jamaican is back."

"Not Terror Pennycooke?"

"The very Pennycooke."

"You had a run-in with him, didn't you?"

"Yeah, and he seems to be back. It's a job I took on for Gloria, a family thing, and I'd like to see this young relative of hers turn up safe and sound. Terror's involved somehow. Anyway, G. Dan probably knows where he is."

There was a sudden scurrying rattle from the hamster cage, and Jack Liffey looked around. "What's this shit?"

Art Castro sighed. "The boss's son, senior VP, says everybody here's got to commit to interspecies association. Man, don't ask me any more than that."

Jack Liffey held up two palms. "Can you get me G. Dan's address?"

"Yeah, Jack, sure. How about you do *me* a favor some day?"

Jack pursed his lips. "So I owe you big time—that's what you want me to say?"

"In a word, yes."

"Dis guy, him my true bredren, same mother, I tink same father, too. Him step it to Englun when I-an-I 12 and we write letters every week and, y'naow, it was always Glenwood who tole me what's what an' tings like. Dese letter real funny an wise. Him get in college for enginyeer."

She could tell he was really proud of his brother, and that made her happy. She placed a high value on family feelings, never having experienced them herself. They had driven from the Malibu Hills to the Valley in the ancient Buick he had found in the garage and hotwired.

Now they were walking along Ventura Boulevard, past the falafel stands and dress shops, with their arms around each other, drawing surreptitious stares. She was surprised how oblivious he was to the gawking.

As Trevor talked happily of his brother's letters home, Luisa Wilson's head turned casually, as if watching the traffic, but she was actually following two stocky matrons with shopping bags, and she caught their disapproving eyes on her as they passed. One whispered to the other with pursed lips. Of course, she thought, home in Owens, there would be an even bigger sensation at the very sight of Trevor, with his chartreuse plaid silk shirt and tricolor knit cap. She hugged him back around the waist as his hand rubbed and squeezed her shoulder. She had a real boyfriend.

Gradually, Trevor let her know that much of what his brother had written home for two years had been lies and self-delusion, and his life on the dole in Britain had been no picnic at all.

"Aw, that's awful," she said.

Three teenaged boys in ski sweaters and penny loafers split to go round them on both sides, and they made faces just as they passed behind them. This time, without warning, Terror Pennycooke reached behind and grabbed the neck of a white ski sweater with reindeer on it and yanked the last boy to a stop. "Who you make dat face at, fuckbwoy? You tink I should stay 'way from white girls?"

"No *sir.*" There was real panic in the boy's face. "I'm sorry, *sir.*"

The other boys turned back and made half an attempt at striking challenging poses.

Terror Pennycooke made a sucking sound between his front teeth that Luisa Wilson had never heard before, but she knew immediately it was pure contempt. With one powerful shove, he threw the boy he was holding into the others, and they all reeled and then ran. A half dozen men nearby watched as if they might have been on the verge of intervening.

"Let's go, Trev."

"I not afraid of dem nor you baldheads neither."

The other men turned away or pretended not to notice. "You're scary," she whispered.

"For you dis man always be protection."

They walked on, and the mood on the street seemed to have changed. A man in a gray suit smiled and gave them a peace sign.

"We at da place," he said.

He led her upstairs, following the address he had on a slip of paper. On the first glass door it said, ambiguously, Van Nuys Business

Office, and there were a number of decals offering services including Discreet Forwarding, and Notary Public. Inside, there was a single small desk where a girl with spiked up purple hair and a lot of piercings was filing her nails.

"We seek for the gem'mun who make Dangerous Games," Terror Pennycooke said, confidently.

She raised her eyebrows and pointed at a wall of small post office boxes. "They live in one of those, man. They're about two inches tall and very quiet."

"Huh."

She set down the nail file. "This is a mail drop, bro'. Send them a letter. That's how it works."

"I see? They got a place, a real place somewhere?"

"I wouldn't know."

Terror took a memo pad off her desk and, sitting on a bench along one wall, slowly and laboriously wrote his name, his cell phone number and an offer to do big-time business with *Dangerous Games*.

"Look, man, I can't get into the boxes to leave something," the girl said. "Really. The address is over the door. Get an envelope and a stamp, write that address on the envelope and drop it in a mailbox."

He held her eyes a long time. "Dis de program, dawta. When man step through that door and him put the mail in dese boxes, you tell him put dis hyere message in Dangerous Games box or I come back and fi real I fuck up dis place bad and you in it crucial."

She offered him an anxious smile. "Yes, sir. I guess I can do that."

"Thank you, sistah. Alls we need between us is a likkle respek."

SEVENTEEN

Till the Wheels Come Off

"Some *carrucha* man," Thumb offered appreciatively from under the VW's dash. "This is a real *classico*."

"Just like me. *Classico* and worn out." They'd already gone over the essay, and the boy wasn't happy at all about being asked to rewrite it yet again. Finally, he'd capitulated after looking over the few notes. It was still structural editing; Jack Liffey hadn't even started on the word-by-word work. "I used to have a real car. A Concord straight six."

"Man, what's that?"

"Sort of a Rambler."

"Like you?"

"Another obsolete model."

"Obsolete?"

"Out of date."

"Hmm. I knew a guy, had to take the back seat out, but he put a big Chrysler V-8 in one of these."

"With that much power you'd need an anchor to keep it on the ground."

"*Listo*. I'm done. Lemme show you." He opened the glove box to show off a tiny new toggle switch fixed to the left side, just in reach of the driver's seat. He flicked the toggle down. Then he turned the ignition key, and it ground and ground without starting. "The coil don't get no spark. I put in a solenoid to cut it off."

He flicked the switch up with a flourish, and the engine started on the first twist of the key. Thumb gave a little pump of triumph, like all the athletes on TV.

"That's great. Let me at least pay you for the parts."

"Man, no need. They all from Midnight Auto Parts."

"Ah." He didn't want to encourage theft, but there was nothing he could do about it now. He got in to let Thumb drive him around a little. He knew Thumb didn't have a car and would probably enjoy the driving. Maybe it would loosen him up some more.

"*¡Hijole!*" He turned quickly up an alley when he caught sight of a heavy-set bald man with hard sleepy eyes and a carved ebony cane.

"Trouble?"

"Not if he don't see me. *Bastón* is an O.G. He's *eme,* too, a real *carnal.*"

Jack Liffey knew by now that *eme* was the Mexican mafia, a prison-run supergang that stood above all the barrio crews, taxed them, and decided who could do what.

"It's all about respect."

"Did you ever think how much nicer the world would be if everybody didn't have to be in warring armies? If we were all brothers. Remember that truce day—the demonstration against the war down at Salazar Park?"

"Yeah."

"Imagine you could walk anywhere in town and people would smile at you."

Thumb shrugged and drove cautiously through the alley onto a narrow street of lovely little bungalows with pots of flowers everywhere, all lashing westward in the insistent wind. "The world ain't that way, man. I just got here. Don't blame me."

"When you think about a better world, what's it like?"

He could see that the question threw the boy a little. Thumb thought a moment and had a little trouble with third gear, lugging the engine before shifting down. He wasn't an experienced driver. "I'm wearing a mask and this bright red and green *traje* like a big hero in the wrestling, and I got a big sword, and when my enemies come after me I just swing them through the guts with the sword. Fwoosh. I want to be so strong nobody fucks with me. I don't bang much, man, but I gotta have the protection, and I gotta be down for my *barrio*. I ain't a pussy."

Jack Liffey wondered what wisdom he could possibly offer to a cosmos so steeped in testosterone. He wondered if any intimacy at all could pass between their worlds, without continual misunderstandings. "I have daydreams like that, too, but only when I'm frustrated and feeling alone."

"Uh-huh." The boy blasted the horn at a car in front of them that didn't start up fast enough on the green light. Jack Liffey glimpsed eyes in its rearview mirror, looking them over. It was a near thing, but the angry driver moved on. Thumb wasn't pushing it and had circled back almost to Gloria's.

"Drive around some more if you want."

They now took a wider circle through Boyle Heights, passing Roosevelt High School with its football squads working out on the field, and a few hangers-on outside smoking and banging their backs idly into the chain link fence.

"Your old lady don't like me," he said abruptly.

"I don't really like the term 'old lady,' Thumb, but there's not much else in English. I don't like 'girlfriend' either. You could say *novia*. Maybe she's pissed because she's thinking about you taking a shot at my little girl."

Thumb went quiet for a while. "I told you I don't know what happened, man. It just went off. It was a accident."

"Yeah, you told me."

"I'll take you home, *señor*," he said resignedly.

"I'm not mad, Thumb. I'm puzzled. I want to be your friend, and I still can't figure out what happened."

"It's so hard. I want to be the wrestler in the mask that fights for *la raza*, you know, but then I'm me, and I do that thing." He looked genuinely confused.

As a gesture of some kind, Jack Liffey held up his left fist and crooked his doublejointed thumb back. Thumb matched him.

"You know, I got sisters, and one of 'em was attacked when she was little. A really bad *pendejo* from another street who's dead now. The other sister is married to a guy who's up in Corcoran for banging, and she's got three babies. They both live with it okay. I'm the one who's angry—it's not right, but sometimes it make me do bad stuff."

"Nobody live out hyere but foreigners, Mr. Two Baldheads, so you no tink dey care one likkle bit." Terror Pennycooke took out the big Webley .455, a British Service revolver from World War II, and held it in Kenyon Styles' unhappy face. Rod Whipple was frozen in midgesture, opening a beer at the kitchen table across the room. The clunky Webley was Terror's weapon of choice, a nice reliable revolver with a big shoulder-busting cartridge that the cops back home in Jamaica still used. He was holding the pistol now with his wrist rotated so the handgrip was parallel to the ground, the way they always did in the movies.

"We haven't got any money here," Rod said. "I promise you that's the truth."

Just a half hour earlier, they had all met in a diner down the street that catered to the whole East Hollywood neighborhood, the hand-lettered menu on the wall offering Armenian *lahmajun* and Salvadoran *pupusas* and four or five other imaginative ways to combine bread dough and greasy meat.

The two young men had patiently tried to explain to Terror that there was no big money at all involved in an appearance in *Dangerous Games*. They never paid their actors more than a hundred bucks, mostly homeless men or reckless daredevils who'd have done their stunts for the challenge and notoriety alone. For some reason, the big Jamaican had stubbornly refused to believe them, persisting as if they were just bargaining hard and would eventually come around.

Finally, growing jumpy, Kenyon had excused himself to use the bathroom and after about five minutes of absence, Rod had realized he was on his own once again, and he had sprinted away into the morning.

Terror Pennycooke had just sat patiently in the diner, grinning confidently, until the two had made their separate ways back to the apartment building in clear view across the street, one of hundreds of similar aging runway apartments in that part of town.

"I-an-I need a discuss byisness some more wit dese buoys," he had told Luisa. "Hey, you dress up good," he said, cocking his head as if just noticing that she was really filling out the skimpy blue velvet dress he had bought her.

"I feel good in this. I like to touch the cloth."

"Mmm, it come off a you fine, too, I bet. You de ongle girl for I, you knaow. You go wait in park dere some time now. Don't fret, Trev come soon."

After pushing his way into the apartment, Terror had backed the taller young man across the spare-looking living room. He paused to admire a Richard Widmark poster, grinning his devil-grin. A lot of the rude boys on Jamaica had taken Tommy or Udo as street names, from Widmark's crazy-giggling gangster in *Kiss of Death*.

Terror set down the shopping bag he carried and patted the poster as if comforting it. "You marked for life," he said softly.

Rod Whipple held his head in his hands at the kitchen table, and then looked up forlornly from the open kitchen, glaring at both of them. "Ken, I've had about enough of all this."

"Here de way it is," Terror said, ignoring him. "A black cat, him run across you pat'. Den your private sector itch you up and you see it Friday 13, and all a sudden, a man like me show up. What you gone say? Just superstitches? Just bad luck? Forget dis guy? He nothing."

All of a sudden he turned and slammed the heel of his palm straight into Kenyon Styles' forehead, like some kind of machine arm hammering a rivet, and Styles fell backward over the coffee table and lay spreadeagled across the table and the sofa, moaning.

"Stay right dere," Terror ordered. He turned to Rod Whipple. "Might as cheap me kill two bird before dey hatch, eh?"

Rod put up his palms. "Don't hit me."

"You say de wiseguys come and dey take away de *Dangerous Games* Numbah One. Dey makes millions, and you two don' make dibbi dibbi. I tink you bwoys thick as two short planks, you no see it, you need a nursemaid to watch over you. I-an-I not greedy like dese yere Eye-ties."

He turned on a cheap stereo beside the TV, found a rap station and got the volume up. Then he turned the TV on, too.

"We be partner naow, dis is de ting for you to see, for sure for sure."

"That's absurd. What have you ever done for us?"

"Lessee. I knaow you be need protection, and you need some persuade still." He retrieved his shopping bag, reaching down into it for a fat roll of duct tape and a fourpack of D&G Jamaican Ginger Beer. He plucked out one bottle and began absently to shake it up. "Who wanna be first? Don' be shy."

"And that's not all!" the TV set bellowed. "With every order we include six stainless steel steak knives . . ."

He stopped for gas at the big dinosaurs at Cabazon, as good a place as any, and at a mini-mart in the gas station, he bought a wrinkled hot dog off an automatic griller that rolled them constantly under a plastic hood. "Praise God," the clerk said as if the twenty Jack Liffey held out to him was something very special.

"What for?"

"For giving his only begotten son." The kid had acne scars and a pompadour that wouldn't stay down.

"Do you think God is more insecure than you are?"

"Huh?"

"Why on earth does he need *our* praise?" Jack Liffey was in a bad mood, engendered by Gloria Ramirez, who had chewed him out for taking too long in the shower that morning. A meaningless fidget of her generalized resentment.

"Bless you, sir."

He relented. "Bless you, too, son."

"Yes, sir."

The hot dog was inedible, and he threw it away. As he drove past the big power-generator windmills in the San Gorgonio Pass on the way to Palm Springs, he saw that the blades were churning away hard, facing out into the desert. And the car, too, was bucking a little and slowing unnaturally, even on the downhill into the Coachella Valley. The Santa Ana was blowing up a gale out of the great basin, out of the violent Mojave. That might account for half his mood right there, he thought.

Just before the 111 turnoff to all those rich white-belt-and-white-loafer cities, he passed a car that was shaped like an old dial telephone, skulking along slowly in the right lane. As he got up his courage to pull the wind-balked VW over a lane to pass, the giant receiver lifted a foot off its cradle and a sign popped up to say, **It's for you!** He kept right on going. It did not seem to be a good idea to answer it.

G. Dan Hunt lived on the edge of a big golf course complex in Cathedral City just past Palm Springs. Jack Liffey had read somewhere that there were 110 golf courses in this 20-mile pearl necklace of gated retirement complexes that stretched from Palm Springs to La Quinta, an area where more land was devoted to the strange Scottish sport than to housing the old and monied themselves.

He didn't want to announce himself at the guard shack and give G. Dan a chance to be out, so he parked at the back of a gas station with some cars waiting for engine work, made sure to flick off Thumb's new kill switch, and walked a quarter mile before leaping a concrete block wall. They weren't all that serious about keeping the riff-raff out. No turret guns, no mines or barbed wire.

The houses were all what Mike Lewis had once called Silent Movie Spanish, with red tile roofs and stucco, all over-large for their retired occupants. Patches were artfully missing here and there to reveal faux adobe blocks. Hunt's townhouse was on one of the greens, with a foursome stooping to eye the level of the grass. Being on a green seemed preferable to being located near one of the driving tees where the houses all cowered behind wire screens and tall plexiglass shields. From the patio you could step over a low wall straight onto the rough grass that bordered the green. It must have been weird, like living in a pinball machine.

Jack Liffey stopped in his tracks on the rough. There was a figure out on a nearby patio who bore a strong resemblance to G. Dan Hunt. But the Hunt he knew from a few years back had been an immense chesty man with a bark that could draw headwaiters fast and chase off trouble all by itself. He had been a fixer at every level for a number of studios and had used the violent Jamaican, Penny-cooke, for his nastier work. The man he saw now had the same colorful suspenders and the same nose and eyes, but he was more than merely older. He had lost a good hundred pounds. Once again, right in front of him, the Grim Reaper was serving up previews of the big feature to come.

The man was sipping a milky beverage that looked more like medicine than a cocktail and baring his face to the sun. Jack Liffey came along the rough toward him, trying to make enough noise in the high grass so he didn't startle the man.

"Hello, Dan. I'm Jack Liffey, remember me."

"I know who you are. If *you* remember, I was impressed enough with you to try to hire you once."

"Can I come over?" He still stood in the rough.

The man shrugged with one shoulder, a gesture of great physical economy. Jack Liffey boosted himself over the low retaining wall and sat opposite him in an expensive-looking patio chair made of wood and vinyl straps. "Your old employee, Trevor Pennycooke, is back in town. I'm looking for him."

"Feel that wind," he said. "It reminds me of all winds I've ever felt. I'm just primary process now."

"I don't know what that means," Jack Liffey said.

"You'll have to ask my *roshi*."

"You're into Zen?"

"Is that so surprising?"

"Yes."

"Zen is practical as shit. Doctor's orders, learn about dealing with pain and shit."

G. Dan Hunt let himself drift for a while, basking.

"You know where I might find Terror Pennycooke?" Jack Liffey asked.

Hunt bided his time. Then he said, "A guy named Levine. He used to work for me, too, and I think Trevor would hook up with him if he's back in town."

"Levine have a first name?"

"Not that I ever knew." Jack Liffey waited patiently. Unless there was more, the trip would have been a waste. He had no need to pay his last respects to G. Dan.

"Levine had a place up on Malibu crest near Fernwood. Someone in the neighborhood might have found Trevor a bit noticeable if he's staying with Levine."

"I guess that helps," Jack Liffey said.

"It doesn't matter to me whether it helps or not," G. Dan told him. Then he stood up, breathed a couple of times and started making some strange slow motion exercises in the air, probably *tai chi*.

"What's that called?" Jack Liffey asked.

"It's called Ride the motherfucker till the wheels come off."

Dear Diary,
Now that I have linked my fate with love I feel different. Trev had some business & he asked me to wait in a little park. I watched kids playing like I was way off the earth above them but I was attached too. Then I got to watching a Mexican man with two little girls on his knees. He talked very serious & then the girls laughed so he laughed & one of them hugged him. God I could of been one of those girls but I never had a man be so nice.

EIGHTEEN

A Little Off Balance and Having to Think Hard

When Jack Liffey got home from the store, he found Maeve's Toyota parked in front. Kathy must have relented and let her venture out into the wilds of East L.A. after all. Or else she'd come on her own. It wasn't unknown for Maeve to violate a parental ban. She'd obviously heard his VW approach—everyone within miles could hear the air-cooled engine—and she came out to greet him. In an instant, he herded her officiously back inside, away from any random events the street might toss her way.

"Three more days of Santa Anas," she predicted. She hugged him. He held on a second longer than she did, but giving Oskar a wide berth. "I predict major wildfires up in the hills."

"Let's hope not. Want a Coke?"

"Diet."

He got them both Diet Cokes and watched her tap softly on the top of the can with a fingernail before opening it—she believed it cut back on the potential for geysering fizz. He wasn't convinced.

"The wind really worries me," she said. "I was thinking of some people I know up in the hills. I hope they cleared their brush." They both knew that he had once lived with a fading movie star in the commanding heights of the Hollywood Hills smack in the middle of a critical fire zone. But she had been dead for several years now, her house leveled by the big Burbank earthquake. It was probably just another empty lot these days. It wasn't really prime real estate any more since the jumped-up music execs and overnight rock stars and drug dealers had moved in. After the quake, he'd never even been tempted to drive past the place on Avenida Bluebird. Nostalgia was no game to play with yourself, he thought, even if places and people had once meant a lot to you.

"You're pretty close to Gloria," he suggested. "Do you know what's eating her? I don't think it's just the Santa Anas."

"Have you ever considered that you might have a wounded-bird syndrome, Dad?" she asked.

He sighed. "Gloria seemed a lot stronger than me."

"You're overreacting. Gloria's going to be fine. It's really just a matter of semiotics."

He laughed. "Lord, I don't think I want you to explain that. I'm not imagining her pain, hon. She's stewing on something, and I just can't seem to help."

They both stopped talking as a noisy VW bug just like his rasped past the house. "Reminds me of an old Warners Cartoon," Jack Liffey said. "I better not look close, I might be in there."

"No, you're in here for sure." She leaned far over to kiss his cheek and set down her can, then noticed what she had set it on. Moving the Diet Coke, she plucked the sheet of paper off the counter and began to read aloud: "There was trouble in Texas and Texas was independent away from Mexico in 1836. US wanted Manifesto Destiny still and wanted all land. California too."

Prickles went down his spine as he tried to remember if there was anything in the essay that would suggest its author was her assailant. He didn't think so.

"What's this?"

"A boy I'm trying to tutor," he said.

"Another wounded bird. You were always trying so hard with Rogelio, but it didn't take. It's too bad, he had a good heart." Rogelio was the nephew of another woman he had lived with.

Maeve was right. He'd tried hard to get the boy into computers, or into anything with a future, but Rogelio just had little interest in applying himself.

"Where'd you find this kid?"

"He lives a few blocks away," he tried out. But it wasn't adequate, and he knew it.

"This needs a lot of work, doesn't it?" she said. She wasn't making fun of the boy; her interest was quite earnest. "Aside from the mistakes, every sentence has a big black line under it, like a death notice."

He had no idea what she meant, but it sounded interesting, and he wondered if she wasn't gradually getting smarter than her old man. He'd always resisted having her IQ tested, on the presumption that if it was even a little low, or just average, she'd be devastated, and if it was really high, she'd get smug and full of herself. He liked her best not knowing, a little off balance and having to work at life. Just the way we should all feel about ourselves, he thought.

She looked up at him innocently. "How'd you pick him out?"

And there it was, he thought, the big ethical question staring him in the face once again. To lie or not to lie? The convenient omission, the shaded truth, the polite fabrication that would save someone else's pain. "His name is Thumb," he said. "His nickname, that is. He's got a double-jointed thumb, like mine." He showed her the bend. "His real name is Tino Estrada, and he's trying hard to get his GED so he can go to art school. He's a pretty fair graffiti artist."

He paused there, watching her, overcome with love for her innate kindness and her so-vulnerable beauty, all her genetic him-ness, too, traits that she would never escape. He wondered if anyone, anywhere, ever, got to embark on the life of perfect integrity you always planned for yourself.

A troop of schoolkids walked past outside the house, full of slurred jokes and laughter, roughhousing, sounding quite natural in their gossip and chatter and challenge. Thinking about them, Jack Liffey no longer knew where to draw the line.

"About a week ago I went to his hideout—a garage behind his house—to kill him."

That got her attention, and he could see her figure it all out in a flash. "Oh, Dad. You're still making yourself my protector and avenger, aren't you, like one of our ape ancestors?"

"It's what I do, hon," he said. "I'm a father. What do you expect? Gloria's none too happy with me, either, since it makes complications with the cops who're looking for this kid. You tell me. I went to shoot him, but I lost my resolve. What should I do with him? You tell me, and I'll do it."

She buried her face against his shoulder. "Dad, you're not being fair. You've got to let me be angry at you for a little while. At least thirty seconds."

He chuckled softly, but couldn't find much relief in it. "Hit me a bit if it helps. Mention your sainted mom."

"I'm not even sure I have a right to an opinion. You *are* the dad, and you do it pretty well. You know, deep down I have this terrible feeling that you can see inside me, that you know everything—past, present, and future, and all my feelings. I'm in awe sometimes. Despite all that, I *really* don't want you fighting my battles for me. It robs me of something I need."

"I'll give you the .45 and you can kill him."

"Be serious," she scolded. "Can I meet him?"

"Oh, Jesus."

"What does that mean?"

"Roughly it means, Oh Jesus. I don't think it's a good idea right now, hon."

"We're connected by tragedy. Who has more of a claim to check out this guy than me?"

"I don't think being shot by accident by a guy, or even half-accident, gives you any claims over his person. He's just a kid with a big chip on his shoulder, crappy friends, a lousy family, and damn little future, plus a tiny bit of artistic talent. You're a very bright girl from the other side of the tracks with the gold spoon and everything else."

"Oh, right."

"What's it going to prove if you meet Thumb?"

"Maybe he'll be able to tell me something he can't tell you."

* * *

"James Dressler, banker—my ass. It's Jack, isn't it?"

"Best I could do on short notice. Nice to talk to you, too, Art. You know a guy named Levine who only uses the one name?"

"Does he pitch for the Dodgers?"

"I sincerely doubt it. But he hangs out with that Jamaican charmer Terror Pennycooke."

It had taken him two tries to get through. Art Castro's receptionists had orders to obstruct and, possibly for good measure, annoy Jack Liffey in any way possible. This time, Jack Liffey had insisted on an urgent callback about a bounced check at Westside Bank.

"Matter of fact, I know Levine. Big guy, bald. I don't know where the hell the name came from. He looks about as Jewish as the emperor of the Manchus."

"People don't *look* Jewish, Art, or at least a lot of them don't."

"Yeah, yeah, Paul Newman in *Exodus*. It's okay, Jack, I look Latino. Glor looks Latino. You look wasted and tired."

"You can't see me. I'm tanned and terrific."

"Glad to hear it."

"So, would you know how I could get in touch with Levine? It's important to me."

"I happen to know he's in Cedars-Sinai. Somebody jammed his accelerator cable with a fishing weight, but whether it was a friend or enemy, you've got me."

"Thanks, Art. You keep saying I owe you a favor, but you never call."

"I'll make you come see arena football with me."

"What is it?"

"They shrank it, put it in a hockey rink—made it sort of a pinball game."

"People actually *pay* to watch that?"

He heard a laugh at the other end. "Watch out with the hard boys, Jack."

Kenyon Styles lay on his single bed, spasm-coughing sputum and a little blood into doubled-up wads of Kleenex that Rod Whipple kept handing him, one after another. Rod felt a bit guilty because he'd been wishing Ken ill ever since the avalanche incident. Then, like a genie out of his subconscious, the big Jamaican had materialized to impose his bizarre torment. In the end, they had shown the Jamaican their rough cut, still in progress, in the makeshift edit bay, and all had agreed that Trevor Pennycooke was now the line producer of *Dangerous Games II,* and some unspecified girlfriend would be cut in as narrator and host.

"We're not really going to give this guy a share, are we?"

Kenyon tried to answer but could emit only a croaking, which set off another paroxysm of coughing. Several empty ginger beer bottles were still scattered in the corner. He'd probably never be able to look at one again. Rod even decided he might never again eat anything flavored with ginger, though it had taken only half of one of the bottles to subdue him. The Jamaican had found out quickly that Kenyon was the one to focus on.

Kenyon tried again to answer but settled for rolling his head back and forth in a broad no. "Rather . . . burn . . . tape . . . not give . . . him . . . anything."

Kenyon started coughing again. He had stubbornly held out through two bottles, and now was paying the price.

Rod's real worry was that Kenyon Styles—despite his present protestations of defiance—had bought into the Jamaican's proposal for a grand climax to the show. Never one to turn down any repellently outrageous new idea, Kenyon was too reckless to be trusted. History had already demonstrated this. Both the snowboarders had ended up in the hospital and, as far as he knew, were still there.

Rod retreated deep inside himself to calculate his chances. He knew he was in way over his head. They both knew this whole production had been Kenyon's idea from the first, and it worried him now that Kenyon, too, seemed to be in over his head.

The cough syrup he had fetched for Kenyon appeared to sooth his throat, and now he calmed gradually and closed his eyes, like a junkie finally sailing on a fresh shot.

"We're not really going to start a Malibu wildfire, are we?"

It wasn't hard to guess where Terror had got the idea: The fire scare had been all over the news for a week, ever since the Santa

Anas had arrived. Six years of drought had already desiccated the hillside brush down to its lowest moisture content ever. There had already been a handful of small roadside fires, but just one spark in the wrong place, one prankster, one malicious arsonist—the local news anchors bleated on and on.

On one news special, they had brought up graphic overlays, one after another, to map the dozen Malibu wildfires of the last twenty years. These showed that fire had, little-by-little, completed a paint-by-numbers map of the entire coast, pretty much burning every square inch of land at one time or another. Almost always, it began inland at the 101 freeway ten miles across the Santa Monica Mountains, from there burning up and over to roar down the Malibu flank right to the Pacific Coast Highway and often through the beachfront homes themselves.

"It's high concept. But if that island nigger is stupid enough to let us film him starting the fire, his black ass is ours."

Cedars-Sinai had been founded as two much smaller clinics, both, in fact, in Boyle Heights not far from Jack Liffey's new home. This had been early in the twentieth century, when that upland area east of downtown had been the Jewish center of L.A. But, by the fifties, both hospitals had moved west—like the Jewish community itself. Then in the 1970s they merged into one gigantic new edifice on the near edge of Beverly Hills, specializing in heart care, cancer, and chronic diseases of the rich.

It wasn't visiting hours when he got there, but Jack Liffey never cared much about details like that. He kept a nondescript smock and a clipboard in his trunk, and he'd found you could go just about anywhere with those as props. He got right up to the patient area on the seventh floor with "insurance examiner" and "just a few questions." The floor nurse indicated the room and strutted away.

Obviously, Levine had money because it was a private room. It was shaped like a trapezoid for some reason, with the narrow end terminating in a slatted window to the world outside. He tried to find a name on the door or some chart left lying around, just to confirm he had the right place, but hospitals were becoming careful about things like that because of federal privacy regulations.

Levine was indeed a big man and bald as a stone, now half asleep. Both his legs were encased in casts and held aloft by a counterweighted apparatus. A TV depended from the ceiling but the sound was off.

"Levine."

The big man fluttered his eyes.

"It's your mom."

The head rolled toward Jack Liffey, and then the eyes narrowed. "Just kidding. My name is Jack Liffey. I'm looking for a girl named Luisa Wilson. Straight dark hair, about eighteen."

It was a long time coming: "Look all you want. Fuckhead."

Levine's voice reminded him of wrestlers you heard trying to sound bored with their opponents but not being very good at it. "She's with Terror. I know you hang with him."

Levine worked his mouth for a while, as if having to chew the words before emitting them. "Understand my position, Annoying Person."

"I do. Supine. And in traction. I could probably make you a lot more uncomfortable before a nurse got here."

"You're very funny."

"If I know Terror, he hasn't bothered sending you any roses. You don't owe him anything."

"You know Terror?" That had his attention at last.

"I'm the guy who got him sent back home a few years ago, if he ever talks about that. I struck a deal with G. Dan so we could all get over. It was a ticklish situation."

"So you were powerful once. You look pretty fucking useless now," Levine said, and he took his eyes back to the silent TV.

Coming from a man in double traction, that counted as tough. Jack Liffey wondered if his anxieties were showing. He couldn't just go on being this feckless and disorderly person and get his work done properly, he noted. He had to do better. "I just want to talk to the girl and make sure she's okay. It's what I do in life, I help kids. I'm not a cop."

"If I tell you where he is, doesn't it put me in a funny position, I mean concerning my loyalty?"

"That would depend on your sense of humor."

Levine smiled coolly. "What do I get out of it if I tell you where to find him?"

"You get me out of your life for good. You probably get Terror out of your life, if you want it that way."

He laughed once, like a predator about to eat something much smaller. "The guy's such a goofball. Point him in a direction and he walks. Kingston, Jamaica, must be the world fucking capital of the terminally dense. I sat through an action movie with the guy one day, and I had to explain every goddam scene. But he has his good points, too. I'm not sure if I don't miss him."

In Terror's favor, Jack Liffey thought, maybe it was hard to sort things out when you were living on your wits, completely outside your own world. But there was no percentage in arguing any of this. Whether he'd been planning to or not, Levine suddenly turned his head and told Jack Liffey the address.

"Thanks." It was a pleasant surprise. He'd been planning some way to steal the medical chart.

"Well, as long as I'm not around, old Trev needs someone to keep him on his toes. It might as well be you."

Exhausted after a day of driving—fighting the wind in the screaming VW to and from Palm Springs and then over to Cedars-Sinai—Jack Liffey, once back at home, got himself horizontal on the sofa. Intending only to doze for a minute, he went out like a light. When he woke, he had no idea what time it was, but it was dark, and Gloria was banging around in the kitchen. He sat up immediately, all his nerve ends firing.

"Glor, I meant to cook. I'm sorry. Let me do it."

There was no immediate answer, and that worried him, so he got up and peered around the opening.

"Bad day?"

She stood at the stove. Silence.

"Please don't shut me out."

"I had a 1.81. That's a public complaint lodged against me." She told him this in a weary voice.

"I'm sorry. What was it about?"

Silence.

He'd bought the fixings for a curried lamb, and now she was just chopping and tossing everything that might possibly result in a passable lamb stew into a big pot. He came into the kitchen and tried to hug her from behind as she worked, but she stiffened and shook him off.

"Now you know why marriages to cops don't last," she said, almost triumphantly.

"Isn't that being a little cynical? We're both doing our best."

"Am I? Hooray for me."

"Will you please tell me about it? Do you want a beer?"

"I already had a beer at the cop bar. In fact, I had several. I broke my own rule and went out for a drink with the boys so they could all tell me their war stories about the 1.81s they've survived—supposedly to make me feel better. Blacks they'd beat up so it wouldn't show. Latinos they'd dragged along the sidewalk on their face. Winos dumped in trash cans. Gosh, how could I not feel a lot better?"

"You're not like that." He tried to hug her again and got a few moments of reasonable tolerance this time before being shrugged off. "Please tell me."

She was motionless for a bit, then she turned to face him and crossed her arms defensively. "It was in the Rancho, you know, the federal housing down at the port."

"I know the Rancho. I grew up in San Pedro."

"Mostly it's black and a little Latino, but there are some Samoans living there, too. This afternoon, the Samoans were having a barbecue out in the grass between the buildings. I don't know how many there were but you can double the number just for the general impression these people give. The smallest adult there was the size of a tuna boat."

She frowned. "I don't mean to be unkind, but they really *are* big. It was a black woman who lives there that called me. I respect her, she watches over the place and keeps kids out of trouble, and she said on the phone that a woman at the barbecue looked pretty drunk. She also said that a kid this woman was holding was screaming, and it sounded like pain.

"The station's only a minute away, so I rolled down there with Rodolfo Robles as my partner, and we had no trouble spotting the uproar. This woman in a blue muu-muu was standing in the middle of things clinging to a little girl and weeping and every once in a while throwing her head back and bellowing something, while a bunch of other Samoans were trying to calm her down.

"*'Que bárbaridad,'* Robles says to me. 'Thank the lord Jesus it's a woman, so it's your problem. *Allá tú.*' So he hangs back, and I have to go up and deal with it. Now a few of these Samoans already have an attitude about cops, I know that, but I don't want to call for backup and get some tear gas lobbed on their party, so I decided to try to deal with it *diplomatically.* I talk to the nearest coherent human being, and I learn that this woman is named Siitu something and her boyfriend has gone off somewhere for good and it looks like she's ingested angel dust on top of whatever else. I get closer and maybe it is dust because her eyes are glassy and she's babbling and weeping, and the poor little girl is going bug-eyed out of asphyxia, she's being squeezed so hard. The woman probably just wanted to show affection for her kid, but she was way past any sense of her own strength.

"The little girl sees me come up and reaches out toward me with these tiny arms, and, unfortunately, when I try to talk to Siitu, the kid wriggles free a little and gets her arms around my neck. All I can do is try to ask her to let me hold the girl for a moment. I was as soothing as I could be; I even think I set a world record for calm in the midst of bedlam—but the woman's holding on like mad to the girl's legs as if I'm Social Services come to take her away, and my neck is starting to hurt with the kid's death-grip. We might have got over still if some asshole cop-hater, with perfect timing, hadn't pushed through the crowd, a guy the size of Catalina, and he starts shouting at me to stop abusing the little girl.

"*'Po*-lice brutality! Leave that little girl alone! Why you trying to rip her from her own momma!' That stuff. Just then Robles sees me in trouble and comes running up with his nightstick already out and threatening everybody. The woman starts to scream some mantra over and over, something like *O le poto* . . . who knows? Turns out later it's from home, it means that I'm just a minor chief that doesn't have to be obeyed."

Gloria offered a half smile. He wanted to touch her, but her arms were still crossed fiercely and he held back.

"By now, some of the other women are trying to calm her down. Robles fights his way through the crowd and clobbers the woman's shoulder with his nightstick to make her let go of the little girl. Which actually works. But now the cop-hater grabs at the little girl, and the result is that between us we dislocate her shoulder as we all go to the ground. I can tell something bad has happened because the screeching goes up about three notches.

"There's plenty of people trying to make peace now, but Robles is going nuts, and he's whaling on the cop-hater next to me. And when the mother grabs at him, he gives her a pop in the gut with the butt-end of his stick, and this gets her to throw up all over him."

She smiled briefly again. "I suppose if I were on the outside and if we hadn't hurt the little girl, it would all be pretty funny. It's just the sort of stuff that happens all the time when worlds collide."

"Somebody filed a complaint over *that?*"

She sighed. "Robles was in trouble now, sandwiched between the woman and the cop-hater on the ground and I had to pry the little girl off me and pass her off quickly and spray the woman and then the guy. It's only pepper spray, but she starts yelling that I've blinded her, and I have to spray a couple more people before I'm through. We made a thorough mess of it, in truth. I felt like Dirty Harry wading into a gang of terrorists. I'm not sure what I could have done different, but I'm not proud of myself. And the poor kid's in Little Company of Mary."

"There's limits to diplomacy."

"Sure, and in the end, I won't really be disciplined, but it's on my record. *Damn,* it was a clean record. I was so proud of my ability to talk people down." She let her folded arms drop, and he saw his chance. He moved in and held her and she cried softly on his shoulder.

After a while she ran down. "I'm not sure why I'm crying." She pushed him back to arms' length and looked at him quizzically. "I think maybe it was something to do with my own rage snapping. It tells me I'm not really a child of the damn New Age. And also, I think you're going to give up on me eventually. It's the fate of cops."

"Don't be such a poop. I love you."

"Yeah, but you don't love what I do."

"That's not true. I respect sorting out messes. You're crying because you *are* part of the New Age, whatever that is. Your own anger got to you and reminded you you're not perfect."

"I thought I had it all figured out."

The pot started to boil over, but he got to the knob first, dropping it to simmer. "Everybody who thinks everything's all figured out is full of shit," he said. "You know that."

She touched his cheek coquettishly and offered a shy smile. They ended up making love, at first standing up in the kitchen, then in the short hall and then in the living room, while the lamb stew boiled off all its liquid and destroyed itself.

Dear Diary,

Trev is asleep now and I am so lonely! Today he showed me how to load his gun. Its a funny thing. You push it & it all just opens up like a book to show you the round thing where the bullets are. Their easy to take out if you got fingernails. Then you just close it up & it clicks. Its very heavy & he tole me that he would take me shooting sometime so I could learn to hit tin cans. I dont truly believe I could shoot at a living thing.

I made him promise to take me to a real restaurant tomorrow. Im tired of always sitting on plastic benches & plastic tables in places like Macdonalds. He said he knew just the place but it was a long way away.

NINETEEN

Meetings

"My view on de ting naow, dawta: My likkel life, I-an-I see so much time be waste wit no gain at all. Skifflin an givin licks an work for dogheart mans—tings like dose be *wrong* an *dred*." He went on for a while about his sense of disappointment at the waste of it all, though a smile seemed to belie much of the regret of his words, his voice rising a little in the hush of the elegant restaurant he had brought her to.

She could see eyes here and there in the room, belonging to men in business suits, keeping track of him as if he were a madman who might head their way any moment. Taylor's was an old and venerable L.A. businessman's steak house—even Luisa Wilson could see that, with its red leather booths and signed photos of local politicos and celebrities near the door. She could tell that Trevor Pennycooke's colorful clothing and his overlarge presence were making the wrong kind of impression, but she didn't care.

"Lisn me, de basic ting wit any man is have a small land wit a gaadin an naa be dependin' on no man fe you keep. *No bosses.*" That last loud proclamation swung the headwaiter around like a punch as he sauntered past, leading two young women toward a booth. The headwaiter frowned, backing a few steps with an eagle eye on the Jamaican, and then he turned and went on. Oblivious, Trevor went on telling her about a beautiful place he knew on a hill outside Kingston, a spot perfect for raising children. It had lush banana trees, and you could look down at a sleepy village on the slope below, and the earth was rich and brown. All that was needed was a bit of money to set them up and build a little house.

"You be one true bonafide to keep me companion dere!"

Luisa was working on a small medium rare steak, with an occasional glower of disapproval from her lover as he talked. She figured it would probably be her last, but she wanted it. The menu had not contained much of interest for a militant vegetarian, so he was eating slabs of an eggplant that he had brought with him, in the pocket of his chartreuse jacket, and had prevailed upon the waitress to have grilled for him, "Witout de assistance of de fat of beasts."

At the nearest table, a man in a cashmere sweater, sitting with two women wearing too much makeup, leaned to whisper to one of them, who rolled her eyes and glanced briefly their way. She said something in reply that made the man chuckle.

Just to show every one of them where her loyalties lay, Luisa stroked Trevor's giant hand on the table. "I want you to take me with you to Jamaica."

He brayed a laugh. "Girl, you only got to stop eatin' flesh like dis an we a oneness in de heart. Flesh of beast make you sick and p'ison de liver. Some Rastas eats of the fish of the sea, but only them with scales like it say inna Bible, but I-an-I don eat of no living beast."

"I'll do my best to please you, Trevor."

"The key to me is peace and *serenitude!*" Trevor Pennycooke announced, his voice rising alarmingly.

"I can feel it in you."

Trevor Pennycooke took a large mouthful of eggplant, and suddenly his eyes went wide. She thought at first it was something over her shoulder that had caught his attention, but then she noticed how much darker and bluer his face had gone. She'd had basic first aid training on the rancheria, and, when both his palms went to his neck in the universal sign of choking, she knew what she was seeing.

He got up and staggered into the nearest table, making an ack-ack sound, and knocking over a bottle of red wine so that an athletic-looking man in a silk jacket rose in barely suppressed rage.

His companion called, "Tommy, don't! Something's wrong with him!"

"He's choking!" Luisa called out.

She was a little worried about pulling off a Heimlich's on someone so much bigger than herself, but she would save his life or die trying. Trevor was already staggering in panic toward a second table, the one with the man sandwiched between the two women, all of whom watched with horror as the flailing apparition approached. Luisa caught up to him and wrapped her arms around his amazingly slim waist. She locked her hands into a double fist and repositioned them until they were just under where she thought his diaphragm was. She prayed once quickly to the Paiute gods, then yanked with all her strength.

It worked the first time just like magic, and a greenish glob of eggplant dispatched like a missile across the table, followed by a similar mass of projectile vomit. The occupants of several tables backed away in horror as Trevor sucked in a slow triumphant breath.

Trevor Pennycooke raised both fists in the air and hollered, "All praise to His Majesty Haile Selassie I!"

Several men rose at their tables and shouted.

"Can't you be civil, man!"

"Get yourself under control!"

Luisa Wilson faced them down. "This man almost died!" she shouted. "But he's still alive, and he's worth ten of you!"

Light flooded the upstairs bedroom. Slowly, they both became aware that they were both awake and drifting. He nuzzled her a little, but she was no longer in the mood.

"Late for work?" Jack Liffey asked. Her schedule was so ragged, he never knew for sure.

"I'm off today. To do with the 1.81."

"Ah. We could do something together. Maybe go for a drive. Something nice, whatever you'd like."

"It is not necessary to be the cruise director. I'll survive this."

"I never doubted it."

"I'd like things to be simpler." She watched him. "But I can't seem to do it by myself. People like you come along and make me want you. And the minute I want you, I realize I want to have had a real childhood and a happy time in school and two little sisters and dolls and a picket fence. Without all that, what have I got to give you?"

Two enormous tits, he thought mischievously, but it would not have been smart to say it aloud.

"My marriages don't work out, Jack. My relationships."

"We're both getting older," he said. "Maybe we can settle for less than perfect."

"That's not the point. I'm not being finicky. It's some kind of grief I'm carrying that kills things."

He rested his hand on her forehead, and it was feverish, but it usually was in the morning. She stored up heat in the night like a dozen cats, and he often had to kick off the blankets on his side. She sat up but clutched the covers modestly. "I can see the treetops whipping out the window. We've got more Santa Anas."

"I'm inclined to try to make the most of the life we have left," Jack Liffey said, unwilling to let the subject go.

She pushed his caressing hand away, rather hard. "If it's not too spoiled."

"I don't think it's just sadness," he said. "You're really angry at me."

"I guess I am."

"Do you know why?"

"No. But I'm glad you notice. You can just orbit in that zone." She pressed a finger against his nose to hold him down. "It'll keep you attentive."

Prozac, he thought. Barrels and barrels of it in her tea.

* * *

Rod Whipple was dozing shallowly, drifting in and out of sleep, when Kenyon Styles came in and sat on the edge of his bed. He was already mostly awake by the time Kenyon stretched himself out on top of the covers. That brought him all the way out of his busy and disturbing dream. It was probably light outside, something like nine judging by the nervous but rested feeling he had—but the room had blackout curtains, and it always felt earlier. A car alarm went off somewhere for a few seconds until someone got the key in the ignition.

Without giving a sign that he was awake, Rod rolled to face away from Kenyon, who seemed to have recovered from his coughing fits, though his breathing was still raspy.

It seemed only a short time ago that it had all been something like a prank, paying some toothless old winos to bare-knuck it in a parking lot. It wasn't exactly something he wanted to boast about to his family, but it wasn't consign-him-to-hell material either, just maybe an extra week or two in purgatory. He wondered where the path had diverged toward serious mayhem. Or did paths always diverge without you knowing it? Was this the way Al Capone ended up ordering all his competitors shot to death by Thompsons, starting out with simple hotfoots and wedgies? He almost chuckled at the thought. Back in Chicago they still talked about the great Scarface.

If they both managed to survive *Dangerous Games II*, there was not going to be a *Dangerous Games III*—at least not for him. He intended to run home to make his independent film with his old friends, even if he was pretty sure Kenyon would do his best to screw him out of as much of his share as he could.

All of a sudden Rod felt a hand resting heavily on his hip.

"Um."

"In the dorm at UCLA, me and Greg used to have this thing. We'd get in bed and talk about our girlfriends, where they were, who they were fucking. We'd go into details. It was just a thing, you know."

He didn't want to hurl the hand off but he didn't know what to say. He was not interested in this new concept.

"How *is* your girlfriend?" Rod asked.

"You know, I've been finding her less and less . . . satisfactory. All she ever wants to talk about is feelings."

"Are you planning to start a fire today?"

"We need to go meet our new 'line producer' and see if he's ready to go. Sort of Smokey the Bear in reverse."

"I don't know, Ken. We've done some pretty dangerous stuff, but this is way past any of that. Why don't we just call it a wrap now? We've got enough material for *II*."

Rod felt the covers tug down a little, and a hand began to massage his shoulders.

"Don't!"

"Hold still. I can feel how tense you are about this."

Rod had his usual morning erection and couldn't get out of bed without Kenyon noticing. He needed to pee badly.

"Stop it, please."

The hand drifted, working its way into the neck of his pyjamas toward his chest. "Ever turn a trick, Rod? I've got plenty of money."

"No, man. This is not for me."

He jumped out of bed and sprinted for the bathroom, doing his best to conceal the tentpole holding out his pyjamas. He shut the door and locked it as discreetly as he could. But now he faced the usual dilemma of how to pee with his morning erection without peeing into his own face. He waited, thinking of baseball, imaging the different pitches, thinking of batting averages he'd memorized, and finally, he felt himself going limp, and he could pee.

"You okay, Rod?"

"I'm fine." He sighed in relief.

"You think we should bring some *American* ginger ale to this nigger?"

"Let's just forget it," he called back. "But I'm never going to listen to Bob Marley again."

Jack Liffey stepped outside to get the *Times,* and he could smell it instantly on the air—brushfire. Astringent, prickling his nose as if the air carried the ash of some acidic trees, though the brushfire was probably a dozen miles away. Everyone in L.A. recognized that smell long before the sky turned dark and cinders blanketed the freshly shined cars. With the prevailing wind coming off the desert, this one had to be out in the San Gabriels somewhere, maybe in the mountains north of Claremont or Glendora. Luckily, he was planning on going the other way later.

He turned on one of the local channels. They'd be covering the fire with their helicopters if there wasn't a police chase circling the freeways.

". . . There's an abandoned cabin up Icehouse Canyon that they don't think they can save, but no other structures are endangered for now."

"Mary Lou, do they have any idea what started this blaze?" A frazzled-looking blonde in a sweatshirt was glancing regularly over her shoulder at a ragged line of fire on a hillside.

"Not yet, Don. I haven't been able to speak with the division commander yet, but I will. Let me tell you something you never hear on TV about one of these brushfires. It's *very* scary."

"I understand, Mary Lou," he said, a patronizing whicker in his voice. "We'll get back to you in a few minutes. Over to Stan Pollard at the second fire in Altadena near the base of Mount Wilson. Stan, are any of the broadcast antennas or the observatory threatened . . . ?"

Jack Liffey turned the sound off, and started making coffee. Gloria was showering. She was finally beginning to worry him. Or rather, he was finally beginning to wonder if he might not eventually lose touch with the tenderness he still felt for her. She seemed to want to crush it out. Something in her was fiercely resisting being loved. He felt he had so few years left that he wasn't sure he could afford to give them all to someone so damaged. Not that he was perfectly balanced himself, but he was ready to make a commitment, ready to try. And Maeve was demanding it.

The water had stopped a minute ago, and he could hear the telltale squawk of the medicine cabinet closing. He waited for her outside the bathroom door with a cup of her favorite tea. The door came open, and she seemed a little startled. She was wrapped demurely in a bath sheet tucked over her breasts.

"Thanks, Jack," she said as she took the cup perfunctorily and walked on.

"I'll track you down like a wolf," he said. "I'll make you accept my love."

She stopped in the bedroom door and sipped. "What if I can't?"

It was the sedated sleep that did it, he thought. The wrong damn drugs. "I'll give you a few laughs, then. Everybody can laugh."

She looked back over her shoulder and smiled. "It's a deal."

> **Dear Diary,**
> After the bad time in the restaurant Trev & I went for a walk. The whole place had signs in some foreign language. I think its Korean. Nobody was very friendly but I didnt feel anger at us. Tho a funny thing happened. This oriental man was walking a big police dog & he broke away & ran straight toward Trevor. I stepped in front of the dog because I have always been pretty good with animals but maybe he don't speak English & couldn't understand me. He jump & bite my ankle. Trevor pulled the dog off & spoke soft to the dogs face & he ran away. At home he bandaged me up & used some Jamacan medicine on my foot. It still hurts pretty bad tho.

On the ramp at Fourth where Jack Liffey usually hopped onto the freeway out of Boyle Heights, he saw a middle-aged, well-dressed man commanding the spot where a ragged Latino ordinarily sold oranges. He was too well dressed to be a Vet begging for a handout, and he held a tidy hand-lettered sign: **I was once a social worker. I lost the impetus. Where did my humanity go?**

As luck would have it, Jack Liffey's car stopped directly alongside him at the metered ramp.

"Pal, I wish I knew."

The man grimaced and flipped the sign over, and Jack Liffey recoiled a little, fearing a trick, but it only said: **Will work for satisfaction.**

"If you find it, give me a call." The metering light allowed the bread truck ahead of him onto the freeway, and Jack Liffey had to inch his VW forward. That allowed him to think for another half minute about the hapless social worker, if that's what he was, before the worries of his own life took over: His woman was trouble, and it was a long damn drive from Boyle Heights to Malibu.

The wind was so strong that the smell of the fire fifty miles away had made it to the Malibu hills before him. There were enough torchable bark-shedding eucalyptus trees and other fire-ready shrubs in the hills that if smell alone could ignite, the place would already be a firestorm. He could almost picture the singed Porsches and SUVs chasing madly down the canyon roads toward the sea. He wondered why people lived up here and risked it.

The address he had was off the pavement onto a graded and graveled road, then off that to a spur lane that was only reddish clay and would be a real hell in the rainy season. The house itself was on a knob about as high as several others nearby, though the Santa Monica Mountains crested behind him quite a bit higher. All the land above him across the road remained unbuilt, probably Conservancy land forbidden to developers.

A paved driveway dipped steeply to a three-car garage beneath the house. He idled down the drive and rested his bumper against the garage door, hoping to block any sudden exits. Across the road on the uphill, a line of eucalyptuses was whipping so noisily that no one in the house would have heard him approach, or so he hoped. He walked back up the steep drive, emerging head-first into the gusty windstorm, and he had to turn his face away from driven sand and twigs. Fragments of shredding aromatic bark sizzled past all around. He had always imagined Terror Pennycooke ending up somewhere far out at the exhausted edge of things, but that hardly described the hills above Malibu, some of the most desirable real estate in the L.A. basin, the playground of movie people and music execs.

This was a High Modernist show house from the 1950s, flat graveled roof and floor-to-ceiling glass with flagstone patios and planters, probably worth more millions than he could grasp. Personally, he didn't like flagstone much. Then a noise inside the structure took all his attention.

He patted the heavy lump in his belt where he kept the .45 under his jacket. You could never tell with Terror Pennycooke. What he remembered best about him was his predator's eyes, and he wasn't sure he wanted to face them again without a reliable edge.

Jack Liffey studied the lay of the house and went around in the brush to find a vantage point from which he might be able to see inside through the wall of windows that faced across the patio. He found a likely shrub to half conceal himself in a squat and peered back toward the house where, obscured a little by reflections on the bronzed glass, he made out two people in the living room. In a moment, he could see it was Terror Pennycooke himself, dressed as flamboyantly as ever in bright yellow tropical silk and the oversized tricolor knit cap. His companion was a young woman with long dark pigtails. She looked a lot like the photo he had from Owens. They sat side by side on the floor against a plain Danish sofa and seemed to be taking turns reading from an immense black leather Bible. He saw the girl heft it with difficulty across to Pennycooke, who started in reading immediately but seemed to be stumbling over the words.

It was about as incongruous a scene imaginable for that house, an unmistakable boast of the triumph of the secular white elite. His feelings were compounded of a grudged respect for Pennycooke's Rastafarianism and vegetarianism and outlandishism, plus a compassion for these two outsiders who had found one another—born light-years from this world and equally far from one another's. You just had to give them a break. He knew it was feelings like that that sometimes led him to make ineffectual and hazardous gestures, but watching them grin at one another satisfied something quite deep inside.

He watched for a while longer and then stood up and sauntered across the patio. Terror Pennycooke noticed him first, managing almost a silent-movie doubletake as recognition dawned on him slowly. He firmed up his jaw with anger and opened a lip, preparatory to a splendid Jamaican tooth-suck of contempt, but Jack Liffey held up the palms of both hands as a sign of peace.

"No harm," he said quite loudly to the expanse of glass.

Her dad probably hadn't noticed but Thumb's address had been printed in the upper corner of the essay, and since her father had

said something about him living in the garage, the rest was just
Mickey Mouse. She wasn't the daughter of a detective for nothing.
She parked her Toyota in the alley and tried to peer in a small back
window of the garage, but it had been blacked over from the inside.
So she went in the gate to the big uncurtained French window, now
open maybe six inches.

For some reason, she wasn't frightened. Whatever angelic protection she got to carry around for being a girl—okay, she thought,
a fairly clueless white girl—seemed to have been intensified by the
fact of her wound. She cupped her hands against the glass to cut
down reflections and peered inside. The inner walls were covered
with arty graffiti but she didn't have much of a chance to look it
over. A young man with a T-shaped mustache-beard was working
hard at a canvas on an easel. It seemed to be a portrait, and aston-
ishingly a creased photograph of her own father was pinned to the
upper corner of the canvas. Unlike the photo, though, the painted
man appeared to be emerging from the sizing in a chest-back
haughty pose. She supposed it was meant to be macho. *El Pachuco*—
needing only some show-off drapes and a big swag chain.

She wondered where he'd got the photograph, and then she recognized it as a vacation photo that Gloria had taken last year in
Sequoia, her father clowning around after setting up a borrowed
tent. It was the only time the three of them had gone away together,
and it hadn't worked too well, with none of them all that accom-
plished at camping and none very pleased with the discomforts.
Especially the fact that a third person in the tent, no matter how big
it was, made sex pretty much a no-no for the other two, despite her
insistence that she would be happy to go for a long night walk if
they preferred.

Thumb stood back, squinted, then dabbed a bit of color up off
his palette and continued on her father's cheek. After a while she
rapped on the big sash window. It didn't seem to startle him, and
she waited calmly until he swung it open and took a good look at
her, not neglecting her breasts.

"*La llorona,*" he observed.

"I know about the famous weeping woman of folklore. But I'm

not, I'm the bag-lady." She raised the side of her blouse to show the ostomy bag, and he winced a little. "Can I come in?"

He offered a hand to help her step over, and she took it. *"Buenas tardes, güera. Sé que tú es Maeve Liffey."*

"Sí, Pulgar."

"No, say Thumb. *Mi sobrenombre* is *Americano.*"

"Don't you mean *Norteamericano?*"

He shrugged and offered her a seat on a beat-up old sofa but she remained standing.

"Am I really a *güera?*"

"Over here, anyone with *pelo* lighter than this ivory black is *güera.*" He held up a tube of oil paint with a deep black smear on its side.

She smiled. "I remember in *The Good, the Bad, and the Ugly* they kept calling Clint Eastwood 'Blondie.' I always wondered why."

"I'm very sorry I shot you," he said abruptly.

"I know. If you meant to hit anyone, it was my dad."

"Is it terrible—that thing?"

"It's not fun. It farts and stinks, but they're going to fix it. I'll be back to normal before long."

"That's good." The intimate details seemed to have embarrassed him.

She eyed the painting. "You're making my dad look proud."

He looked at the painting, frowning. "Isn't he?"

"I don't think of him that way. Not in a puffed-up way, anyway. But I'm not criticizing your work," she said quickly. "It's fun to see him a different way."

"How do you see him?"

"He's proud in a quiet way, kind of private and fierce. Whatever he believes in, he . . . goes for it." She left out any criticisms she might have made. Stubborn, a little gullible sometimes, falling for the wrong women, walking into danger too often . . .

Thumb had a funny stare, and it made her a little uneasy. It wasn't menacing, just full-bore earnest. *Un homme sérieux,* she thought, but that was the wrong language. She didn't know if *un hombre sincero* had the same connotations.

"Aren't you afraid to come into the *barrio?*" he asked.

She couldn't help grinning. Trying to help her dad, she'd been through the center of the Ibrahim riot in South Central, and another time she'd been held prisoner by a motorcycle gang in Fontana. "You mean because I think some gangbangers are going to jump out of an alley and rape me? Nobody gets raped with a bag of her own shit hanging off her. And I don't really think this part of town is as bad as my scaredy-cat schoolmates think. People are just people. I like it over here. There's more life on the street."

Just then Oskar took it into his head to fart noisily.

"I can't control that," she said with equanimity, or at least a good simulation.

"*Chica,* you are very pretty."

"Don't come on to me, mister. I didn't come here for that, and I don't even know you. I wanted you to see what you'd done, and I want to make sure you're going to be good to my dad."

He appeared a little crestfallen. "Your father has been *muy amable.*"

She hoped that meant kind. "My dad is the Lone Ranger. It may not be very smart sometimes, but it's all he knows."

TWENTY

Wildfire

Just outside the big patio window, Jack Liffey studied the tableau inside and could see now that Luisa Wilson had an Ace bandage wrapped inexpertly around her ankle, and a square of bloodstained gauze taped to her elbow. She collected the big Bible onto her lap as Terror Penny-cooke stirred himself to unlatch the door and trundle it open. There was no screen. Perhaps flies were not allowed into Malibu.

"Hello, Trevor. Luisa Wilson?" Jack Liffey stepped inside.

She didn't answer him, but he could tell the name startled her a little. "Your mother up in Owens hired me to find you. I have a hunch that mutant named Clyde molested you, and I promise I won't take you back to the rancheria if you don't want to go."

"I intend to stay with my beloved forever. We have plans." This was one strange development, he thought. Talk about odd couples.

"I-an-I *nah* wan you hyer, bal'head."

"What happened to your ankle?" If Terror was beating on her, there was no question of letting her stay here.

"We were minding our own business walking on Eighth Street, and a big German shepherd came after me. He bit my ankle and made me fall and scrape my arm."

"Have you had a tetanus shot? Antibiotics?"

"We nah need no lowtal medicine. Dat not from roots."

He turned to Pennycooke. Rabies was unlikely from a pet, but tetanus was another matter. "I assure you tetanus is no respecter of Rasta medicine. It will kill her. It will freeze her muscles into spasms and clamp her throat shut so she can't breathe. Get her a shot. I'll pay for it."

It was enough to ruffle the angry flat glare in the Jamaican's eyes, and made him turn to look at her. He really did seem to care about the girl. "Tet-a-nus, you say."

"Mr. Pennycooke, we need to make a separate peace. I know we had our troubles, but I think we both care about this young woman."

"Den you jus' trod away, mon. Naow. An dis mon say Jah go wid you."

"I can't leave her like this. I'm not kidding you. She needs the shots. How long has it been since the dog bit you?"

"Yesterday," she said. She was starting to get a little worried, too. "I washed it good."

Jack Liffey held out a propitiating hand to the Jamaican. If she was in love with him, it would do Jack Liffey no good to antagonize him. "Mr. Pennycooke, I apologize for any wrongs I did to you. I sincerely do."

A whole series of emotions crossed Pennycooke's face, the wheel of colored cellophane rotating unhurriedly to reveal one after another, until his attitude came to rest on a kind of amusement. The smile actually seemed friendly, with no malice at all. "Blessed, how strange dis life turn, Mr. Lif. Mebbe we do mek peace. Mebbe dis be de rebolution till de rebolution come along."

The girl gave a little squeak of delight. "That's so deep," she said.

Jack Liffey could feel that they were about to shake hands at last—after the initial glacial approach toward one another—when Pennycooke abruptly raised both hands. He turned to the big sliding door that he had left open. "Hush, mon."

He went straight outside, and Jack Liffey followed. The brush-fire smell was now much stronger, and there was a slow crackling on the air. It was out of sight somewhere, apparently uphill behind the house.

"Badness." Pennycooke sprinted to the edge of the patio, looking back around the house. His expressive eyes widened out.

Jack Liffey didn't wait for an explanation. He was beside the man in an instant and saw the low line of fire licking slowly through ankle-high weeds down the slope toward the road. Incongruously, like hallucinations, two widely separated men on the safe side of the fireline were aiming video cameras toward them. One was much taller than the other.

"You dead men!" Pennycooke bellowed.

The taller one of the cameramen waved cheerfully without taking his eye off the little camera before him. The fire downhill of them grew rapidly as he watched, strewing sparks ahead on the wind. Now and then a whole flaming, floating islet of undergrowth levitated by its own heat and whisked itself away like something from a nightmare. A sparse line of shaggy-bark eucalyptus trees waited ominously along the dirt road, ready to go up like bombs. The fire was no accident. It had obviously been set alight along a wide front, and there was a definite gasoline smell mixed with the thin smoke gusting past them. A felled tree had been placed across their access road, and Jack Liffey saw in an instant that their cars were useless. They'd never get the tree out of the way before it was engulfed.

"You Danger Games!" Pennycooke shouted, pointing angrily. "You be fuckin' cook an curry!"

"Time to run, folks!" the tall one shouted amiably at them. "Make it look good!"

Jack Liffey grabbed Pennycooke's shoulders before the man was completely possessed by his need to shout down the tormentors. "Can Luisa walk?"

Her name brought him most of the way back from his blinding rage. "Nah, mon. Slow by slow."

"Let's get her out. This house is going up."

They both sprinted for the glass door. Terror ran straight into the back of the house. "We've got to go now," Jack Liffey told Luisa.

She nodded, without any evident alarm, and picked up a small pink notebook from the sofa, which she tucked into her shirt pocket. He took her hands and pulled her up, and he could see the wince when her ankle tried to take her body weight. Then Pennycooke was back with his big Webley revolver in his waist and both his pants pockets bulging with something else. At least he hadn't taken time to collect his ginger beer.

Jack Liffey slipped an arm around the girl's waist and grabbed the belt of her old jeans, leaving her good leg on the outside. "We'll take turns helping you walk."

They heard a big *whoomp* like the gas igniting suddenly in a wall heater. "They should never plant eucalyptus up here," Jack Liffey said. He got her out the door in a three-legged stumble, and Pennycooke ran immediately to the edge of the patio and fired a few wild shots toward the cameramen. Jack Liffey steered the girl toward where Pennycooke stood—it was the shortest drop off the patio, maybe three feet. Already he could see sparks and crisping leaves floating past the house.

"De worm done turn!" Pennycooke exulted, gazing up the hill with his arms on his hips.

At first, Jack Liffey thought the Jamaican was referring to his own gunfire, but as they helped the girl under the railing and down onto a dirt path, he glanced back where Pennycooke had been looking. Much higher up the slope, a single tiny figure was making its way along the crest of the hills, along what must have been Mulholland Drive, dragging something like a stick through the tangled underbrush alongside the road. It was as if whatever he carried tore minute holes through the fabric of the day to some brighter world beyond. It could only have been a traffic flare, and it had already set another line of brushfire behind the cameramen.

"What the hell is going on?"

"I tink dat Keith, de coke-a-moke cowboy."

And as the name registered, Jack Liffey recognized the tiny figure, limping along favoring his groin. The cameramen were on their stomachs sheltering from Pennycooke's shots and keeping the cameras going, so they hadn't noticed the danger behind them.

They were almost invisible in the heat dance above the first line of flames.

It was like being trapped in one of *Mad Magazine's* Spy vs. Spy cartoon, Jack Liffey thought—every assailant more insane than the previous one.

"Forget shooting at them, man. Come on!"

He half-walked Luisa along the path past a few ornamentals and then down into a dry wash that ran downhill in the chaparral.

"Jah go wid us."

Pennycooke caught up and took Luisa's other side. The bottom of the wash was wide here, and free of vegetation, and they went so fast that her good foot barely tapped down at each stride. The gusting wind blew their clothes hot against their backs, shoving so hard that they had to fight a tendency to run out of control.

"Is there another road down below?"

"Yea. Mebbe it take us to Rambla or Malibu Canyon to get down."

"Great." He saved his breath for the heavy work of hauling the girl along. Sparks looped past like fireflies, and he heard the woosh of another dry tree igniting. Only a week earlier, he had read in the *Times* that a single acre of dry chaparral was the equivalent of seventy-five gallons of aviation fuel. A pleasant fact to remember. At least the brushfire hadn't turned into a firestorm—not yet. He'd read about firestorms, too—Dresden, Tokyo, Hiroshima, the Oakland fire in 1991, Laguna in '93, and at least one of the previous Malibu fires. No one outran a true firestorm.

There was a deep concussion far behind, so visceral it rang in his sinuses. It was either a rifle (no pistol sounded like that) or the brushfire had come upon something explosive. They all craned their necks back. The tall eucalyptus that loomed across the street from the house was catching fire down low among its shaggy bark, but it hadn't been the source of that boom. They had to watch in horror for a moment as the wind tore strips of flaming bark off the tree and sent them toward the house, air-borne rafts of flame. One firebrand caught on the roof but died out slowly on the gravel.

"The house is history," Jack Liffey said. "Let's go." And his car, he thought. Another trusty vehicle lost.

The canyon narrowed and became entangled with dead brush. Somebody had to take charge.

"Trev, go ahead for a minute and kick a path through that dry stuff."

"Fe real, mon."

He ran forward and kicked away at the impassible barrier of dry chamise plants, releasing medicinal smells into the smoke, until finally he had kicked a path through, then he ran forward again and furiously attacked another blockage of the chest high shrubs. Faint yelps of fright carried down with the ash and smoke, and he figured the cameramen had finally discovered their predicament. The smoky wind grew thicker and darker, full of grit, the eye-smarting teargas of a campfire shifting abruptly into your face. Once in a while, a driven spark stung the back of his neck like an angry insect.

"Oh, de debbil!" Trevor Pennycooke came to a halt and turned with spread arms to catch them both against their hurrying momentum. For the first time Jack Liffey noticed the Jamaican's ripe smell, stronger than the fire itself when you got this close. Pennycooke had backstopped them at the lip of a sheer drop down a crumbly cliff. It was nearly fifty feet down and would have made a lovely waterfall if this wadi ever ran with the winter rainfall.

Jack Liffey looked back and saw they would have to retreat forty or fifty yards to find a slope they could manage out of the ravine, returning into the teeth of the fire.

"Ay! Ay! Ay!" somebody back there behind the shimmering heat wall was yapping like a dog.

"That fucking guy!" somebody else yelled, the voices tiny, panicky, like very small men trapped in a bottle. The fire itself had begun a kind of growl and crunch like some unseen predator eating.

"Let's go folks," Jack Liffey said. "I see a deer trail up there."

"My ankle is killing me."

It was about to kill all three of them, he thought, and it would for sure if this turned into a real firestorm.

"Sorry," he said. "It doesn't get any better for a while."

* * *

Maeve went to the window, where she could hear several sirens all around the compass. "They coming for you?" she asked in jest.

"That's fire," Thumb said.

"*Bomberos.* You can tell just from the siren?"

A nearby firetruck gave a series of deep trucklike hoots, and then she could tell, too. They seemed to be all heading westward, and she had a terrible premonition. They should have been going eastward to the Claremont fire, or north to Altadena. "Got a TV?"

He was already turning it on, patting it gently on one side, then shaking it and giving a bigger whack.

"Just don't say it responds like a woman, okay?"

It took him a moment to get her joke, and then he frowned. "Only *cobardes* hit women."

A lopsided picture finally emerged from the streaks and static on the old TV, far too green, and he fiddled with the knobs until the image straightened up. Channels eleven and five had the Claremont fire. He twisted the old rotary dial to thirteen and what appeared to be a helicopter shot of a hillside fire, with a house already burning. A small logo said **13 Live**.

". . . Not one of your ordinary Malibu fires. Several phone tips have reported that shots were fired, but we've been unable to get confirmation from the sheriff's department. It may have begun up here with a drug deal gone sour or even a domestic dispute. This one is certainly arson. Only fifteen minutes ago Air Thirteen captured this scene above Mulholland near Cold Canyon Road."

TAPED EARLIER came up over the logo, and the small foreshortened figure of a man could be seen scurrying along the edge of a paved road with a roadway flare, setting fire to the weeds. The camera panned over to a downhill line of fire that was already threatening a flat-roofed house on a dirt road. A couple of men seemed to be filming this fire. The cameras were smaller than the usual news cameras, so the men appeared to be ghoulish homeowners recording the death of their own homes with amateur equipment. The announcer babbled away, but Maeve was only half listening. ". . . hot flare . . . amazing calm . . . maybe twenty years old . . . we may be watching pure evil at work . . ."

"*Madre,*" Thumb said.

The screen flickered and the words in the corner returned to **13 LIVE.** The flat-roofed house was ablaze. A sunk driveway led to a big garage, and a car seemed to be parked down there, half charred and smoldering.

"Oh, **NO!**" Maeve shrieked.

"*What?*"

She could feel her face burn in sympathy with the flames, and her hands stretched out involuntarily toward the TV, all her muscles stiffening. A VW Bug with two primered fenders, left front, right rear. Her father had said he thought the girl he was looking for was in the Malibu hills.

"That's my dad's car!"

The camera pulled away from the car, and she tried a desperate act of will to make it go back. As the helicopter circled, the camera panned around and tried to stay on a prone figure on charred ground that had obviously been overtaken by fire. The person was too thin and too tall to be her father, and he seemed to be clutching a little video camera. One arm was still moving a little. She felt an immense relief and then a momentary guilt at being thankful for someone else's misfortune. While she watched, begging the helicopter camera to come around again to the car, to show her some detail that would belie what she knew, the TV set broadcast the sound of two gunshots. Instantly, the man in the helicopter began to jabber, and the helicopter scooted outward and higher, losing sight of the house.

"Are you sure?" Thumb said.

She nodded dully, and they both watched as they could hear the pilot shouting "We're taking fire!" and all they could see was a chaotic streak of landscape as the helicopter retreated in a tilted circling evasive maneuver, the cameraman bravely struggling to find a target.

"I owe you two a life," Thumb said. "Let's go get your father."

"You didn't kill anyone."

"I have."

She wasn't sure whether it was rueful or proud, and just then she didn't care. "We don't even know where that fire is."

"Mulholland and Cold Canyon," he said. Obviously, he had listened more carefully than she had. She tried to picture a route. To get there, she'd have to drive east along the 10 and, when it hit the ocean, up the coast highway, but by the time she made the turn onto PCH the traffic would be a nightmare—or blocked by the police. By then most of the traffic would be fleeing the other way, but, anyway—Thumb was right—she had to try.

"Let's go."

"I got to get something."

He turned his back to her and, trying to hide it, he tore open a small box and yanked out a black pistol that he stuck in his waistband.

"Is that the one . . . ?" she asked.

"*Claro que* yes. I'm sorry."

"That's over. I forgive you. But it's dangerous for you to be keeping it."

Trevor Pennycooke had halted momentarily when they finally boosted the girl up to the deer trail. Without warning, he drew his big ungainly revolver and fired a couple of shots back into the flames. Jack Liffey could only think of the man-of-war at the beginning of *Heart of Darkness,* standing off the coast of the Congo and firing its cannon into the endless jungles to punish some nameless indiscretion of the continent. This pistol fire would have about as much use, but maybe he discerned a target back there in the dancing heat.

"Bal'heads tink dey beat on me like a drum. I-an-I a snake fe squeeze dem dead."

"Yeah, okay, Trevor, but not *now.*" Jack Liffey could feel the heat pouring down the hillside like an avalanche from an open furnace door. The fire had become a steady roar now, an animal poked into authentic rage. "Let's get her out of here." The dear trail was only wide enough for one, but he struggled slightly off trail on the downside to offer the best footing he could to her one good leg. Just as he got the pace he tripped on some outcrop and lunged forward, dragging her along, before he caught himself. She whimpered with pain, but he could tell she was trying her best not to. Pennycooke followed close behind, as if to protect them from the fire. Before long, the trail tilted down at quite an angle, and he had to find a new cadence, his heels hitting the steep dirt hard. His own ankles were starting to hurt.

"I-an-I take over naow," Pennycooke insisted, and Jack Liffey felt a strong hand on his shoulder. The live sparks and firebrands streamed past, and he hated to slow down even for the changeover. It was a miracle that the fire hadn't leapfrogged ahead of them on the flaming debris.

Pennycooke picked her up and put her over his shoulder like a long sack of grain. Jack Liffey was amazed at his strength and balance as he started to jog heavily down the trail, the girl's dark pigtails jouncing behind. Even unburdened, he had to hurry to keep up. A minute earlier, there had been a news helicopter but no evidence of fire department aircraft—all those angelic water-droppers you saw on the news. He supposed they were busy on the other fires or charging up with fire retardants somewhere. If the fire hadn't been so loud itself, howling behind them, he figured he would have heard sirens from the fire trucks. But there hadn't been a one. He wondered if they'd all been sent to cover the fires in the east.

He saw a flame lick upward out of the brush to his right, an offspring of the main fire. He'd read that wildfire raced uphill faster than a man could run, climbing on its own heat and the grasp of its taller flames, so he supposed they were lucky to be chased downhill.

Trevor Pennycooke stumbled ahead, and Jack Liffey lunged forward to help catch him before he went down heavily. The Jamaican gasped once. "Thankee, mon."

Somehow, they had lost the deer trail, or it had petered out on them, and they were kicking and high-stepping their way through chaparral now, waist-high dry weeds, wild grasses, and concealed stone outcrops. It was pure brute strength that kept the Jamaican tearing through the weeds at almost a trot, carrying his limp burden. Jack Liffey was having trouble himself getting a breath, with the smoke and the exertion, plus one lung still weakened by its recent collapse. An echo of Dickens entered his weary mind: somewhere nearby there is pain. And exhaustion.

A hundred yards ahead, and well below, they could see the dark scar of a paved road, two lanes without shoulders, a guard rail along the lower side. There wasn't a single vehicle escaping along it. Why?

Maeve drove fast, too fast for the little Toyota, which was starting to feel floaty at about 100, losing traction on the freeway as she wove grimly in and out between other cars in the faster lanes of the 10, and she had Thumb dial star 3 again on her cell, the speed-dial for Gloria's house, but it was still busy.

"Please don't get us busted with a *cuete* in the car," he said, one hand clinging hard to the shoulder belt next to his neck and his palm flat against the dash.

It was *Calo* slang, but she could guess. "Put it in the glove compartment. I'll take the blame."

He did just that, and then redialed and by his expression she could tell he'd got a ring. He held out the cell.

"Gloria—don't talk—this is Maeve. Dad's caught in that fire in Malibu. I saw his car on TV—that big house off Cold Canyon was the first one to burn up." She grimaced as she swerved around an SUV full of kids. "I'm going there now. Do what you can." She rang off before Gloria could argue, then switched the phone off completely and dropped it into her shirt pocket.

Thumb pressed both palms hard against the dash now, wincing silently from time to time—but he didn't want to admit a girl's driving was frightening him.

"You drive pretty good."

"Hope I don't hit a slowpoke. If I do, there's going to be a fine spray of my own shit all over the inside of this car."

"I'm not sayin' nothin', *chica*."

They slithered down the weedy bank to the road, and it felt good to stand on pavement. Trevor Pennycooke lifted the girl off his shoulder and set her down to rest stork-fashion on her good leg. The six-foot cliffbank protected them a little from the blast of heat that was visible as a speckled wavery wind passing overhead. Jack Liffey guessed that they had actually gained on the fire.

"The road's no good," Jack Liffey said. "I think this is Piuma. I came up it once, and it switchbacks like crazy for miles." He pointed straight across the road back into waist-high yellow grass and sighed. "Straight down is the way."

In the end, it was a different issue that settled it. Jack Liffey happened to be hanging his head, staring down at just the right spot in the roadway to see the startling and baffling spark of a tiny collision, instantly inhabited by that weird sound of a high-velocity ricochet. A few seconds later, they heard the crack of the rifle far above. He pointed to the white gouge where the bullet had come in at a shallow angle and then ricocheted away.

"Who bust dat cap?" Pennycooke stood out fearlessly in the road and squinted back toward the fire, visible as a solid wall of billowing flame.

"That was a rifle, probably with a scope on it. I think it's your friend Keith—the guy you circumcised."

It was just possible in one spot to make out the break in the weedline far up the hill where Mulholland ran. A fire captain's sedan and a pumper truck were parked up there, but no one was visible. Trever Pennycooke aimed his big Webley uphill and fired several shots blindly into the fire before cursing and discarding the empty revolver. Jack Liffey realized he had lost his own pistol long ago. Farewell, old friend.

Pennycooke hefted the girl onto his shoulder again, and they stepped over the low guard rail and back into the chaparral. Jack Liffey felt guilty letting the Jamaican do all the heavy lifting, but he knew he was too near his own limits.

A noisy helicopter came high along the hillside behind them, dangling a swaying firebucket on a cable. Jack Liffey caught a glance of orange mist falling away from the bucket. It didn't seem to him it would do much good against a fire this size. The helicopter warped away toward the ocean, its bucket swinging in a big arc with the turn. He remembered a half dozen of his friends once trying to piss out a roaring campfire. Even with beer-engorged bladders, they'd done no more than give the fire a short hissy fit and engulf themselves in an unpleasant smell.

There was a much bigger Canadian flying boat that could scoop up tons of water, and the city had borrowed a couple of them one year but had never sprung the money to buy one. There were no freshwater lakes convenient, and there was intense objection to using sea water on a chaparral fire. Better to let the land burn than despoil it with salt water. Some environmentalists also objected to building homes for the rich up in the fire zone in the first place, as argued by his friend Mike Lewis. Inevitably, the fire departments would have to commit to defending these homes, and inevitably they would burn, the city spending millions to make vain and dangerous stands on back roads for a handful of high-rollers.

He pounded along behind Pennycooke and Luisa. He could tell that his mind was doing its best not to think directly about the inferno at their back. It was like the sound of a thousand cigarette packs being crumpled, plus a deeper roar, under that, like the steady howl of a bear the size of Nevada.

TWENTY-ONE

Zor the O

He was wrong about gaining on the wildfire. It was starting to flank them now, perhaps just a twitch of wind direction or maybe a bedding of some faster-burning plant that gave a yank to the flames so they sped forward to the right of their deer trail. Now, the three of them were running for their lives. Or two of them were running; the girl was still draped over Trevor Pennycooke's shoulder. Jack Liffey couldn't keep his eyes off the errant thrust of the flame, kinking his neck that way again and again. It was like a living thing, hanging back unexpectedly, then lunging forward in attack, taunting them— vile orange slaps of fire, sudden mouths that engulfed a dry bush at one bite, the flames creeping low for a moment and then taking a ballet leap. His hands and neck were covered with grass cuts, stinging himself with his own sweat.

For a while, he had heard sirens and airplanes, but now he could hear only the crackle and thunder of the living fire that was determined to outflank them. Luckily, the dear trail trended away from the flames, but then it dropped steeply into an arroyo that was too dangerous to enter, and they had to set out across the open brush, weeds slashing at their ankles. Trevor Pennycooke was visibly tiring ahead of him, but if he set the girl down, so they could triple up, it would only slow them up.

"Can I help?" Jack Liffey called.

"Trod on." The man was gasping for air. "We all ruff necks, mon."

They must have been spotted by the fire department helicopter because it made a low pass from in front and hit the chaparral just ahead with a faint orange spray. The edge of the mist cloud drifted onto the threatening flame to their right and gave the beast a momentary surprise. It reared and smoked a pure white emanation, as if in a rage, then lay back down and carried straight on, more determined than ever. Get a bigger plane, he thought. There might have been another gunshot from behind, he wasn't sure, as a kind of sizzle seemed to pass near his ear and then the crack of a shot.

Running for his life, Jack Liffey became lightheaded, and in the steady rhythm of his run and the muddle of his thoughts, he began to stew on Gloria's sullen rejections, and to wonder why so many of his relationships with women ended so badly. He had an over-whelming urge to lie down and let his thoughts swirl over the problem, nap on it.

Was it him, he wondered, some perfectionism he carried or some way he pushed women into dissatisfaction? Was it the types of women he chose? Wounded birds, as Maeve had said? Or was it just, after all, a matter of luck? Or maybe all his life he'd been trying to reproduce some relationship from his childhood, as a psychologist he detested had once suggested, and get it *right* this time.

He really thought he was doing his damnedest with Gloria, trying as hard as he could to make her feel loved, but it just wasn't working out for her. His own feelings aside, he didn't want his failure to disappoint Maeve once again. How many potential step-moms had bailed out on him? His thoughts piled one on another in the chaos of stumbling and running, all accreting into the urgent rhythm of nightmare. He did his best not to let the danger take him that last measure over into panic.

He was running now on some automatic impulse that had carried him beyond the point of exhaustion, his legs turning rubbery with fatigue. Even stranger musings began to clutter his mind, as if he were drifting toward a kind of running sleep. Indignities made him wince, faces he didn't know sniggered. A sudden sense came over him, that there had always been something beckoning him from just beyond the bedroom window, and he had never opened the window, never climbed out there. A flash of clarity: Perhaps it was simple, after all—he had clung too hard to women who offered him comfort, who soothed something in him, who made love cheerfully.

Smoke made him retch then and drove away the clarity. It was those early years after Viet Nam, the first ones with Kathy when he had lost the instinct to raise hell. Had he forsaken some energizing principle then so that all women—like wolves—ended up sensing his weakness?

As he ran, he worked his way through every breakup, working forward through hazy images of their faces, seeking primal causes: Kathy, his Kathy, née Fitzgerald, so scornful about his lost employment, his retreat into drink, his outrageous and unacceptable new profession as some kind of character out of a pulp novel. The image of her scowl made him wince even now.

Eleanor Ong, fastidious, anxious, the emotionally simmering ex-nun—he remembered she had offered an epitaph for him as she gave him up and planned her retreat from the world, back to the convent: "I don't think you're going to make it, Jack." Could she have been right?

Lori Bright, the once-and-nevermore movie star who died in the Burbank quake but only after seducing him with her mercurial sexuality, a kind of effervescent and constant role-playing. And there had been his own complicity in some deep iniquity of the spirit—the corrupting power that her celebrity had worked on him.

Marlena Cruz, stolid, sentimental and ordinary, resourceful, insanely jealous, drawn like a moth to gimcrack religion and finally to a sympathetic co-believer, a big male doofus that she could count on.

Rebecca Plumkill—a bit like Kathy, he realized now—career headmistress too prim and conventional in the end to put up with what he did for a living, tarring his fingers in the world's back alleys. And now Gloria Ramirez . . . Gloria Ramirez, a Native

American orphan, studying him with eyes as hard as black dia-
monds, cynical as any cop, her life pitched like a tepee over the vent
of some volcano that was gradually coming to life, steaming and
rumbling. He wanted to know what it was all about. *Why me?*
Why so many *kinds* of failure? But his mind was as weary as his
legs, jumping from image to image, never staying.

Trevor Pennycooke stumbled and fell forward with a cry, toppling heavily with the girl over his back, and Jack Liffey hurried
forward to help. The fire still raced along behind and beside them,
running forward on its bright fingers, a deadly race to some finish
tape. "Shoulder-to-shoulder," he insisted. "We're the three muske-
teers. All for one, or all for one." He was so woozy, he didn't know
what he was saying.

"I glomm it," Trevor Pennycooke said as they hoisted the girl to
her feet.

She drove on the shoulder to get around an accident between two
mini-vans in which whole families seemed to be arguing right there
in the lane. The traffic was lighter than she expected going north on
Pacific Coast Highway through Santa Monica, past the bulk of the
Jonathan Club and the rows of beach houses, past the cliff where the
Pacific Palisades began, and past the big wall of railroad ties and
steel they'd erected against landslides, a near permanent condition
along the highway. It was amazing they hadn't blockaded the road
yet. The fire department and all species of cops hated lookie-loos.

They could see two water-dropping helicopters dangling buckets
far ahead as they shuttled to and from a hot zone. A massive plume
of gray smoke was billowing off the land and far out to sea, not
rising much until it hit some wall of cooler air out there.

"I never been here," Thumb said. He was staring across her at
the ocean, at the three-foot swells that were rolling up the narrow
beach.

"It's just a short drive from Boyle."

"I never seen the ocean."

She was flabbergasted. She couldn't imagine growing up in a
coastal city without having seen the ocean. She wondered what else

he and his friends had never seen. Then, she wondered how many Anglo kids had seen Boyle Heights or City Terrace or the wonderful Latino murals on Estrada Courts and Ramona Gardens, all things she had only seen since her dad moved to East Los with Gloria.

"Have you seen the Watts Towers?"

He shrugged.

"Have you been to the snow?"

"I got no car, Miss . . . can I call you Maeve?"

"Of course you can. I don't have some cool nickname."

"Maybe we find you one."

"You can think about it, but I don't want it to have anything to do with my shit-bag."

"I'm really and truly sorry I did that."

"I know you are. I'll get over it, Thumb."

They passed under the pedestrian bridge in the Palisades beside the arcaded hulk of what had once been Thelma Todd's Sidewalk Cafe. She knew it had been a popular restaurant in the forties, when PCH had been known as Roosevelt Highway. Her dad had told her some Catholic TV company used it now to make upbeat films for teens—exorcising the ghost of one of L.A.'s most notorious murders of the 1930s.

"It'll be easy to get over," she said lightly. "Like you get over anything. Time passes, and then you're somebody else, and the stuff you were so worried about is in the past."

He gave an embarrassed laugh. "Don't change. I think you pretty good the way you are."

"Don't go there, mister."

His gravity rushed back, like an inner nature asserting itself. "Have you been so tough all your life?"

She almost smiled. "Not yet."

The front of the wind-forced fire had finally turned on its flank and pressed them down into the gully to escape, but it was still pacing them implacably up above. The ravine gave them partial relief from the Santa Ana-driven smoke and ash, but only partial. It was still hard to see, hard to breathe, with the fiercer gusts shoving them into stumbles as they took turns supporting the girl. Trevor Penny-cooke no longer had the strength to carry her over his shoulder. Judging by the terrible crunching sound just above them, the forward edge of the brushfire was running just behind them but staying at the top edge of the gully. Unless there was a drastic shift of wind, fire didn't usually spill downhill. At least that's what Jack Liffey told himself.

"Mon, there someting bad luck hyer." As if the Jamaican had sensed his thoughts.

"We're alive. We're not burned. That's good luck."

"All men are hostages to fortune," Luisa said in a daffy earnest voice, and he wondered where she had read that.

"What dat?"

"Don't even think about luck," Jack Liffey insisted. "It's nothing to do with this. We're getting out of here for sure." He knew if they kept going downhill, and if they could stay ahead of the flames, they would have to hit PCH and the ocean eventually.

He nearly shouted when he felt something squirm underfoot and his spine tingled. A jackrabbit, a little singed on its long ears, did a contorted little leap sideways from his oafish foot and then took off downhill, rapidly outdistancing them.

"My ankle is killing," Luisa complained.

"We know."

"No, it *hurts!*"

She had her arms over both of their shoulders now, and she barely touched down as long as they could move in coordination. But the bottom of the arroyo was so uneven that they kept breaking apart and then she'd have to take her weight unexpectedly on the bad foot. He could sense her gasps, though the howl of the fire itself outbid just about every sound but shouting.

Then they were all bowled forward at once by a tremendous force, as if a linebacker had blindsided them from behind. Jack Liffey scrambled to pick himself up, overwhelmed by a musky smell, and something sharp hit him in the forehead and knocked him back down again. There was a shrill bleat just as he was getting himself oriented again and found himself lying in a pile of arms and legs.

"You two okay?"

Hoofbeats hammered away down the ravine, and he glanced in time to see the rump.

"Evil badness, mon! Dese fire spirits is bona *fide*." Pennycooke was up on all fours, shaking his head. He was bleeding from the arm where a hoof must have grazed him.

"It was a panicked mule deer. We're on a game trail."

"Praise Jah, hyer be no rhinos."

Jack Liffey laughed once, liking Pennycooke a lot better for the spunk. Luisa sat rubbing her ankle where the Ace was coming undone.

"Up, up. No time, folks," Jack Liffey mother-henned.

As they helped one another to their feet a fat possum waddled rapidly past, pausing just long enough to hiss at them. It was like being trapped in a children's book, he thought—next we meet *Mister* Tortoise—but without the children's book guarantee that it would all turn out well in the end.

For just an instant's lull in the gusting of fire and wind—was it imagination?—he thought he heard mariachi music. He hoped it wasn't some strange presage-of-death phenomenon peculiar to Southern California. The smoke grew whiter for some reason, and then, with a new chill on his spine, he heard a crackling directly behind them. The wildfire had made the leap to the bottom of the arroyo. All he felt for an instant was a tremendous desire to live, to abandon any assistance to the others and run—his entire moral universe succumbing to fear.

Terror Pennycooke lifted the girl over his shoulder again, huffing a little with the effort. A gopher or some other fat rodent thumped past quickly, as if the humans didn't exist, his flank singed pitifully into dark curls.

"Let's step. Truss wi' me, mon. Good knowin you." He held out a hand and Jack Liffey gave him an ordinary handshake, no banging or twists or Masonic embellishments.

"We're getting out of this. Don't doubt it."

"Good on you."

Jack Liffey took the lead, holding the tail of his shirt across his mouth and nose to filter a little of the smoke. He pressed small boughs aside and tried not to let them whiplash back on the others. He was the lead now, and his heart missed a beat when he realized that the bottom of the arroyo took a hard turn to the right, directly into the worst of the crackling roar where the fire had got well ahead of them. He saw how steep the bank was but he didn't even hesitate.

"Up the hill, folks. Sorry. Fire to the right."

He leaned into the angle of the hill, and a few yards up he caught at a tough-seeming shrub with one hand, reaching back with the other. Pennycooke made a face and caught at his hand, nearly pulling the arm out of its socket as he lunged uphill with the extra weight of the girl. They picked their way up, using rocks and clumps of low weed as footholds. Jack Liffey let them go ahead and slipped in behind to push on Pennycooke's rump like a helper engine on a heavy train. Luisa's head dangled as if she were unconscious.

"Tanks for de boost-up, mon."

The fire hissed and crackled directly below them, very near, as they crested out of the ravine. It was like something gaining on you in a nightmare. It was a nightmare. The hot smoke was much worse now, blanketing and blinding them, and fear caught him up once again, nearing panic. He didn't even know which way to run. The panic was oddly voluptuous, almost sexual, and it was all he could do not to abandon them and run on alone. The howling of the fire was so close that he expected it to reach out and tap him on the shoulder.

She could see three big black-and-white CHP cruisers parked criss-cross, completely blocking the highway. The cops had set up just beyond the turnoff for Rambla Pacifico, and she followed a big Ford Expedition up Rambla along with most of the traffic, largely sports cars and SUVs that all seemed to want to U-turn right away on the wider spots of the road, making a tangle of vehicles at every angle. They were backing out of driveways, making three-point U-turns, just trying to get around so they could drop back down to PCH and return toward Santa Monica. It took her a while to get past the jam, honking away to still the cars, like threading a convention of first-time drivers.

Thumb had her Thomas Bros. open on his knees. "This will get us there," he said.

"If it's not blocked, too." When they crested the higher spots of the road, they could see a curious mix of dark and light smoke, a whole cloud bank of it, peeling away from the hillside perhaps a mile farther on. She pulled carefully around an abandoned ladder truck on the side of the road, the front tire flat, and dozens of storage doors on its side standing open, as if insatiably ravenous children had descended on a candy truck. They passed a small development of homes that all looked abandoned, two of them with lawn sprinklers spinning slowly on the roofs. There was a turn onto Piuma Road, heading west, the way they wanted to go but it was blocked by what looked like an Eagle Scout standing beside a light green pickup truck. He turned out to be a very young Forest Ranger and Maeve handed him one of the business cards she'd had printed—one of the last few her father hadn't found and destroyed. It said **Liffey & Liffey, Investigations.**

"Insurance investigation," she said without hesitation "There's evidence of arson up here."

"You can't go up yet."

"Captain Watson in the arson bureau called and told me the fire was knocked down enough up on top to have a look." She'd heard firefighters use the term "knocked down" on the radio before and had always found it weird, as if you put out a fire with boxing gloves.

The young man seemed unsure of himself.

"Come on, we're in a hurry," she insisted

At last, he stepped aside. She waved a thank-you and drove around the truck. Thumb was awestruck.

"*¡Hijole!* You're *loca*."

"I've seen my dad work. He always says a clipboard and a sense of entitlement will get you anywhere."

Thumb watched out the rear window, just in case the man gave chase. "Man, that was like Obiwan Kanobe—that trick you did on Mr. Smokey the Bear."

"You know, the forest service insists he's called Smokey Bear. Isn't that's nuts? Everybody says Smokey *the* Bear. Names are what people think they are."

"Sobres." He smiled. "Ain't no Zor the O."

She smiled. The roadside was empty for a mile or so, but she started seeing pumpers pulled half off the pavement, linked from one to the next by fat hose with water runnels darkening the asphalt at the joints. When the map showed they were only about a half mile from Cold Canyon Road, they passed abruptly into fire country. Here the land was burned black and still smoldering in spots on both sides of the road. Then their path was blocked by fire trucks parked side by side. The fire fighters all seemed to be off somewhere. She backed a ways and pulled well off the road onto a gravel patch that didn't look hot.

"We can walk it from here."

Maeve noticed him retrieve the pistol and stick it in his waist but didn't object. They could always dump it if they had to. She grabbed an old pair of binoculars her father had given her and slung them around her neck. Stepping up onto the berm at the edge of the road, she could see that the hills were charred all around, smelling that tingly fire smell, with small trees and bushes reduced to upright black sticks and hardly reacting to the gusty wind which whisked ash eddies up off the ground. A few spots fumed like volcanic vents, but the active fire was far below them, an almost continuous arc of red flame flickering and surging at the base of the smoke column.

Not far off the road, down a lonely gravel drive bordered by a little surviving iceplant, there was a sooted-up slab foundation with a rock chimney and a few blackened studs sticking up, all of it still smoking angrily in the wind. It was painful to look at, it was so definitively destroyed. She examined the hills nearby with the binoculars but reminded herself that the house they had seen on the TV, the one with her father's car, must be higher up near the origin of the fire, probably out of sight. Thumb found an address painted on the curb at the driveway, which wasn't far off the one they had worked out from the Thomas's.

They waited on the berm for a time, watching a helicopter with a water bucket on a cable and a fat old two-engine propellor plane dropping chemicals on the fire.

"There's no point trying to get up to that house," she said. "If Dad was up there, they'll have got him out already." Dead or alive, she thought, but superstitiously she didn't say it aloud. "If he's . . . okay, he'll probably be down there, ahead of the fire. Let's go."

"What if they see us?"

"They've got other stuff to worry about. The fire's not going to turn back on us."

"How are you going to be?" he asked, still hesitant, pointing to the ostomy bag under her loose blouse.

"If I have to, I'll empty it. I hope it won't upset your stomach."

"Uh, okay."

So they set out across the charred rolling land, directly past the dead house, heading diagonally down toward the part of the long fire line that she guessed would be immediately below the house where her father's car had been. It was the only thing she could think to do, and she prayed she didn't come upon a charred body. Her nose wrinkled up as they hiked down through the charred land. The smell off the burn was abhorrent, acrid and choking, and she could actually feel warmth from the earth through her shoes.

Jack Liffey felt himself poisoned by both fatigue and fear, but the wind had backed off a little, and they had finally gained a lead on the fire. He knew his batteries were running dangerously low, near the point where the machinery of his body would just quit on him unexpectedly, but he still hurried Pennycooke along, carrying Luisa. Jack Liffey wasn't sure what had knocked her out, maybe just exhaustion or a combination of the shock and pain and smoke. He knew they couldn't be too far from the Pacific; the hot wind was fighting some colder air near the ground so the smoke was beginning to lift upward. It grew thin enough that he could actually see flames, maybe fifty yards back, fingers of red billowing up into the smoke. They could see better ahead of them, too, a series of transverse benches between them and the ocean which was just discernible as an abrupt gray texture. He tried to guess how far and could not.

"The wind's letting up a little," Jack Liffey gasped.

"Hole it down so de debbil no hear."

They were nearing the edge of the first bench where the land dropped away, but they couldn't see yet how steeply. They might have to do some serious shinnying and sliding. It was the kind of slick-weed hillside that in his youth he and his friends had recklessly tobogganed down on opened cardboard boxes. He wished he had some now.

He'd been hoping to blunder into an expensive hillside home. One of those rich-man's enclaves in the fire zone where the fire department, however reluctantly, always set up a perimeter with fire hoses awash and backhoes tearing out the shrubbery to make a stand. But there were no houses, only wild coastal chaparral. As luck would have it, they had chosen a pure wilderness descent from the hills, and he guessed they were blundering across one of the Santa Monica Conservancy's land purchases. The environmentalists had been buying what they could for years, trying to save a patchwork of wild coastal land.

His heart skipped a beat when a speckled sagehen burst from cover just ahead of them and ran first laterally and then back toward the fire. At least there was no tiny brood of chicks following her toward sure death.

With the wind letting up, he began to think they might just make it out, despite their fatigue. Pennycooke reached the lip of the bench first and sat hard, gasping for air. He set the girl across his lap; her eyes looked glassy. The Jamaican pressed one hand gently under her head to support it. Jack Liffey stopped to breath heavily with his hands on his knees, but he dare not sit because if he did he doubted he would ever get up again.

The dropoff was steeper than he'd thought: it would be a dangerous slide but probably just manageable and it gave them a sense of momentary safety against the crackling fireline approaching behind. At any moment, they could go over the lip and quickly outpace it.

"I'm near done," the Jamaican said.

Jack Liffey sat, despite himself, and got a good look at Trevor's face, and every blood vessel in his eyeballs had burst so they were bright red, giving him a demonic look. Jack Liffey reached over and squeezed his shoulder in affection.

"How's she doing?"

"She wid us in body. De spirit weak." In his voice there seemed a remarkable sensitivity, like something retained from his own childhood. "She only a child."

"Remember when you were little," Jack Liffey said, a memory appearing out of the whirl of his thoughts. "And the barber put a booster seat across the arms of the barber chair? Did they do that in Jamaica?"

A smile flickered and died away. "Sure, mon. Wid a leather pad on one side. De first t'ing to being a mon was when day turn de pad downside and you sit on wood."

"And then they moved it down to the chair as a booster . . ."

Jack Liffey would never work out where he had been going with the reminiscence—he was sure there had been some point to it all. All of a sudden Trevor Pennycooke arched his back hard with a startled look and a bright red orchid bloomed from his chest. Was this all a dream? Trevor opened his mouth to say something but no sound would come. A crack from behind, louder than the fire, echoed and echoed over the hills and Jack Liffey looked back through the shimmer of the flames but couldn't make out a thing.

Trevor Pennycooke slumped to one side, the exit wound of a rifle shot in his chest unmistakable now, pumping arterial blood.

Jack Liffey immediately pushed the Jamaican and the girl together over the edge of the escarpment, but they were dead weight and stalled only a few yards down. He slid down and got on his back between them, his head pointed downslope. Grabbing each unconscious weight by a shirt, he began kicking off against the land to propel his little convoy into a slide. Pennycooke's silk shirt was wet with blood, a little hump of it pumping out of his chest, which there was no opportunity to try to staunch. Once the land tilted steeper and they got up a little speed, they broke friction on the weeds and he had no trouble keeping up the slide. He had to hold up his head to avoid small rocks slamming past. The dry grass flailed at his ears and neck and he went on autopilot, his emotions frozen by everything that had happened, kicking and kicking the earth behind him like a backstroke swimmer as they tobogganed down the bench.

Maeve and Thumb picked their way down the burnt-over land to a point of rock where they had a pretty good view back uphill through a canyon. From here it was easy to make out what was left of the house they'd seen on the news. Something about it must have defied the fire because firefighters were still pouring water onto it But flame licked out of what was left, and it looked soon to be a dead loss like the foundation they had seen. Nearby, smoking blackened trunks stood up where eucalyptus trees had been. The firefighters were too busy to notice two people far below in the great blackened emptiness, two people who were slowly turning black themselves, covered in the ash their passage raised.

"Can I?"

Thumb lifted the binocular strap off her neck with some urgency. He'd seen something below. They were junk binoculars made of beige plastic, 10X20s, too powerful and wobbly to hand-hold properly, but he lay down and braced them on the rock.

"*¡Chale!* I don' believe it."

"What do you see?" Maeve's eyes darted over the blackened universe below. The wind had let up a little, and the smoke was rising to seaward now, boiling off of a long arc of red flame. There was a big area of rocky outcrop like a paved field far below. It provided a gap in the fire line through which she could see to the hillsides below and even to the empty highway and the gray ocean. Thumb dropped the binoculars and took off running downhill hard, and she picked them up immediately.

She looked first at where Thumb seemed to be running, the rocky outcrop. It was like an electric shock hitting her: a young man lay on his stomach there with what was clearly a sniper's rifle braced on a granite boulder. He looked strangely like the boy she had glimpsed for just an instant rolling out under the Malibu garage door and sprinting away. She swung the binoculars immediately toward where he was targeting. They had such a narrow angle of view that it took her a while to find his target. Finally, through a wavery haze of smoke at the edge of the fire, she saw two men sitting with their legs dangling over an apparent cliff-edge, one tall and black, one white. Someone else was there, too, lying across the lap of the black man, but it was the silhouette of the white man that took her full attention. Amazing how little visual information the mind required, she thought: It was her father. A kind of relief welled up in her that he wasn't lying dead in the burning house up the hill, or somewhere in between. Then she felt a confused panic. Who was the man with the rifle? And was he, in fact, aiming at her father?

She sat up and dropped the binoculars, surprised how much she now could make out with her naked eye. Thumb was more than half way to the sniper, sprinting recklessly downhill. Strangely, the sniper was so focused, or the noise of the fire and the wind and the helicopters was so loud, that he didn't seem to hear her new friend coming.

She jolted as she saw the rifle recoil and a few moments later she heard the bang of the shot rolling back and forth across the hills. In a panic she scrabbled for the binoculars and focused immediately on the figures at the edge of the cliff. Her father seemed okay, and the big black man, too. Then, slowly, she saw the black man lean and fall to one side. Thank God it wasn't her father! she thought— with a tiny addendum of guilt for once again wishing to shift misfortune on someone else.

Again she abandoned the narrow field of view and used her naked eyes. Thumb was running hard and drawing close to the sniper. The young man turned abruptly, having become aware of Thumb, and started fighting with the bolt on his rifle. Thumb drew the pistol out of his waist and fired again and again, and she couldn't help cheering. She even found herself thinking with pride that it was the very same pistol that had wounded her, and now it was defending her father. The sniper's body was flung back on the flat rocks and the rifle bounced away. He had clearly lost the duel with Thumb.

By the time she looked back to the cliff where the three figures had been, the brushfire was approaching, making it hard to see. They seemed to have disappeared. She took off running herself.

Bless you, Thumb, she thought, as she leaped, light as air, down the charred slope. That's worth any number of old bags hanging off my body!

TWENTY-TWO

Saving the Kids

"Oh, little sister," Gloria cooed gently, consoling the weeping girl as she sat heavily on a tangled coil of firehose and held Luisa's head in her lap. "You're a long way from home, girl. Shh, shh. I'll take care of you, don't you worry. Shh, now."

Gloria Ramirez had hitched her way there on a police helicopter from Harbor Division that had been sent Code 8A—working a fire—to replace a Westside chopper that was down for the afternoon for repairs. She was still a little shaken by the white-knuckles trip flown by a cowboy who obviously liked to hotshot when he had a woman riding shotgun. She wondered if it was in her Paiute genes to stick close to the earth. She didn't like flying much under any circumstances, and there was something too mystifying about whatever it was that kept you aloft in a helicopter.

After landing, she'd ridden out to the scene with some sheriff's deputies and helped with what she could, settled a battered and wearied Jack Liffey down to rest on a foam pad provided by the firemen and tried to talk down the inconsolably weeping girl, the very Luisa Wilson they'd been searching for for weeks. Gloria had deciphered bits and pieces of the tale sputtered out to her, details that half explained, among other things, the red-eyes-open Jamaican who lay ten feet away from her in an unzipped body bag.

Gloria was there, in the midst of the bedlam, but, the truth was, she wasn't temperamentally ready to be there. She felt like screaming at Jack to please normalize his life a little, please just give her a chance to adjust to one big change at a time and not hit her with so much at once.

Jack Liffey was slashed about the neck, though a few butterfly bandages seemed to have stopped the bleeding, and he was finally over a wave of paroxysmal vomiting, trying to clear the smoke from his lungs. He'd had oxygen for a while but didn't like the mask and pulled it off, keeping it by his side, just in case. He was just beginning to get himself oriented again after all the ruckus. He was surrounded by chugging firetrucks, pumping water from one to the next, and fat canvas hoses running along the pavement, blooming fine sprays from their the metal collars. Somewhere, not too far, a successful fireline was apparently holding its own, protecting a clutch of valuable beach houses. Firemen came and went quickly, with their usual calm and competence, extracting tools and equipment noisily from the trucks.

He watched Gloria's back, seeing how tenderly she sat and cradled the girl. There was an unzipped olive green body bag near the women, with Trevor Pennycooke's head and shoulders exposed. The Jamaican was decidedly dead, making Jack Liffey feel surprisingly bereft. He'd begun to like the poor hardcharging Rasta gangster quite a lot. He understood that Trevor had been doing his best to infuse a kind of makeshift hope into Luisa Wilson's sad life.

A small detachment of sheriff's deputies trooped down off the hillside to join them, leading a couple of kids, and Jack Liffey decided he was hallucinating for sure when he saw that the shamefaced pair looked a lot like Maeve and Thumb. One of the deputies carried a black Walther PPK in a big plastic baggie, its magazine removed.

He sat bolt upright, realizing it was no mirage, and sure enough Maeve ran to embrace him. Before he could say a thing, she whispered:

"A guy up there was trying to kill all of you with a sniper gun. Thumb stopped him."

He looked at Thumb, who had turned his back to one of the deputies, submitting to handcuffs. How on earth had these two met? How had they got here? *You're going to rewrite that goddam essay another million times for this,* he thought.

"The *vato* up there was trying to kill these guys," Thumb objected.

Maeve jumped to her feet. "I shot the sniper. He was trying to kill my father."

A deputy—a shrewd middle-aged man wearing the department's street tans—looked at her skeptically. His aging eyes looked like they could see right through rock. "Everybody please make use of their right to remain silent."

"No, *I'm* Spartacus," Jack Liffey said, and the deputy's eyes wrinkled up in suspicion. Jack Liffey didn't even know who the sniper had been, but he had long ago decided it was always a good idea to confuse the issue as thoroughly as possible whenever his daughter was involved. "I shot the sniper a half hour ago," Jack Liffey insisted. "That's my pistol you've got. You think it's hers, go ahead and ask her the make and caliber."

She glanced down furiously at him.

"It's a Walther PPK," Jack Liffey volunteered. "Nine millimeter. I took it as payment for a job years ago."

"That's *my* strap," Thumb said indignantly. "It cost me six hundred dollars, *ese.*"

"Shut. Up," Gloria commanded, seconding the sheriff.

"Yes, would you all please can it," the deputy said. "Detectives will be here soon to take your statements. In the meantime, is everybody here okay? Any hidden wounds? No more confessing, okay?"

The deputy walked away to his car, reached in the window for a microphone on a coil-cord and began a conversation.

Jack Liffey felt himself gathering some form of coherence slowly out of his wooziness, sobered by the need to protect Maeve. He forgot completely about his stinging cuts and strained hip muscles. The arrival of his daughter had sharpened up his protective instincts no end. "What the hell are you doing here?" he asked softly.

"Thumb saved your life," she explained.

He looked at Thumb and guessed that the pistol the detective held was the very one that had wounded Maeve, even though he claimed he'd thrown it away, and if they ever ran it through ballistics, it was going to get a whole lot tougher to protect the boy. He couldn't let himself lie there any longer like a slug, so he cocked his legs and sat up stiffly to try to get a handle on things. The wildfire smoke was arching over their heads out to sea, billowy white with large seams and inclusions of dirty ashy gray. He didn't fear the fire anymore. He had to assume the firefighters knew what they were doing, and he guessed the whole covey of fire trucks had massed behind some safe fire line.

"Glor," he called softly.

Her face was far less anxious than he had gotten used to seeing. Luisa seemed to have passed out again across her lap, but she might have been in shock. For the moment they were almost alone.

"And how are you doing, Jack?"

"Do you really think we can save the kids?"

She smiled. "All of them?"

"Every one of them," he said, thinking of Thumb. "No exceptions."

"It's going to be rough getting all the stories straight. Let me talk to the deputies. I'm out of my jurisdiction."

"And get the girl a tetanus shot and a rabies shot. She was bit by a dog."

"After all the cuts, you'll probably need one, too."

"Do you think we can save you and me, too?"

"Us?" she said neutrally.

"You do have a tendency to see failed love as the norm."

"It's been my experience."

"How about this time you look at me hanging around your place as just desirable enough to console you for all the negatives. It might be enough."

"We're getting old, Jackie, aren't we? Maybe we should try and make do with what we got on the shelf."

"That's all I want. And save the kids."

Dear Diary,

I just cant get over how much I miss Trev once I got accustomed to the idea of him being around. I think he kind of went to sleep in that slide down the hill & I hope his last time was without pain. I hope he is meeting Highly Slassie right now.

I am luckily fallen among good people. Mr. Liffey says Trever & him were really enemies when they first met. Im sorry about that. Gloria and Jack are letting me live with them for now. The house is so full of books I can read forever as long as I am here. They are all trying very hard to get the other boy out of jail & I hope they find a way. Maybe if I had never existed Trev would be still alive.

I know I can't go back to Owens & they said fine. They say I can be a daughter to them if I want. I can see it is something they seem to want a lot especially Gloria. Maybe I will do it.